Ann Scott is deputy editor of the *British Journal of Psychotherapy*. She is author of *Olive Schreiner: A Biography* (with Ruth First) and collaborated with Mary Barnes on *Something Sacred: Conversations, Writings, Paintings*. She lives in London.

Real Events Revisited

FANTASY, MEMORY AND PSYCHOANALYSIS

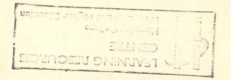

ANN SCOTT

A *Virago* Book

First published in Great Britain by Virago Press 1996

A CIP catalogue record for this book
is available from the British Library

ISBN 1 86049 263 0

Typeset by Palimpsest Book Production Limited,
Polmont, Stirlingshire
Printed and bound in Great Britain by
Clays Ltd, St Ives plc.

Virago
A Division of
Little, Brown and Company (UK)
Brettenham House
Lancaster Place
London WC2E 7EN

For Hilda, again, and for Herbert Lass

Contents

Acknowledgements

This book is the product of an engagement with questions of fantasy stretching back nearly ten years. It began with a request from *Feminist Review* to address what has often been called 'the real event debate' in a special issue of the journal on child sexual abuse, and I thank the journal for that beginning. I wish to thank two other formative settings as well: Free Association Books, and Bob Young, for an editorial atmosphere in which I was privileged to work with and learn from experienced authors over a number of years; and the editorial network of the *British Journal of Psychotherapy*, which continues to provide me with valuable ideas, stimulation, and 'thought about the field'.

For her discerning comments on the whole manuscript, I am deeply indebted to Meira Likierman. I have also benefited from the expertise of Parveen Adams, Jean Arundale, Andrew Barry, Lesley Caldwell, Prophecy Coles, Andrew Cooper, John Fletcher, Cora Kaplan, Diane Middlebrook, Mica Nava, Rozsika Parker, Susannah Radstone, Barry Richards, Lynne Segal, Barbara Taylor, and Cathy Urwin, who generously commented on individual chapters at different times. For their encouragement and many acts of intellectual kindness, I must thank Pete Ayrton, Christopher Cordess, Isabel Menzies Lyth, Mandy Merck, Marilyn Pietroni, Jean Radford, Andrew Samuels, Martin Stanton and Jenny Taylor. I have also been supported by Georgina Born's perceptive and enduring friendship.

I particularly want to acknowledge my gratitude to Bob Hinshelwood for his unstinting engagement with my ideas, and facilitation of my work, over a number of years; and to Dr Michael Parsons for a space which enabled me to complete this book.

At Virago, my warmest thanks to Ruthie Petrie and Melanie Silgardo for their astute overview of the text; and to Sarah White for her relaxed forbearance with an author who, not surprisingly, found it hard not to be a back-seat driver of the publishing process. Sue Kemsley prepared the bibliography; Beth Humphries copy-edited, Jane Horton proofread, and Klara King indexed the book; I am most grateful to all for their rapport with the work, and their meticulous skill.

For permission to quote from 'Are Incest Victims Hated?' I am grateful to Dr Brendan MacCarthy and *Psychoanalytic Psychotherapy*. Advertisements on p. 114 and p. 117 are reproduced by kind permission of the National Society for the Prevention of Cruelty to Children (© 1995). For permission to reproduce advertisements I am also grateful to the Children's Society and the YMCA. The cover design of the catalogue 'Child Sexual Abuse: Books from Sage' is reprinted by permission of Sage Publications Ltd.

Chapter 1 was originally published in *Feminist Review* no. 28 ('Family Secrets: Child Sexual Abuse') (1988, pp. 88–102. Chapter 2 was originally published in *Women: A Cultural Review*, vol. 1 no. 2 (Summer 1990), pp. 127–34. Chapter 3 was originally published as a review essay, part of *History Workshop*'s special feature on 'Psychoanalysis and History', no. 26 (Autumn 1988), pp. 143–52. Chapter 4 is developed from a lecture, 'Real Events Revisited', to THERIP (The Higher Education Network for Research and Information in Psychoanalysis), London, February 1992, and a panel discussion with Jean Laplanche at the Institute of Contemporary Arts, London, September 1992. Chapter 5 is based on a lecture given in the Philadelphia Association 'First Sunday' series, London, December 1993. Chapter 6 was first given as a paper to a joint Freud Museum/*British Journal of Psychotherapy* conference, 'Hysteria Today', London, February 1994, and published in the *British Journal of Psychotherapy*, vol. 11 no. 3 (1995), pp. 398–405. Chapter 7 is in part based on a presentation, 'In Conversation with Diane Middlebrook', at the Institute of Contemporary Arts, London, November 1991. Chapter 8 went through several revisions as a paper given to the Social Work Research Seminar, Brunel University College, February 1995; then at Middlesex University Conference, 'New Sexual Agendas', July 1995; and, most recently, to the MA in Psychoanalytic Studies, Tavistock Clinic, February and May 1996. I am, lastly, most grateful to the editors of these journals, the institutions which invited me to speak, seminar leaders and members of seminar groups for their comments and – often – the disagreements with me that enabled me to think afresh. Naturally I alone am responsible for any errors of judgement that remain.

A note on fantasy/phantasy

I have followed the 'ph' spelling of phantasy when writing about Kleinian work or quoting from Kleinian authors, since here 'phantasy' signifies a specifically unconscious activity. As authors in other schools of thought in psychoanalysis often use 'fantasy' for both the conscious and unconscious process, distinguishing the meaning being given to the word as the context arises, the reader will find both usages in this book.

Introduction

'Language is a skin', in Roland Barthes's memorable phrase,[1] and in this book I am exploring some of the ways in which the language of psychoanalysis clothes and displays psychic life. In its classical setting, the consulting room, psychoanalysis allows the subject a new lexicon. Here, for example, is the American writer and radical Agnes Smedley, author of the autobiographical novel *Daughter of Earth*, writing in 1924 to a confidante about the possibility of a return trip to the United States. She had then been in psychoanalysis in Berlin for two years.

> The memories of my childhood will perhaps be understandable by the time I return, but they will be dark ones nevertheless . . . I have left a world of misery, a world of poverty, of prostitution, of ignorance, of dirt. Shall I go back and look upon it once more without being able to help? And then once more go away, with the wounds reopened, with the pain sharper than ever? I cannot forget, and yet I cannot rationalize such things, which were the earth in which I grew.[2]

Of this time she was later to write, in *Battle Hymn of China*:

> My psychoanalysis began, and continued tortuously

> for two years. During this infinite suffering one image haunted my sleeping and waking: I held a small Chinese vase in my outstretched palm and contemplated its beauty. A crack kept growing down the side, the vase broke, and the fragment rolled out of my outstretched palm. It seemed a symbol of my life.[3]

Agnes Smedley's life and work hauntingly – if unwittingly – pose the questions with which this book is concerned. I am looking at events, the materiality of life, the place of memories: how and to what end are these represented psychically? What does psychoanalysis, as an approach, do in engaging with the past? What is meant by this past – a personal past, a social past? What is meant by 'fantasy', and indeed by psychic change? The lexicon that the clinical setting makes possible is intended to make free, or confer distance, usually in conferring meaning and a sense of psychic truth. This talking cure is also expected to remove symptoms. In the example I have chosen Agnes Smedley herself offered a symbolic reading – 'A crack kept growing down the side, the vase broke' – in place of the raw confusion of 'the wounds reopened . . . the pain sharper than ever'. The image of the vase belongs within an analysis; the wounds and pain belong within a remembered past that is, at times, all too vividly present. And uncannily, it seems, the Chinese vase also prefigures a future, which took Smedley to China as a special correspondent for Western newspapers and inspired in her a lifelong advocacy of the nationalist cause.

It is a commonplace of psychoanalysis to argue that 'meaning' is what matters in the psychoanalytic dialogue. My suggestion is that the much greater social, cultural and clinical awareness of trauma, and of sexual trauma in particular, in the last decade or so, has enabled a fresh focus on the question of the 'event' in psychoanalysis. The period since the Cleveland crisis of 1987 provides a setting within which these complex questions of fantasy, memory and the event can be newly thought. The frame has altered; and this changing perspective is mirrored in the book, which shifts between an involvement in the wider world of cultural and social debate, and (to invoke Freud's own notion of *ein anderer Schauplatz* – another place) the more sequestered world of the clinical. But that world is sequestered in a narrow sense only; for it is one of the defining features of our time that the initially private dialogue between a male physician and a female hysteric, once public – in the sense in which Barthes wrote of 'giving publicity' to relations of speech[4] – initiated a body of literature, a movement, and then, in the phrase often attributed to W.H. Auden, 'a whole climate of opinion'. That climate of opinion, however, has recently been tested by debate and controversy, in the public domain, around seduction and memory.

Because we are increasingly familiar with child sexual abuse as the 'event' – and the disturbing event – *par excellence* it can be difficult to pose questions about actuality in psychoanalysis from other vantage points. Indeed the importance of the debate about child sexual abuse is that it rightly reopens debate about fantasies of seduction. It is not, however, the only route and in the book I look at other aspects of the 'real': at the terrain of 'event', 'fantasy' and 'memory'. The objects of memory are events, naturally, but thoughts and fantasy as well, along with a most complex interweaving of the two; an interweaving for which psychoanalysis has traditionally had a vocabulary that includes screen memory, family romance, construction and reconstruction, and, more recently, transgenerational haunting.[5] All imply a certain way not just of thinking about the past but of looking at, or *seeing* the past, a stress on vision to which I will return.[6] I am asking, then, what could be seen as constituting the distinctive voice of a psychoanalytic perspective on the event. How does psychoanalysis – in its various schools – address the issue, theoretically and clinically? Has feminism (including feminist psychotherapy) found a place in these debates? And what of trauma, considered more broadly?

* * *

Let us stay for a moment, by way of introduction, with sexual trauma. At the heart of the problem of sexual abuse is to be found a series of questions about children's and adults' minds: about denial, repression, memory – and fantasy; terms which are to be found, too, at the heart of the psychoanalytic conception of the mind and its conflicts. Let us recall that the psychoanalytic conception is of fantasy as having a relatively stable nature, in which fantasy scenarios may bear little or no relation to what is commonly referred to as 'external reality' or the 'outer world'.[7] Indeed the idea of a 'real event' haunted much of feminism's initial engagement with psychoanalysis – in the fascination with Freud's 'Dora', for example[8] – for the psychoanalytic conception of fantasy was frequently perceived as being at odds with the 'real-life events', with relations of power as a kind of event, which explained or inflected women's place in the culture.

Events in the public domain in the 1980s then brought into a new and more urgent focus the question of fantasy, conscious and unconscious. First came Jeffrey Masson's and Alice Miller's widely publicised critiques of Freud's move away from the 'seduction theory' of neurosis to the theory of the Oedipus complex, which put sexual fantasy at the centre of the formation of the personality and of the origin of illness. Next came the increasing recognition of the extent of child sexual abuse – focused by the crisis in Cleveland in 1987 and now a constant issue of public debate and social concern. It was the publicity around Cleveland which enabled people to talk about childhood memories previously suppressed or repressed, and which enabled a fresh focus on definition.[9]

At this time the most widely accepted definition of sexual abuse was 'the involvement of dependent developmentally immature children and young people in activities which they cannot fully comprehend, to which they cannot give informed consent, and which violate the social taboos of the culture'.[10] Child sexual abuse is thus not synonymous with but is closely linked to incest and the transgression of the incest taboo.[11] The incest taboo proscribes sexual relations between family members of specified degrees of closeness;[12] statistics (along with anecdotal evidence) consistently show that father–daughter incest, empirically, is the most widespread.[13]

By the time of *Working Together Under the Children Act 1989* (1991), the mandatory guidance to all professionals using the Act, sexual abuse had been defined as 'actual or likely sexual exploitation of a child or adolescent. The child may be dependent and/or developmentally immature.'[14] However, the field of research into child sexual abuse is generally understood to be fraught with difficulty because of definitional problems. Indeed as definitions become more restrictive, there is some evidence that prevalence appears to fall.[15] A recent review of the epidemiological research on child sexual abuse, surveying the empirical research since the late 1970s on the prevalence of sexual abuse among adult clinical populations, shows that the rates reported in the studies are highly discrepant and vary from 3 per cent to 90 per cent.[16] Complicating the picture is the observation that little is understood of 'why some women are more profoundly affected than others – what may be the protective factors?'[17] And that although it is known that poverty and reconstituted families increase the risk, it is still only in a tiny minority of families that abuse actually takes place.[18]

These discrepancies in definition became a matter for governmental concern in England in the summer of 1995, when the NSPCC announced its most recent finding that one in six adults claims to have suffered sexual abuse in childhood. No distinction had been drawn between reports of rape, molestation and indecent exposure. In defence of the NSPCC's data, one expert in the child protection field said that a narrow definition of abuse denied children's rights.[19] But as Suzanne Moore pointed out in her *Guardian* column at the time, as a qualifier to her concern that 'we refuse to believe statistics on the sexual abuse of children even though they are presented time and time again', 'the word abuse is now so over-used that almost any situation can be constructed as abusive'.[20]

Despite these difficulties, our awareness of the prevalence of sexual abuse and of the representation of sexual abuse informs our thinking about the child's registration of the sexual. In Chapter 6 I quote Jean Laplanche's prescient observation, in a psychoanalytic panel discussion on hysteria in the 1970s, that 'the body now appears to us as the locus for a communication which is potential, implicit, veiled and fixed'. This notion of the 'veiled and fixed' resonates also with the way the body of the child has become newly invested. Our current preoccupation with the child's body shows that whereas the discussion of the incest taboo in 1970s feminism turned on woman as sign – in Juliet Mitchell's discussion of exogamy and the incest taboo in *Psychoanalysis and Feminism*, for example, which turned on the exchange of women and rules of marriage – it is now the child's body which is the sign.[21]

It is also interesting, with hindsight, to observe how the discourse on incest in *Psychoanalysis and Feminism* differs from that today; in some cases the public discourse on it, in some cases psychoanalytic discourse. Mitchell's exposition is passionately concerned with a deep structural issue, a meta-perspective, to which questions of subjectivity 'appear' to be subordinated. Yet we may be being offered a structural framework within which such questions could be placed – and may still need to be placed. As Mark Cousins and Parveen Adams put it:

> The very idea of a taboo against incest situates the taboo on the side of prohibiting action, while

> implicitly recognizing a desire on the side of fantasy and representation. The incest taboo is therefore not a random injunction against a particular relation. It is the very moment of the inauguration of *the difference between representation and event.* (my italics)[22]

* * *

I am aware that in these papers, collected (and in some cases revised) from work I have been doing since the Cleveland crisis, and presented in the book in roughly chronological order, my vocabulary is diverse. Sometimes I speak of reality, sometimes of actuality; sometimes I use the conventional psychoanalytic phrase 'external world' to mean just that – the world outside the subject (people, discourse, networks, political forces), assuming in so doing that there is a meaningful distinction to be drawn between interior and external states. Clinically this is often termed the distinction between narrative and historical truth, and one of the enduring lines of debate in this has, after all, been over the role of language in establishing and interpreting that relationship, especially as it concerns questions of fantasy.[23]

Jacques Lacan and Melanie Klein are often taken as standing for an 'argument' about 'reality' – and certainly its representation in language. For the Lacanian analyst Eric Laurent, for example, unconscious phantasy implies the presence of a subject linked to otherness, rather than innate knowledge.[24] Yet the links between Lacan and Klein are there. Darian Leader, among others, has pointed out that both Lacan and Klein are suspicious of distinguishing between fantasy and reality too readily. This exposition of fantasy is intimately linked to the question of the traumatic, if the bodily crisis of weaning can be seen as exemplifying subsequent 'external' trauma. Laurent points out that Klein saw weaning as the first fundamental crisis of the subject, and that Lacan linked her text with Freud's concept of negation – the judgement which accepts or refuses. Klein, in 1936, said 'the superego does not begin at two years, but at weaning, and linked with the traumas that it implies'.[25] Here, for Laurent, Lacan is incorporating Klein's approach to the presence of a subject linked to an otherness. It is, incidentally, a reminder that the notion of the traumatic is of an initially unavoidable event, an intimately familial one.

The notion that subjectivity is unavoidably traumatic is indeed linked, in Malcolm Bowie's words, with 'the traumatic event proper, which is as extrinsic to signification, as unassimilable to the pursuit of pleasure, as any foreign body encroaching upon the human organism'. Bowie points out that 'it would be too simple to say that here Lacan is traumatizing the unconscious', but that in Lacan's account of trauma there is a sketch of an extremely wide area of application for a term that for Freud had had precise clinical uses linked with the effect of external trauma. Yet for Lacan, as for Freud, he suggests, 'it made much more sense to suppose that a single set of rules governed all mental events and that the pathogenic ones were a lens through which the structure of subjectivity at large could be viewed'.[26]

The absence of language – of words – to depict traumatic experience is crucial in thinking through the questions with which this book is concerned; for running as an underlying problematic within it *is* a question about that 'single set of rules'. But for the moment let me note that the Real, when defined as that which lies outside the symbolic process, is to be found in the mental as well as in the material world: 'a trauma, for example, is as intractable and unsymbolizable as objects in their materiality'.[27] Links with the language of psychiatric classification have been tracked in a fascinating commentary by Aisling Campbell, who notes that in DSM-III the stressor must be 'an event, which lies outside the normal pattern of human experience and which would clearly cause suffering in virtually anyone'; by the time of DSM-IV, however, 'the subject has, as it were, insisted; it is no longer the observer who determines what should or should not be traumatic, but the patient's own reactions to the event'.[28] Campbell suggests

> that [post-traumatic] disorders represent a certain hysterical presentation; implicit in all of them is a kind of demand, and a problem of putting something into language . . . trauma always represents an encounter with something that cannot be spoken about, which cannot be symbolized . . . Clearly, something has happened to language for these patients. Trauma resists symbolization; its horror makes us literally speechless. Any traumatic event is one which confronts us with the inadequacy of language . . . The real is not something independent of the symbolic register, or for that matter, of the imaginary. They are all bound up with each other . . . Accidents, catastrophes, traumas represent encounters with the real.[29]

Language thus runs as a constant through all the debates with which this book is concerned. And language, incidentally, is seen at its most fraught in the recent crisis over false or recovered memories – indeed it almost negates Lacan's axiom that

> speech is *mediation* between subject and other, and it implicates the coming into being of the other in this very mediation. An essential element of the coming into being of the other is the capacity of speech to *unite* us to him.[30]

Here many concerns are in play, not least temporality. For the 'coming into being' of which Lacan speaks denotes the child's acquisition of language rather than the adult's retrospection. Yet the two cannot be altogether severed.

* * *

Freud's 1896 paper, 'The Aetiology of Hysteria', which lays such stress on the traumatic nature of the environment, especially the intimate environment, has become a point of reference in these debates. Roger Kennedy, in a recent discussion of the effect of sexual abuse in childhood on the adult mind, points out that this paper 'outlines a complex picture of the nature of memory', with trauma acquiring new meaning by deferred action. Kennedy considers that

> Freud's emphasis on the role of the arrival of genital maturity at puberty is the extra factor needed to create symptomatology [and this] is matched by my experience at the Cassel Hospital with young abusing adults, most of whom have been themselves abused as children . . . My impression is that there was often a threat of an adolescent breakdown, perhaps related to the flooding back of conscious or unconscious memories of abuse.[31]

Alice Miller and Jeffrey Masson regard the paper as of crucial importance, and Freud's move away from it a move in bad faith (to paraphrase). The paper appears fleetingly here in Chapter 1 but at more length in Chapter 4. This early paper asserts the principle that the traumatic effect is not sudden, instantaneous or irreversible; it has its effect over time. Masud Khan pointed to this in his concept of cumulative trauma, in which (developing Freud's formulations in *Beyond the Pleasure Principle*) the mother is pictured as a protective shield, with cumulative trauma resulting from breaches in the mother's role 'over the whole course of the child's development, from infancy to adolescence'. These breaches are not traumatic singly: 'they have the quality of a "strain" . . . [they] cumulate silently and invisibly', and are not traumatic at the time; they achieve the value of trauma only cumulatively and in retrospect.[32] But, without wishing to erase the significance of deferred action, clinical evidence does seem to be pointing to a *specific* quality in the psychic effects of sexual abuse (literally a breach in a protective shield, this time that of the child's body surface). To quote Roger Kennedy again:

> One could perhaps wonder whether or not there are certain early experiences, for example where there has been massive and repeated abuse, that remain constantly pathogenic, with rather little rearrangement in the memory.[33]

The point is amplified:

> The abused adults I tend to see in analysis have somehow managed to wall off their traumatic experiences to a greater or lesser extent . . . One may wonder what is the effect on the mind to have to keep such experiences walled off or hermetically sealed. My impression is that the consequence is that certain 'imaginative' elements of mental life such as dreams and fantasy life may also have a sealed off and unavailable quality to them. These elements may be felt as persecuting or as almost inanimate objects, split off from the rest of the mind . . . the analysis of the abused adult is perhaps less concerned with the issue of recovered memories of the past as such than in confronting the emotional impact of their abuse, and the effect of the abuse on their mind's emotional functioning.[34]

At the moment, when a lot of work has been done on the effects of catastrophic trauma, it is clearer that certain events may be on such a scale that their impact is impossible to process at the time. Even so, part of what has made the debate on sexual abuse difficult, elusive even, is that evidence is less easily obtained and less unambiguous, despite an agreement in principle that its effects are destructive. Less is known about precise effects.

Some years after Chapter 1 appeared as a contribution to *Feminist Review*'s special issue on child sexual abuse, I returned to the issue of the 'real event', in a paper which gives this book its title. By this time, 1992, there had been a proliferation of papers, conferences and working networks, inside the profession, on the topic. But what of the traumatic itself? This was the question I set myself to explore. Freud's model is of the exact repetition of traumatic events. In what has echoes of Lacan's generalising of 'the traumatic', Laplanche offered a 'general theory of seduction', a map of a relationship between parents and infants organised around the message, an enigmatic signifier. Laplanche looked at both the Kleinian and Lacanian traditions and proposed a new way of thinking about 'seduction' in the relations between parents and infants, rather than what he calls 'event-based realism'.[35] In Laplanche's recent work children receive adults' projections but the 'mute' child of Alice Miller is replaced by the child facing an enigmatic signifier – an important difference. A world hangs on it – a world of comprehension and misreading. How do children understand their parents' messages, and particularly their parents' sexuality? Laplanche poses the question: under what conditions is an adult gesture a seduction? He suggests that it is the presence of a sexual fantasy in the adult.[36] It is an important development, given that the dominant analytic tradition in Britain (including feminist therapeutic practice) has, broadly, been Kleinian or object-relations in its orientation, following Klein's focus on the pre-verbal mother–infant relationship, seen as saturated with phantasy on the infant's part.[37] Discourses of seduction have thus been shifting in relation both to the internal evolution of psychoanalysis and to wider public debate.

These are highly complicated matters. Language and the absence of language are crucial. But the debate about 'seduction' continues, and must continue, because it touches on an ethic as well as a psychic state. The analytic real is contingent on the work of analysis itself, as we see in Chapter 1; but seduction, as we see there too, has its origins in the Latin 'to lead away'.

* * *

Questions of truth and memory in biographical writing – and their link with the question of narrative in 'False Memory Syndrome' – inform Chapters 3, 5 and 7. Definiteness, as Carolyn Steedman has reminded us, is an elusive goal in autobiographical and, by implication, biographical writing. Kathleen Woodward's testimony, for example, in the working-class autobiography *Jipping Street*, is one of 'seduction and betrayal by beautiful words'.

> The sonorous repetitions of Jipping Street give the violent events she describes the ambiguous qualities of a dream, and the reader asks, against her will, was a grandmother *really* swung round the room by her hair? Did her mother *really* split the mad grandfather's back open with an axe?[38]

Here a liminal space resonant of psychoanalysis – by which I mean not just the sequestered space of the consulting room but the psychic space that psychoanalysis takes as its own, more widely – is in play. How do the categories of psychoanalysis – overdetermination, ambiguity of the event, the haunting quality of memory – find a place in language outside the consulting room? R.D. Laing, for example, interviewed for Phyllis Grosskurth's biography of Klein, observed in connection with the language of 'reparation' that he would have liked to see more discussion of the relationship between some of the mental states Klein postulated and states of mind for which ordinary language already existed (remorse, sorrow, contrition, and so forth).[39] It was a wish to link a specialised vocabulary with a lay one.[40] But when in 1993 a new development burst on to the Anglo-American stage, 'False Memory Syndrome', Freud's legacy, at least in terms of the theory of repression, was less benignly centre stage. Originating with the False Memory Syndrome Foundation in Philadelphia, parents were coming together to protest against what they believed to be their grown daughters' false accusations of sexual abuse. Memory – its reliability, its nature, its formation, its dissipation, its susceptibility to distortion – became an urgent matter at every level, from the intimately familial to the more public stage and ultimately the US courts. The culture had moved from an initially nervous but increasingly steady acceptance of the extent of child sexual abuse – in Andrew Cooper's words, discussing social work's situation at the moment: 'arguably we have assimilated awareness of it [child abuse] into the wider culture in a manner which suggests that the initial social trauma of its disclosure has been mastered to some degree'[41] – and now the terms of the debate had moved on to a new terrain.

Prompted by the tendency (on the part of some radicals and some feminists) to see the organisations of parents opposing their adult children as primarily or merely a backlash phenomenon, I was suggesting that the development needed to be taken seriously.[42] Why had there been such defensiveness about memory? (I did less to this paper, now Chapter 5, to refine it or bring in more recent sources than to any other in the book, preferring to let it stand as a response to a moment of cultural anxiety and ferment.) I look at the way in which memory is invariably seen as a construction within psychoanalysis, and at the concept of 'false memory' itself, almost implicit in psychoanalytic thinking in the notions of screen memory, reconstruction, psychic truth, and in the biographical writing that is discussed in Chapter 3.

Here it is worth looking back again to *Psychoanalysis and Feminism*, which concerned itself with the laws of culture, the event of human society. The forward movement – of ontogeny repeating phylogeny – takes place very fast in the structuralist account. These laws cannot be established *de novo*; that is, after all, the point about each child *as* an Oedipal child. And the notion of 'ontogeny repeating phylogeny' speaks to us about memory, for it is based on the existence or history of a past. Impressionistically, we could say that we are now faced in general with another 'event in human society' – the transgression of the incest taboo. But with this shifting focus of debate – at least in public life – from the child to the adult woman, the organising principle had become the denial of a (psychic) past, not the acquisition of a past.

My own aim in Chapter 5 is to notice a significant change. We start with memory and the recovery of memory, in Freud's writing, as primarily benevolent processes, an idea brought home to me by the work of the textual critic David Krell:

> Freud's famous 'talking cure' . . . rests on the confidence that there is something in the patient which, in spite of all resistance, wants to *express itself* and *to know* . . . Freud encourages the analyst to have faith in the ultimate fidelity – and also the benevolence – of memory . . . In an address to his dubious medical colleagues in 1905 Freud assures them that the remembrance induced by analysis cannot cause more emotional and somatological damage than the amnesia. If the unremembered reminiscence is *thanatos*, remembrance is *eros*, and *eros* will prevail.[43]

But in the situation False Memory Syndrome configured, memory became a site of contest and disruption. The dichotomy, I propose, became that between the benevolence of memory, and the disruptiveness of memory. The clinical – ever since Freud's key papers on construction and reconstruction in analysis[44] – had always been an arena of personal truth. Now things were altered, because adults convicted on the basis of adult children's charges faced a prison term. This literal imprisonment amplifies all that has been carried in the notion of psychic imprisonment, the 'enslavement' implied in the etymology of 'seduction'. It is an overdetermination on a grand scale. It also returns to the point about the disruptiveness – rather than the nostalgia – of Smedley's memories with which I began this Introduction, and is a point which recurs throughout the book.

When False Memory Syndrome first began to be reported in the UK, it was seen by one commentator as 'the latest engagement in the debate about child sexuality'.[45] To my mind it is more accurate to see it – in discursive terms, irrespective of the truth or falsity of the daughters' claims – as a displacement from a debate around *adult* sexuality – and certainly a debate about *parental* sexuality – which was not taking place in public life. By this time child sexual abuse had left the privacy of the family, but the child was still being represented as the site of sexuality, although it is the child who is abused. So it may be possible for the notion of enslavement to be linked – perhaps as a switchword – with the question of perversion, the perversion of parental sexuality. Perversion, as Jonathan Dollimore has pointed out,[46] was originally linked to crimes of knowing. It is, I would add, widely accepted that incest entails precocious knowledge and so we might speak of a return to an earlier notion of dissident knowledge, and see incest as a crime *about* knowing if not *of* knowing, with the child as fetish, its body as a part-object for the other. (Incest is, after all, still seen as one of the '"basic" crimes', along with murder.)[47]

The difficulty of knowledge is clearly at stake. Indeed, the controversy over False Memory Syndrome raised, among many other things, the very difficulty in establishing any sort of consensus, or shared view of the past, that could be validating. In the last couple of years the social as well as clinical commentary on False Memory Syndrome has become extensive,[48] in part coinciding with a fresh controversy, around memories of ritual abuse. In an explicit link with the controversy over real and false memories of childhood maltreatment, Peter Fonagy, for example, has refuted the analyst Roy Schafer's principle that analysts make use of a mixture of psychic reality and an approach which takes for granted 'certain biographical data and events . . . so highly conventionalized or consensually validated' that an analyst would take them as criteria of what is 'real' and 'actual'.[49] Psychobiographical constructions are the result of a dialogue, Fonagy responds, arguing that it is impossible to separate a historical and a narrative truth. The analytic stance requires scepticism. This is his rationale for treating recovered memories as hypothetical constructs rather than historical events.

> Psychic change . . . is a process of 'becoming' through the psychoanalytic dialogue. Looked at in this way, the question of the nature of the relation between the real and the constructed past is poorly stated. It can have no unambiguous conclusion.[50]

But at the same time this whole debate about memory has thrown up a vivid insistence, which we see in the media debates especially, on the importance of 'telling one's story to survive', but also in the work of the Women's Therapy Centre with incest survivors.[51] It is set against the culture's 'commitment to amnesia', in Beatrix Campbell's evocative phrase.[52] The letters and agony columns of women's magazines are now full of discussions of the remembered past, and a conflict over how to remember and whether to remember. Take the following example, from *She*:

> I am a survivor of childhood incest abuse – at the hands of both parents. For years, I lived in a world of shame and fear, attracting predatory, damaged people like myself. At age 47, I felt strong enough to start looking within. It meant going down into the depths, which wasn't easy . . . but I feel reborn.

> I just want to say to others, it can be done – provided you are willing to face whatever comes up. Contact your local Rape Crisis Centre, as I did, and things will start to move.[53]

This popular concern with memory, and with the sense of a past, is paralleled in the academy. At the scholarly level, research into memory and its nature has begun to demonstrate that traumatic memory may indeed be of a different type from the usual, and perhaps takes a non-linguistic form.[54] Clinically, too, there has been a groundswell of opinion and writing on 'memories that seem to be held in the body';[55] 'as if' held in the body; or perhaps held in the body because an experience took place before there was speech. It opens up a debate about memories and their transmission and, equally importantly, also about the way in which one generation can unconsciously transmit its secrets, which exert their traumatic effect even though they are not spoken of. But when memory is released from the body into speech one notices the imperative that many incest survivors have felt, as I say in Chapter 6, to articulate experience in language.

André Green has said, in the context of the early work on hysteria, that Freud tried to re-establish communication between representations; affects had been blocked in the somatic, and now meaning could newly circulate.[56] Through verbalisation, links that had been broken were re-established. Barthes's notion that 'affective space contains dead spots where the sound fails to circulate' strikes me as being about something similar.[57] It seems to me that in the familial and social arena of sexual abuse, in which silence is being replaced by speech, communication between representations – which is seen in the proliferation of clinical articles on the psychic meaning of different incestuous linkages, a form of writing which obliges frankness about a discourse hitherto untouched if not outlawed[58] – is leading to meanings that may heal. And this because child sexual abuse (although the phrase itself seems to be fast becoming emptied of meaning) implicates the body and the affects. Sometimes the words used to describe it by those who have recently emerged from the experience are formal, distancing, almost medical terms; as individuals they are just starting to 'own' language as their own.[59] It is indeed also because sensitive clinicians believe that, as Valerie Sinason puts it, 'you have to be the voice, with someone who has little speech'.[60]

All told, then, I am interrogating talking – what it is to talk, whether in a clinical setting, or in print, or on television – what is set in motion by different kinds of talk. Sylvia Fraser's autobiography of incest, *My Father's House*, which we meet in Chapter 6, is a good example.[61] It is because our culture has moved sharply away from the traditional secrecy about incest that such autobiographical literature has doubtless been growing in recent years. Jessica, whom we also meet in Chapter 6, brings her body-memories to 'Freud' in London in 1938, in Terry Johnson's play *Hysteria*, first performed in 1993. Jessica is a fictional character but Anne and Linda Gray Sexton are not, and one of the most remarkable expressions of this writing has been Linda Gray Sexton's account of her relationship with her mother, the poet Anne Sexton, which I look at in Chapter 7: here the 'enslavement' appears to be explicit. Here too the power of memory to torment and 'tug',[62] and of words to bind, to freeze, and ultimately to set free, is displayed.

The predicament of the two women has been brilliantly captured in a biography and an autobiography. Culturally, the initial reaction to the biography was focused on the ethics of Anne Sexton's therapist releasing 300 hours of audiotaped therapy sessions with his patient. For my part I think we might want to see the books as a dyad, intimately revealing of a disturbed mother–daughter relationship. My suggestion is that the sexualised relationship the mother had with the daughter produced a kind of incorporative identification on the daughter's part, analogous to a melancholic identification.[63] That is the analytic language; what of the language of publishing? In its account of lives lived in therapy, the daughter's autobiography 'broke the silence that normally hung over the American family'.[64] Here the relationship between psychoanalysis and public life, or at least psychotherapy and public life, is once again laid out.

* * *

The talking cure is, by definition, a linguistic cure but it is also about looking, or 'looking at'. One of the features of the analytic space, a sonorous space in which the visual environment is intended to be unchanging but in which the sightlines for analyst and patient are indirect, is that through altering conventional lines of sight new perspectives come into view. These fall in the domain of representation, and one can model 'what happens between the spectator and the art object . . . on the relation of analyst and analysand',[65] as Parveen Adams has recently written:

> the space of representation . . . can no longer be thought of as only physical, architectural or institutional. We must introduce the idea of psychical space.[66]

As the book closes, I look at the image of abuse in two forms of media: print advertising and a television soap opera. One of the striking changes in the urban environment since the events of the late 1980s around child sexual abuse has been the intensification in the image of the abused child. And although the actuality of this abuse is now recognised, facts may not be 'so radiant with their own clarity', to invoke Mark Cousins and Parveen Adams' felicitous words:

> The space of communication and argument between different domains is a space of representation, the space in which one domain is represented, translated, for another . . . 'representation' does not rest upon the relation between a theory, a word, or an image and a *thing*, but upon the equivocation between one word and image and another word and image.[67]

The 'street' has many, many resonances, and urban architecture, in at least one commentator's mind, is already linked with the body.[68] Representations of child sexual abuse are not the only images of sexual violence we find on the streets now but in the massive extension of the use of images and words of abuse, something is being lost; perhaps the emptiness of the experience itself. In a complex discussion of a photographic installation, Adams proposes that

> the spectator's relation to the image is disturbed. This detachment constitutes the object as object of loss, a loss that it is the very function of representation to deny.[69]

Sexual trauma has posed questions not only for psychoanalysis but for the wider culture – as Andrew Cooper argues, the social work profession has had to face difficult and important questions about its contribution to the way abuse is represented in the public domain; should it now seriously 'attempt to influence public perceptions?'[70] I make some observations on the current climate of opinion in social policy and cultural life. This greater visibility is important, but is obscuring as it reveals; it is loss which is denied. But because of this very tension the public arena becomes a fruitful site for further thought about the relationship between fantasy, reality and memory. And to the extent that the 'external world' becomes represented in the 'inner world', clinical psychoanalysis will continue to be permeable to these wider debates, contradictory and compelling as they must inevitably be.

Time and again we have been coming back to the question of the mind and its porousness; and from there it is a short step to the body and its porousness. In what way, then, does the immediacy of this actual, this event, find its place within the psychic life of the subject?

I

Feminism and the seductiveness of the 'real event'

Some ten or fifteen years ago, when feminists began thinking seriously about psychoanalysis, the most common expression of doubt was: but isn't Freud culturally specific? Weren't the illness and disturbance he described true for the period, but times have changed? Today we have the appearance of a reversal. Now that the extent of child sexual abuse is increasingly recognised, some people are asking the other side of the question: if Freud was so mistaken about the reality of the 'real event', does psychoanalysis have any credibility at all? In one sense nothing has changed: there will probably always be rational and irrational forms of ambivalence, not to say scepticism, about the validity of Freud's theory of the mind and its motives. In this chapter I want to look at the implications for psychoanalysis, and the varieties of feminist response to psychoanalysis, of these specifically new terms of discussion. For there is no doubt that the current, unprecedented concern with the reality of child abuse must lead one to look again at the methodological implications of Freud's work during the period which resulted in his writing, of the women patients who spoke of having been seduced as girls by their fathers, 'I no longer believe in my *neurotica*'.[1]

There has always been a debate inside psychoanalysis

about the status of 'real' and 'fantasy', but nothing compares, for events in the public domain, with the recent furore over Freud's seduction theory, and I'll begin by sketching the facts of the Malcolm–Masson controversy. In December 1983 the *New Yorker* ran a two-part article by Janet Malcolm, author of *Psychoanalysis: The Impossible Profession.*[2] 'Trouble in the Archives' went over, in Malcolm's elegant and intelligent way, a sequence of events between 1974 and 1981 with three main protagonists: Kurt Eissler, a senior New York analyst and secretary of the Sigmund Freud Archives, established in the 1950s to secure a collection of posthumous and Freud-related material; Anna Freud, then working in London and living in the Freud family home in Maresfield Gardens that was to become the Freud Museum after her death; and Jeffrey Moussaieff Masson, a young Canadian Sanskritist who had trained as a psychoanalyst and was being groomed to succeed Eissler at the Archives.

While researching the origins of psychoanalysis in Freud's personal papers at Anna Freud's home, Masson came across discrepancies between the original and published versions of correspondence which led him to the conclusion that Freud had suppressed his knowledge of the extent of childhood seduction. When Freud abandoned the seduction theory, Masson argued, he was acting in bad faith and did so in order to protect his standing as a respectable member of the scientific community. The ensuing conflict between Masson, on the one hand, who went public in articles in the *New York Times*, and Eissler and Anna Freud, on the other, resulted in Masson's being sacked as projects director of the Archives, in an atmosphere of raw and unbearably intense feeling.

'Trouble in the Archives' raised a storm of interest at the time and later appeared in book form.[3] Meanwhile, Masson had published *The Assault on Truth: Freud's Suppression of the Seduction Theory.*[4] There his view, briefly, is that Freud's understanding of hysteria, up to and including the 1896 paper 'The Aetiology of Hysteria', was important and compassionate. Masson cites Freud's cry, 'Poor child, what have they done to you?', as an example of this work.[5] When Freud 'abandoned' the seduction theory, however, he did a disservice to psychoanalysis with which all subsequent analysts have colluded. Psychoanalysis, as a theory and clinical practice, has denied the reality of sexual abuse, and in so doing has sentenced thousands of patients to confused, guilty silence while exonerating the abusers.

The chronology is complex, fastidious even, as is often the case with such public rows. In the introduction to one of the later editions of his book, Masson states that the individualistic focus of Malcolm's articles obscured the more substantial issues of psychoanalytic theory that he had tried to raise in the book.[6] Then, shortly after his book came out, *Mother Jones*, the American radical monthly, gave Masson the opportunity to argue his case.[7] Here he concentrated on two issues. One was the disillusionment he experienced as an analytic trainee in North America: an embarrassing intellectual level, an exaggerated reverence for Freud, etc. (He is not the first to venture such observations.) The other was the similarity he believed he had uncovered between how *his* discoveries were misbelieved and denied by the analytic establishment, and how women's reality is denied. In this way he linked his work on sexual abuse with the feminist issue of male supremacy most directly. Moreover, many of Masson's warmest acknowledgements go to the 'speaking bitterness' women's literature of recent years – autobiographical testimony, empirical data on abuse, campaigning writing – which serious feminists do take seriously.[8]

What should we make of this constellation of views, ideological positions and hurt feelings? Let me start by attending to the character of these two sets of writing. Malcolm's articles fizz along, sophisticated in the best *New Yorker* way, sharp, observant, framed by the usual gloomily understated cartoons. Malcolm has her detractors, though I am not among them. 'Trouble in the Archives' succeeds well in documenting the appalling personal suffering experienced by all concerned – the slew of idealisations, careerism, insults, disappointment, ostracism among any group of people falling out – without trivialising the issues (though the deeper merits of the issues, in scholarly terms, are not her topic). Masson's book and *Mother Jones* article, by contrast, have an alternately bludgeoning, now self-justifying tone, despite the significance of the issues that he raises and the evidence he adduces in their support. Permeating the whole book is a quality of muddling, muddled thought – with confusions of logic and caricatures of others' positions – which of necessity weakens the force of his argument. For Masson would have been on to something important, if he had been fully justified in his critique. It is a tautology, but worth setting down. If Masson's accusations had been accurate, then the psychoanalytic community would justly have been on the defensive.

I shall quote a typical passage from his book, to give the reader the feel of his thought, but before going any further it is worth making the general point, as many have done, that it is what Freud put in place of the seduction theory – the theory of infantile sexuality, which attributes unconscious drives and desires to infants and children – which got him into much greater difficulty with the orthodoxy, professional and intellectual, than the seduction theory had ever done. It was because Freud either had to abandon his work when he came to doubt that actual seduction was a necessary precursor of neurotic illness, 'or realize that what he had been doing was only a beginning: respecting what his patients said really did matter in a way he could not have appreciated before',[9] that he was able to work out the distinction between historical and psychical truth which informs all thinking about fantasy as a structure.

To return to *The Assault on Truth*. Taking up Freud's

1916 view (in the *Introductory Lectures*) that stories of childhood seduction in which the father figures regularly as the seducer involve 'an imaginary . . . accusation', and that (in Freud's words) 'up to the present we have not succeeded in pointing to any difference in the consequences, whether phantasy or reality has had the greater share in these events of childhood',[10] Masson writes:

> But in actuality there is an essential difference between the effects of an act that took place and one that was imagined.
>
> To tell someone who has suffered the effects of a childhood filled with sexual violence that it does not matter whether his memories are anchored in reality or not is to do further violence to that person and is bound to have a pernicious effect. A real memory demands some form of validation from the outside world – denial of those memories can lead to a break with reality, and a psychosis . . . in fact psychoanalysts have always shown a greater interest in the fantasy life of a patient than in real events. Freud shifted the interest of psychoanalysis to the pathogenic effects of fantasies, putting less emphasis on the pathogenic effects of real memories in repression. The ideal analytic patient has come to be a person without serious trauma in his childhood.[11]

One of the most obvious criticisms of this way of thinking is that it leaves no room for the possibility that Freud could make an error of judgement, perhaps a grave one – in this case about the after-effects of a real seduction – without this compromising the whole fabric of psychoanalytic thought and its development by subsequent generations of analysts. It is noticeable that Masson's overriding interest is in probing the motives for Freud's alleged disingenuousness (my words, not Masson's; the writer Marianne Krull shows a similar concern with Freud's personal motives for dropping the seduction theory),[12] rather than exploring what becomes of key aspects of psychoanalytic theory if the nature of the real event and its consequences is being reconsidered. I am thinking of the concepts of repression, transference, unconscious conflict, secondary gain in illness, repetition compulsion, working through, projection, projective identification, and so forth. For Masson does not address the issue of how much or how little, at the level of mental structure, depends on the reality or fantasy of a special kind of experience.

Another observation. Psychoanalysis is often criticised on 'genetic' grounds, that is, for inappropriately treating an account of the origins of something as an adequate form of explanation of it. Masson, ironically, is constructing a genetic type of argument, for he writes as though everything of significance about psychoanalysis takes the form of an original betrayal. It is a confusion at two levels. Between internal and external, in the first place, for in one sense Masson is right to say that 'psychoanalysts have always shown a greater interest in the fantasy life of a patient than in real events' – but only in the sense that psychoanalysts cannot assume that an (external) event bears within it an unalterable (internal) meaning. It is this confusion, too, which allows Masson to draw his caricature of a conclusion: 'the ideal analytic patient has come to be a person without serious traumas in his childhood', because he is mistakenly ascribing to psychoanalysis the view that it is *only* fantasy which has an impact or an effect: indeed that there is no relationship between fantasy and event. In psychoanalysis, however, all events *become* invested with fantasy, conscious and unconscious, and may on occasion by potentiated *by* fantasy.

In the second place, Masson confusingly identifies 'real memory' solely with 'the event' – as though people have real memories only of their status as object for the other. 'Real memories' can be of thoughts, too, and thought may sometimes take the form of fantasy, and fantasy may be unconscious. Such thought demands its own validation: thus for many people in analysis, it is the very complexity, indeed inaccessibility of their own 'personal store of memories' (to borrow a phrase of Masson's), with its interweaving of accuracy and distortion, which is at the centre of the analytic process. Of recent work Ronald Fraser's *In Search of a Past* is probably the most convincing and haunting reconstruction of such a process of mapping.[13] Fraser explored his own childhood and the memories of the servants he had known as a child, combining the practices of psychoanalysis and oral history, in the attempt to come to terms with his deep sense of having been split as a child. It is just such a 'deep sense' which structures his reality,[14] and forms the strongest possible contrast with Masson's notion of the event as the real.

Put simply, I believe *The Assault on Truth* is misdescribing the place psychoanalysis attributes to real events, whether in general or in the specific form of sexual abuse. I will return to this in the wider context of the analytic community's response to Masson's work. Here I will note the interestingly similar trajectory in the writing of the Swiss psychoanalyst Alice Miller, although one of the significant differences between Miller and Masson is that Miller practised clinically for more than twenty years before giving this work up to write and campaign about child abuse. (Masson acknowledges Miller's influence on his work, and says he owes her 'a great deal'.[15])

In their original German-language editions, only two years separate her first three books, *The Drama of the Gifted Child*, *For Your Own Good*, and *Thou Shalt Not Be Aware*.[16] That period charts Miller's explosive turning away from her enlightened but orthodox psychoanalytic view of disturbances, within and between people, to her current, fiercely polemical work on parental power over children (*For Your Own Good* and *Thou Shalt Not Be Aware*), with its combination of hostility and respect for Freudian thought. *The Drama of the Gifted Child* is not just different in rhetoric, but conceptually very far from the two more recent works. *Drama*, still embedded in the psychoanalytic, and widely influential within that world, is a delicate, Winnicottian exploration of the way in which the mother–child relationship, often in the case of gifted, sensitive children, can fail the child because the mother is herself narcissistically deprived.

The originality of Miller's thesis was striking. Separating the analytic notion of narcissism from its pejorative connotation, she posited a child's narcissistic needs as authentic, first distinguishing between intellectual development – which could survive maternal failure – and emotional development – which could not, for the mother would be using the child to meet her own unmet needs. Next, and more radically, she compared this relationship with the analyst–analysand relation, suggesting that analysts too could use patients for their own narcissistic purposes. I have drawn this out in order to illustrate the point that Miller's initial stance took up the problem of parental failure in a wide-ranging way – implying, in so many words, that destructiveness, intrusiveness and failure to observe boundaries (all key terms in the literature of sexual abuse) could take a number of forms, many of a subtly interactive kind.

For Your Own Good and *Thou Shalt Not Be Aware* are both more ambitious works. *For Your Own Good* chronicles eighteenth- and nineteenth-century German approaches to child-rearing in an attempt at explaining social cruelty and sadism on the basis that what was done to children is what these children, as adults and parents, later do to others. *Thou Shalt Not Be Aware* is a sustained polemic against all forces in society – ideological, psychiatric, psychoanalytic – which attempt to deny or minimise the extent of child abuse. A number of Miller's reviewers have noticed the absence of a distinction, in her work, between sexual and non-sexual forms of abuse, and I need not go over it here. What is especially relevant, I feel, is that where *Drama* took up the experience of some children, some mothers, *For Your Own Good* and *Thou Shalt Not Be Aware* are universalising. Stemming from their need for 'power' and 'revenge', parents have a 'compulsion' to use their children as an outlet. The outlet is all too frequently sexual, only society denies it, and when it is, parents are acting from an unconscious compulsion to repeat their own experience as children. But notice that the experience that is re-enacted is real in the literal, narrowly empirical sense of the word.

Nevertheless, I have said that Miller's recent work includes a psychoanalytic orientation of a kind. It is shown in her deploying one form of the notion of the repetition compulsion, her respect for the arduousness of analytic psychotherapy, and the cathartic power of this one-to-one relationship to release the damage of the past. If my vocabulary is reminiscent of the language of early Freud, it is no accident, for Miller shares with Masson a commitment to the Freud of 'The Aetiology of Hysteria' – that is, to the period in which Freud attached to real seduction the power to traumatise.[17] By the same token, she adheres to the 'cathartic' model of therapy – that it is repressed memories of real events which create symptoms, or create the compulsion to repeat, and that when these are worked through the patient will cease to be ill.

This is not to say that Miller's descriptions lack poignancy or force. The reductive theorising of the two recent books – for her argument is essentially in the form of the cycle of deprivation, and she seems oblivious to the acknowledged difficulty with theories of that kind – is inseparable from an extraordinarily powerful indictment of a 'climate of cruelty' in child-rearing: from contradictory messages, deception and taboo topics, to outright physical violence and sexual abuse. Miller is also skilful on the 'denial of psychic reality' in children who can so little acknowledge their hatred of their parents that the hatred is split off and projected, and both parents and childhood are idealised. But to develop this argument she has had to make children into wholly good and innocent objects – as she puts it in her critique of the psychoanalytic theory of the drives, children are the mute receivers of adults' projections. Thus, paradoxically, although Alice Miller is such an opponent of the idealisation of childhood, she has ended up idealising the child.

Miller's theoretical approach to child sexual abuse could be described as asymmetrically psychoanalytic. I put it this way because she does make use, as I've said, of certain parts of a 'Freudian model'. The past is determinant of the present. The parents have the greatest influence on the child. There is repression. Repression cannot be undone without the assistance of psychotherapy. But what are the implications of her view of the small child, for example, for a picture of mental structure or a theory of sexuality? Put simply, there is no sense of agency on the part of the child, in the most general sense. The notion of 'infantile sexuality', in Miller's work, is a defensive (adult) construct projected *into* the child to enable the adult to be relieved of (his) guilt about having sexual impulses towards (his) child. Yet it is a one-way process. With the child as recipient, there is no stage at which the child becomes a project*ing* child; or where there is a pre-existing mental structure which enables the process of repression to take place, thus providing the basis for the compulsion to repeat in later life. In short, the child has no unconscious mental life; only the adult does.

Actual seduction and analytic practice

Masson expected his work to lead to a deep crisis of confidence within the analytic profession, but it did not. This is only partly because his scholarship was seen as so easy to fault that his credibility was undermined.[18] Analysts of more or less all schools have been concerned, since the inception of psychoanalysis, to establish general criteria for distinguishing between real and fantasied events,[19] and specifically to go on exploring the conceptual relationship between the seduction theory and the theory of infantile sexuality. This is not to say that the balance was always evenly maintained. John Bowlby, for one, believed that the Kleinian emphasis on unconscious phantasy masked the impact on children of real-life experiences of separation and loss, and he regarded children's subjective experiences as largely a matter of accurate perception of an external reality rather than as derivative of unconscious processes.[20]

But however divided the analytic schools have been about attributing causal or semantic significance to real or fantasied events in a general sense, none, to my knowledge, have been casual about the effects of real seduction. Take Anna Freud herself – ironically, in view of her later role in the Masson conflict – writing in the 1960s on child development:

> It is extremely unlikely that a child will outgrow his or her Oedipal fantasies in situations where father or mother, either consciously or unconsciously, elevates the child to a substitute sexual partner or commits real acts of seduction with him.[21]

Or, in stronger and more recent terms: 'Nothing could be more disturbing to a child than to have a parent attempt to realize these [Oedipal] wishes by attempting a real seduction.'[22] Hanly, by no means a maverick within analysis, went on to dispatch Masson, in the *International Journal of Psycho-Analysis*, in part for his distortion of the psychoanalytic view of the analyst's role. 'It would be painfully humiliating, confusing and profoundly detrimental to the progress of an analysis,' he wrote, 'if an analyst were to treat even a distorted memory of a real event as though it were a phantasy.'[23] For one can believe in the existence of unconscious fantasy – and the notion of infantile sexuality and its effects is an instance of such fantasy – without being committed to the view that real seductions do not take place.

But psychoanalysis, as well as being a theory of the mind (or of mental structure, or the psyche) is a clinical practice, and the status of real seductions, for that practice, is pathogenic, for its impact on the individual at the time, and for its subsequent place in the work of treatment. Winnicott's view reflects both aspects of this dynamic:

> The greatest difficulties [in therapy] come when there has been a seduction in the patient's childhood, in which case there must be experienced in the course of the treatment a delusion that the therapist is repeating seduction. Naturally, recovery depends on the undoing of this childhood seduction, which brought the child prematurely to a real, instead of an imaginary, sexual life, and spoiled the child's perquisite: unlimited play.[24]

Leaving aside for a moment the exquisitely Winnicottian emphasis on play as constitutive of a child's reality, these remarks strike me as representative of much of the analytic writing about real seduction. Childhood seduction is destructive because it is not appropriate to a child's sexual, physical and affective development, and it is the parents' task (or that of the child's carers if they are not the parents) to take responsibility for their own sexuality, and for getting their (adult) emotional needs met without using the child to do it.

But Winnicott's juxtaposition of 'real' and 'imaginary' takes the issue one step further, for it is a reminder that in psychoanalysis, the 'real' is always a paradox: it can be tangible or deeply intangible, observable or more purely internal. Most importantly, as Fraser's *In Search of a Past*, among other work, reveals, it is contingent upon the work of analysis itself.[25]

Let me take one clinical example, which shows what

was 'real' for one incest victim. It is taken from an article by an American analyst discussing issues of psychotherapy with hospitalised patients, including a young woman of twenty-four. The woman had had a sexual relationship with her father for ten years from the age of eleven, and was now hospitalised as a result of suicide attempts:

> I began to interpret to her that her self-mutilations and suicidal wishes could be understood as her attempt to punish herself for participation in the incestuous relationship with her father and to express her rage at him for crossing boundaries and taking advantage of her. She was perplexed at my line of thinking and explained to me that her father had made her feel very special and loved, in contrast to her mother, who she felt had rejected her. She went on to elaborate that she had become depressed and suicidal because her father had *stopped* his sexual relationship with her.[26] (author's italics)

It is taken for granted that the incestuous experience is transgressive and pathogenic. In a situation where the young woman is attacking *herself* – her aggression is introjected – the analyst's focus is on working through an unconscious compulsion to repeat, here in the form of repeated self-mutilations, at a time when part of the patient's conscious experience is of depression and deprivation. Indeed Winnicott's point about the necessary reliving of a seduction, within analysis, finds an echo both in Gabbard's description of the seductiveness *of* the patient towards hospital colleagues, and in a lecture on incest in the Freud Memorial series at University College London a couple of years ago, given by Brendan MacCarthy of the British Psycho-Analytical Society, an analyst who has worked with incest victims for many years.[27]

'Why do you want to give the woman five-times-a-week analysis,' I recall him describing one analytic colleague saying to another (both men) about a prospective patient, 'when her father's been fucking her every night for years?' That is, why couldn't the analyst 'leave her alone', why did he want to *repeat* the seduction, even if such a repetition were inevitable? There is thus a fine line, I think, between the arousal of narcissism or omnipotence on the part of the analyst (as is suggested by this example), and the space the analyst (or the analytic setting) offers for a sustained process of working through, not just of the pain from the past, but of what may have become a pattern of, for example, addictive relationships in the present – or no relationships at all.

Perhaps because it just rang true in an intuitive way, I have always remembered one other vignette from the same lecture: the incest patient who said to her analyst something like 'I had sex with my father for seven years, and it will be seven years before I can begin to get over it.' It is the notion of a process which cannot be forced and has its own tempo of resolution. It is only superficially akin to the cathartic as therapy, although it concerns damage at the level of the real event, for it eschews the notion of an immediate release of symptoms when a truth is realised (the patient is in no sense unaware of the real event in question).

One of the conclusions this leads me to is that analysts since Freud, far from blurring the distinction between real and fantasied events, have been *more* sure than Freud was himself of the destructive effects of sexual abuse. (Laplanche and Pontalis have provided what is probably the definitive account of Freud's uncertainties and attempted resolutions of his conceptual doubts on this score.[28]) It is true that they work at a different level and with a different vocabulary from the language of a feminist analysis of power. They do routinely speak of 'actual seduction', not, routinely, of rape/violence. Equally they speak of seduction *into* the fantasies of the parents;[29] seductive*ness* as a form of parental intrusion; and, in the words of a French analyst of, I would say, Lacanian persuasion and with an interest in etymology, of actual seduction as ending in psychic enslavement.[30] They speak in a way that Masson never does, for in Masson there is what I can only call fetishism of the event – that is, of the physical or external event. As Laplanche and Pontalis, among others, have pointed out, Freud's original theory distinguished between event and trauma.[31]

When Masson and Miller replace 'seduction' with 'assault' or 'rape' or 'violence', an important distinction of meaning is introduced. Seduction always implies suggestibility,[32] or, in Masson's words, 'some form of willing participation on the part of the child.'[33] To counter what they see as the invidious effect of the word 'seduction', feminist writers like the Australian Elizabeth Ward,[34] who have documented the experiences of incest survivors, engage in this language shift deliberately:

> Freud moved from an initial awareness of Father–Daughter rape, to create an entire superstructure of metaphysical concepts in order to protect himself (the Fathers) from having to face the truth about the rape of girl-children by their Fathers.[35]

We have returned to the problem of unconscious motivation, and thus of its description. Jane Gallop's formulation is apt, noting that 'as with all seductions, the question of complicity poses itself. The dichotomy active/passive is always equivocal in seduction, that is what distinguishes it from rape.'[36] For it is always provocative to speak of complicity when sexual abuse is discussed.

I am reminded of the conflict between Erin Pizzey and the Women's Aid Federation, some years ago, about the legitimacy of speaking of battered women's complicity in 'addictive' relationships with husbands and lovers.[37] Because children and their parents are in an unequal power relationship it seems doubly provocative to invoke the notion in matters of child sexual abuse.[38] In the words of Virginia, from Ward's *Father–Daughter Rape*:

> Now I understand it as a power thing: I was obviously totally powerless to repulse this person that I was completely reliant on at the same time . . . I can see, as an adult looking back, that a child is quite unable to make choices about that contradiction.[39]

In general I would say that the only way one could legitimately speak of complicity in such matters would be by describing it as unconscious, and as part of a most complex family dynamic. Take Gabbard's patient, who experienced her sexual relation with her father as in some way compensating for the absence of a relationship with her mother. It is almost a truism to say that the notion of a repetition compulsion makes sense only as an unconscious drive, for the repetition is so often of something psychically painful. Moreover, it is probably significant that the 'seductionists' in these debates about Freud do not seem to pay much attention to the later Freud, of *Beyond the Pleasure Principle*, in which the compulsion to repeat is posited as a cardinal attribute of mental life. In Miller the compulsion to repeat is a straightforward meting out to the next generation, a replication of one's past as a child. In analytic writing in the tradition of *Beyond the Pleasure Principle*, the compulsion to repeat is a more nuanced form of self-destruction or destruction of the other.

I said earlier that Masson's view involved a caricature. 'That is the worst thing that analysis has left the world,' he said in conversation with Janet Malcolm: 'the notion that there is no reality, that there are only individual experiences of it.'[40] It is a caricature because it inscribes a view which only the most solipsistic, relativist analyst could hold – and indeed it is a view which not many analysts show signs of holding. More common is the view that there is a reality out there, but the analyst's task is to enable the patient to understand how she or he is construing and misconstruing it, constructing it in such a way as to enact a role, such as that of victim, that the patient most wants to be free of but feels in thrall to. When I looked through the past few years' analytic journals to get a sense of the discussion of childhood seduction and its effects, I found little evidence to support Masson's view of a calculated indifference to the issue. It goes some way to explaining why analysts have on the whole appeared untroubled about the possible effect of his work on their practice, professional and intellectual.

2

Melanie Klein and the questions of feminism

I suspect that when the name of Melanie Klein comes to many women's minds, their first association is to a complex web of sensation. Loosely, the stress is on 'the mother and the infant'. What is it to be a mother? What is it to receive a mother's love? What is it to be newborn and so utterly dependent, for survival, on feeding and being cared for by others? What is it to be 'before speech'? What is it to register, dimly perhaps, the existence of another who has claims on the mother? What is it to *wait* for food? Those who are already familiar with Melanie Klein's writing will know that my list of questions is not a random one. Each of them bears on a concern of Klein's, and in this chapter I hope to indicate some of the terms of the debate, for British feminism, around Klein's work. I also want to provide a preface to Chapter 3, which takes up Klein from another perspective – that of her biographer, Phyllis Grosskurth.

But I want to begin by stressing that the questions that have traditionally been asked of Klein's work have been asked within the clinical psychoanalytic community. There was a psychoanalytic critique of Klein long before there was a feminist engagement with her. For Klein assumed the existence of the unconscious and of a rudimentary ego from birth; she assumed the existence of unconscious phantasy from birth. She believed that knowledge of the vagina and of the mother's womb was unconscious and innate. Thus there have always been questions about the validity of her model of the psyche; questions about whether tiny babies are able to make the sophisticated mental moves that she posits. It is also a commonplace of criticism from within psychoanalysis that her theoretical model can be confusing, and her grasp of the rules of logic tenuous. And yet there is no doubting the power and force of her work. Lacan's objections to her clinical technique, for example, which are to be found in the early *Seminar* (and spring from his theoretical critique of her work on the ego),[1] did not preclude his respect for her 'precious' work. So where does the work of Melanie Klein, so central to the evolution of clinical psychoanalysis in Britain, belong in feminism's trajectory?

As is well known, the gradual shift from a feminist affirmation of sisterhood and the collectivity of women to the more recent concern with difference – and the representation of difference – has seen both a variety of psychoanalytic theorisations of women and the 'feminine', and a move into individual psychoanalysis and psychotherapy.[2] How might we think about such a development, and how might we place Klein's work within it? In the first place, and simplifying what are extraordinarily complex matters, I would say that the move from a 'Lacanian feminism' to a 'concern with Klein' (a move in which there are many subgroups of themes) represents a shifting locus of perspective: not just from Oedipal to pre-Oedipal, as it is so often termed, but from the constitution *of* the subject to the subject's constitution *of* its 'world'. A rough chronology might look something like this. Initially one sees feminism's engagement with theories of patriarchy and with Lévi-Strauss's and Lacan's contributions to an understanding of how kinship structures are internalised; it is a concern with the oppression of women as a distinct social group, and with the 'negative entry into culture'.[3] Then there is a rush of works on mothers and daughters, and what we know as the 'mothering debate' within feminism: a project of understanding the lived experience of women; from a concern with 'the chains that bind' to a focus on attachment and nurturance, to the 'primary' relationship of mother and infant; a concern to theorise the difference between the mothering of girls and the mothering of boys. In the work of Dorothy Dinnerstein there is an important use of Klein herself;[4] in Nancy Chodorow an overview of the Kleinian and non-Kleinian object-relations traditions.[5] Then, at the level of clinical practice and roughly paralleling these texts and their influence, there has been the emergence and consolidation of the Women's Therapy Centre in London, with its own, eclectic intervention in the question of the relationship between the unconscious and the external world, between 'inner' and 'outer'; an intervention in which the place of Klein has been taken seriously though not uncritically.[6] Now – or so it feels – there is an intensification of cultural and feminist interest in the work of Klein herself;[7] although it could be noted that this is happening at a time when Kleinian clinical practice is in part 'post-Kleinian', significantly concerned with the work of Bion, Meltzer and, also, with the implications of Winnicott's rather different mode of thought.

These shifts within feminism have in part been reactive: at each stage the felt impasses or gaps within one approach have led, as it were organically, to an engagement with a different body of work. From verbal to pre-verbal; from Oedipal to pre-Oedipal; from lack (in Lacan, the phallus as privileged signifier) to plenitude (in Klein, the mother of infancy who is the source of all good). For example, it seems to me that the 'turn to Klein' can be seen to be related to at least three strands of thought: one, the sense of difficulty around the question of the cultural or biological valorisation of the phallus; along with a subjective perplexity at the consequences of the location of the 'place' of language and power in the culture as male; and the growing awareness that Britain had its own, though importantly marginalised, psychoanalytic tradition, very different from the European 'rationalist' tradition of Lacan.[8] But this movement of thought remains dialectical, to-and-fro; Juliet Mitchell and Vivien Bar have reinstated the commentary on Klein from a Lacanian perspective and remind us that all theorisations within psychoanalysis set up their own counterpoint.[9]

Within this setting I want to draw a contrast between the feminism of the mothering debate and the current concern with Klein. The mothering debate has had two central and inseparable concerns: the nature of the mother–daughter bond, and the possibility of change within and, most importantly, *for* women as mothers and as social beings. Klein's work, at its most profound, is a model of the psyche and its contents. It is not an account of 'being' a child, 'being' a mother; or of being in a mother–infant couple in the way that Winnicott describes it; the adult world is viewed through the eyes of an infant/child, whose perception is initially of 'parts' of bodies, 'parts' of relationships and only in time of 'whole objects'. Thus the more recent involvement with Klein's work is, of necessity, an engagement with the world of an infant, as yet unspeaking, faced with a mother who can nourish or withhold. By splitting the (feeding) object, the baby has, in a sense, 'created' it, though defensively.[10] These early responses to the feeding situation, based as they are in Klein's thought on the postulated innate capacity to oppose 'good' (feeding breast) and 'bad' (depriving breast), provide the terrain for all subsequent taking-in, all internalisation. Very roughly, the infant is (in this sense only) the agent of her own destiny. What Lacan might call the 'punching-in of words'[11] is, for Klein, subverted by an infinitely earlier, determining dynamic of (infantile) projection and introjection.

This stress on the determinative power of the earliest of experiences is also an account of the possibility and limits of internal, individual change. For it presupposes that our perception of the world[12] is always and irreducibly inflected by unconscious phantasy; but, by the same token, it becomes an account of the way in which change in the 'inner' world lays the basis for a more benign perception of the external world – and thus, by extension, for the attainment of one's goals in that external world. These goals could, in principle, be socially egalitarian, as the long tradition of Kleinian public sector work, focused largely on the Tavistock Clinic in London, attests.[13] But Klein's own theories, despite her early critique of phallocentrism in Freud, were in no sense the product of an attempt to marry psychoanalysis with feminism, as the 'mothering' writers of the 1970s and 1980s have done, or as an analyst like Klein's contemporary Karen Horney did, up to a point, in the 1920s.[14]

Klein wishes rather to take as her object of study only 'what is', and sees 'what is' as an intrapsychic world of primitive emotion, in which the earliest relation to the mother calls up a lifelong yearning for an understanding without words. Here we see one of Klein's attractions for feminism: the great primacy of the mother as a powerful force within the personality, and alongside this her status as a nodal point for debate around the determining character of the symbolic order of language. But Klein always did more than idealise primitive emotion, or this early pre-verbal relation between mother and infant. At the time of her death, she was working on a paper on the 'sense of loneliness' in both children and adults, which, by its status *as* a last paper, acts as a kind of farewell. It is a poignant statement of every individual's aloneness in the world, a psychic loneliness born of the recognition that full, permanent integration of all the parts of one's psyche is unattainable:

> Some polarity between the life and death instincts always persists and remains the deepest source of

> conflict . . . the pain which accompanies processes of integration also contributes to loneliness. For it means facing one's destructive impulses and hated parts of the self, which at times appear uncontrollable and which therefore endanger the good object.[15]

These, then, are some of the givens of Klein's theoretical model in its maturity: the positing of a continuous interplay of (unconscious) mental processes; the significance of the subject's destructive feelings, the power of envy and jealousy, of persecutory anxiety, on the one hand; and the notion of the good inner and outer object, to whom reparation can be made and gratitude expressed, on the other.

'On the Sense of Loneliness', a short, incomplete paper, exemplifies all that is compelling about Klein's work. She had a great capacity to cut through conventional representations of childhood to a sadness, and of course at times more serious disturbance, within the youngest of children. In 1927 she wrote of the 'immeasurable suffering' of small children,[16] and her empathic solidarity with what one might call the child's life instinct – what may also be termed his or her capacity for insight – runs through her writing. And yet, as I said earlier, Klein also embodies a view of the innateness of knowledge;[17] of what in the next chapter I call the innateness of the darkest emotions; and of the 'constitutional factors' at work in every newborn which could seem, on the face of it, to refuse the most basic environmentalism.[18] It is hard to know how to work within such a texture of thought, especially when the focus is on such very early experience.

In an early discussion of psychoanalytic theorisations of the family, Barrett and McIntosh took their distance from this 'biological' dimension of Klein, while acknowledging the power of the Kleinian and object-relations tradition of thinking about nurturance and attachment.[19] They took from this tradition its emphasis on the 'caring' dimension of mothering as a form of relationship not usually valorised on the Left or in feminism in discussion of the family.[20] It seems to me, however, that the challenge of Klein is not that she presents us with a view of a powerful maternal role and a valorisation *of* that role. This brings me back to my (retrospective) concern with the concept of sisterhood, with its celebration of identity; implicit denial, at times, of generational difference; and commitment to positive identification with the 'other' – be it individual (other) women, or women as a group. For the world of the infant that Klein describes is a world of innate, envious attack *on* the mother by the child, girl or boy; but, by the same token, a world in which the innate capacity for love is able to harness the destructiveness of instinctual life. A world in which good things are not, at the outset, 'only' cherished, but sadistically and enviously attacked, albeit in unconscious phantasy. Klein's infant is, in this sense, in the grip of a dystopian fantasy. And as such, if one finds her portrait of infancy persuasive, and believes, with her, that the infant world is retained throughout adult life, then such a representation of the early months of life will have unavoidable repercussions for one's view of group processes, family life, political identifications and social organisation. And it is important always to remember that this is not an account of the impulse to destroy that which is bad in the external world (although Kleinian thought in no sense precludes doing so), but that which is *good*. That is the disquieting feature of Klein. Among other things, it led to disquiet within the British Psycho-Analytical Society when she introduced 'Envy and Gratitude' in 1957.[21]

It is hard to know how one would start to integrate such a perspective on psychic processes with the more 'familiar' projects of feminist commitment, or with a vocabulary of gendered subjectivity involving issues of passivity or deference. It is one thing to de-idealise women. It is another to say that life begins in sadism and paranoia, innate forces as powerful as love. Even more fundamentally, there is the very question of 'gendered subjectivity' itself, which, as I have mentioned, exists for Klein from birth; and the notion of a developmental sequence which finds its echo again and again in the structures of adult life. The centrality of these questions lies at the heart of the Lacanian critique of Klein and the object-relations tradition. This is at times a critique of the way in which Klein is seen as departing from Freud's view of psychic meaning as a retrospective construction, at times a set of questions about how to read the death drive: whether, with Klein, it connotes aggression or, rather, conservatism, as in Freud.[22] Then there is the question of how we wish to think about psychic structure; about the formation of the subject, of the unconscious. For Lacan the unconscious is set up by a refusal (at the level of forbidden wishes, organised through the law of the father). For Freud, writes Mitchell, the object is a lost object; for Klein the objects are, in essence, taken for what they are, biologically and socially.[23] Sexual difference, then, ceases to be constituted; not a representation, but a given of biology.

The resolution of such issues will not, I think, be settled by an appeal to a 'pure' or 'true' psychoanalytic model of the psyche and its effects, for psychoanalysis is not a unitary object. Its foundations are newly in question, and at the level of, among others, both Lacan and Klein.[24] The question, for feminism, of femininity, of the mother and of mothering, will be settled at another level: what does feminism want from psychoanalysis? What representations (or experiences) of the female subject do we wish to theorise? I would suggest that Klein, for all the difficulties of her work, offers an account of our primitive mental states (however we might develop it) which allows us to maintain that break from the narrowly empirical so beautifully identified as psychoanalysis's radicalism by Jacqueline Rose in her seminal 'Femininity and Its Discontents'.[25] To track back to Klein's quiet observation in 1927:

What we learn about the child and the adult through psychoanalysis shows that all the sufferings of later life are for the most part repetitions of . . . early ones, and that every child in the first years of its life goes through an immeasurable degree of suffering. It is not to be denied that appearances speak against these statements.[26]

3

Unconscious explanations

> Bion states . . . what I have been trying to state for two and a half decades but against the terrific opposition of Melanie.
>
> D.W. Winnicott to John Wisdom, 1964[1]

I am not sure why I find Winnicott's fierceness so evocative for thinking through issues raised by Phyllis Grosskurth's biography of Melanie Klein. I suspect it has to do with the sense it gives of Klein's force, power, sheer capacity to impinge, dominate, elicit strong feelings – protective, hostile, loyal – in those around her. For although Grosskurth interviewed many analysts in the course of her research for the book, the most haunting description of Klein in it remains a diary entry of Virginia Woolf's, which she reproduces:

> a woman of character & force some submerged – how shall I say? – not craft, but subtlety; something working underground. A pull, a twist, like an undertow: menacing. A bluff grey-haired lady, with large bright imaginative eyes.[2]

'A pull, a twist, like an undertow: menacing': Grosskurth gives us a woman whose *Psychoanalysis of Children*, published in 1932,[3] so excited Winnicott that he reread it as soon as he finished it for the first time; whose clinical effectiveness was so striking that it won over a sceptical visiting psychiatrist; who was remembered as dowdy by one, beautifully dressed by another; dogmatic by one, receptive by another; who appears to have demanded unquestioning loyalty from colleagues at the same time as she could inspire a sense of 'wonderment' in them with her insight into children's thoughts and feelings; who had difficulties with motherhood, but is warmly remembered as a grandmother.

If this is the quality of the person, then Klein calls for a biographer who can do justice to the complexity of her ideas without reducing her character to the memories of others, or to the wild analysis of motive.[4] *Melanie Klein: Her World and Her Work* is an elusive, difficult biography to review, for it presents a series of paradoxes – a study of one of the most historically significant psychoanalysts in Britain to date, written in a style that to my mind combines inappropriately deep interpretation of unconscious motivation and pellucid clarity about events reconstructed from archival material; an ostensibly 'factual' narrative – or rather, a narrative based in large part on the empirical data of reports, minutes of meetings, publications – of the life of a woman whose contribution to psychoanalysis is centrally identified with the belief that 'external' and 'internal' realities are in a constant state of interplay; an account which argues for a close relationship between the practices of biography and of clinical analysis. 'Displacement', 'condensation', 'evasion': these are the processes Grosskurth sees at work in family correspondence, and they become the terms through which she sees the biographer constructing meaning or the shape or personality within a fabric of relationships. It is a view of biography which goes beyond an impressionistic sense of kinship with clinical psychoanalysis, to the stronger claim for something structurally very close to it. Implicitly, then – for Grosskurth does not address issues of method in any depth – the book also raises the issue of the history of psychoanalysis,[5] and of how one might reconstruct a psychoanalyst's life.

I have said that Grosskurth does not address issues of method, but this may be too strong. She does, at the outset, identify the provisional nature of the biography, the provisional nature of psychoanalytic knowledge. The biography is 'not definitive', it is an 'approximate composite'; each of us presents 'multiple personae' in our commerce with others. On the other hand, since Grosskurth takes it as her aim to present a more balanced view of a professional woman, to evaluate the connection between the woman and her work, how does she go about doing this? In part by eliding distinctions between biography and writing, reading off Klein's inner state at different times from her theoretical writings; in part by inferring the nature of Klein's character from discrepancies between her manuscript 'Autobiography' (written late in life) and early family letters; in part by respecting what she describes as 'the total silence surrounding certain episodes of Klein's life' and focusing on the evolution of the British Psycho-Analytical Society between 1925 and 1960 and the part Klein played in it.

Melanie Klein was born Melanie Reizes in 1882 in Vienna, the fourth and youngest child of a Polish father and Slovak mother. Her father was a doctor who never quite achieved the professional success he sought, and Klein's early years saw the family's efforts to make ends meet. As a young girl she seems to have had both ambition and self-confidence (Grosskurth invokes Klein's description of herself as a child – 'I absolutely was not shy' – as a leitmotif of character throughout the book).[6] However, her marriage in 1903 to a chemical engineer, Arthur Klein, followed by the birth of three children and a series of moves within central Europe as her husband found work with different companies, put paid to her hopes of studying medicine and qualifying as a psychiatrist.

By the time Melanie Reizes married, two of her siblings, to whom she had been very close, had died. Her marriage was unhappy, and she became deeply depressed within it; she was to remain susceptible to grief and depression throughout her life. In 1914, when the Kleins were living in Budapest, she had her first encounter with psychoanalysis when she read one of Freud's papers and, largely for personal reasons, went into analysis with Sandor Ferenczi. Five years later she became a member of the Budapest Psychoanalytic Society and within a few years, now living in Berlin and separated from her husband, was dedicating herself to what became a lifetime's work.

Klein's work with children, encouraged by her second analyst, Karl Abraham, came to the notice of British psychoanalysts in 1924 via Alix Strachey, and she was invited to lecture in London. Within three years she had become a full member of the British Psycho-Analytical Society, having decided to make England her home. She had already achieved a position of eminence within the British Society when European analysts began to emigrate to England and the United States in the 1930s, and it was the arrival of the Freud family in London in 1938 which laid the basis for conflicts between Klein and Anna Freud, and their respective groupings, which threatened to split the Society.

Simplifying somewhat, Melanie Klein had evolved a view and technique of child analysis which differed in important respects from Anna Freud's, and entailed theoretical differences over infantile mental life also. But the conflict was as much – or perhaps was at a deeper level – about power, the inheritance of Freud's mantle, and the ownership of a training and a tradition as it was about the resolution of intellectual or technical difference. Between 1942 and 1944 there took place a series of 'Controversial Discussions'[7] in which the theoretical issues were set out – among others, the relationship between the concept of 'instinct' and of 'phantasy', the place of mental structure in Klein's thought, and the implications of interpreting a child's (unconscious) anxiety at the outset of treatment rather than the defences a disturbed child might make use of in his or her relationships. What resolution there was took the form of an agreement, in outline still in operation today, to organise the training in such a way that analysts of the different schools would teach according to those views, but that candidates should come in contact with all views within the Society (for instance in the personal supervision of their clinical cases).

Once Klein and her colleagues were free from the pain and rancour of the Discussions, there was a renewed opportunity for work, and Klein remained active within the Society and in her own practice, latterly more as a writer and a supervisor of colleagues' work, until her death in 1960. The 1950s saw the publication of *Envy and Gratitude*, still probably her most controversial work, and in many ways the strongest formulation of what one might call her view of the *innateness* of some of the darkest emotions. A year after her death came *Narrative of a Child Analysis*, an intensely detailed exposition of her wartime analysis of a nine-year-old boy. Klein had always planned to write the case up as a way of exemplifying her approach, weaving into the narrative a commentary on her mature views, especially on the nature of the transference and on the analysis of symbolism in work with a child;[8] she was working on the proofs during her last illness.

Taken in the round, the innovations in Melanie Klein's contribution to psychoanalysis could be seen as threefold. She believed that the vicissitudes of the earliest, feeding relationship – that is, infant–mother – set the stage for the way the child and, later, the adult responded to/made sense of/literally 'took in' all subsequent experience. She believed that unconscious phantasy began at birth, and that a relationship with an (external) object began then too. She believed that the infant was born with innate capacities for love and hate, and that the nature of the resolution of its phantasised destruction of others (primarily the mother) was the motor of its development. These views implied departures from the classical privileging of, respectively, the Oedipal triangle; the notion of a phase of primary narcissism, in which the infant is not, at the outset of life, thought to be in a relation with others; and of a view of development in which the libido is organised in successive stages (oral, anal, phallic, genital).[9] They were bound to bring her into conflict with the Viennese.

Clinically Klein's work stemmed from the analysis of very young, speaking children (although one or two were what might now be called autistic), and thus of primitive states of mind; it laid the basis for analytic work with psychotics, previously thought unanalysable. In addition, and undoubtedly brought into focus by her own repeated experiences of loss (after her divorce, a severe disappointment in a love relationship with a married man; the death of one of her adult sons in a mountaineering accident; and, perhaps most arduous of all, a long estrangement from her daughter, also an analyst, who had become one of her most hostile opponents in the British Society) she wrote a series of deeply original papers on mourning, manic depression, guilt, reparation, anxiety and loneliness. Here she developed her thinking about an 'inner world' of objects, 'part objects', 'whole objects': unconscious mental representations of significant others, now persecutory or persecuted, now benign. It was this imaginative focus on the inner world which proved so enabling for later developments in the British object-relations school of psychoanalysis.

Phyllis Grosskurth creates her Klein in a variety of ways. The narrative proper begins with a full description of family life, and Klein's childhood and marriage, reconstructed from early family correspondence, as well as what is known about Klein's first encounter with psychoanalysis. Her early work with children, and the atmosphere of the early psychoanalytic societies in Budapest and Berlin, are explored in some depth, and with sensitivity. Once Klein enters the world of British psychoanalysis, and particularly when the conflicts in the Society spill out in the open, there is an enormous quantity of material – memoirs, interviews, records of meetings, and so on – which Grosskurth organises exceptionally well. The third and last part of the book – with Klein as an older woman, perceived through the eyes of a new generation of analysts, and with a new phase in the Society's history, including the emergence of the Independent (neither Kleinian nor Anna Freudian) group – is largely refracted through the memories of family, friends, colleagues, and clinicians who chose not to be associated with her. Here the book is invaluable as a work of reference, but the sense of a dynamic is absent, and the narrative is at its most fragmented.[10]

My difficulties with *Melanie Klein* concern the way in which Grosskurth uses the evidence of memoir or memory, probes motivation, writes about the unconscious. So let me begin with the book's strengths. Grosskurth sustains the narrative well for long stretches with what I would call a powerfully descriptive ordinary language. There is a succinct, crisp description of Klein and Alix Strachey's social life in Berlin: 'The two incongruous companions, one tall, angular and Bloomsbury, the other squat, Jewish, and *déclassée*, must have made a curious pair.' There is Klein's 'heavily accented voice', her 'rushed, breathless delivery'. Grosskurth has a persuasive grasp of the complex role, often devious, played by Ernest Jones in the British Society – promoting and at the same time undermining Klein's position within it. She writes memorably of the dynamic between Jones and Freud – 'Their relationship was always to be one of wary fencing' – detecting 'cunning flattery' in one of Jones's letters to Freud. She keeps ahead of the protagonists in the tactical ins and outs of the Controversial Discussions, conscious of the manoeuvrings on both sides.[11]

Also there is an attractively straightforward quality of

exploration when Grosskurth speaks in her own voice. In the book she is able definitively to establish that one of Klein's first child patients, 'Fritz', was actually her son Erich disguised: 'Several commentators have already detected the parallels, yet when I mentioned the identity of Fritz-Erich to a number of English Kleinians, they expressed shock and dismay.'[12] She achieves the same even, gently moving tone when reporting her meetings with Richard (the boy in the *Narrative*), now in his fifties:

> I myself met Richard through entirely fortuitous circumstances . . . At first I assumed I had made an awful mistake. Then I had a sudden inspiration. 'Do you remember the bus conductress?' 'Do I indeed!' and he then imitated her voice . . . he had no idea that he was the subject of a book . . . Quite simply, his life does not touch the analytic world at any point.[13]

It may be no accident that Grosskurth is at her most effective when, as here, she deploys an 'ordinary language' of emotion, of people's impact on one another in social situations.[14] None of it is superficial, but nor is it an attempt at deep interpretation. It is when she tries to work as a clinician *might* that the book, to my mind, is least satisfying, and gets into most difficulty.

The problem begins with the status of Melanie Klein's 'Autobiography'. The whole book is in a sense framed by an initial discussion of it, and the way in which Grosskurth reads the Autobiography is typical of her uncritical and somewhat moralising use of psychoanalytic theory. Grosskurth describes the Autobiography, written during the last seven years of Klein's life and for years in the possession of the Melanie Klein Trust, as an official record of Klein's life, as 'cautious . . . ingenuous, and evasive'. In the light of the discovery of a large store of early family letters in a loft in 1983, Grosskurth says, new interpretations of the Autobiography can be made.

For Grosskurth, however, the Autobiography is treated as a fiction, so that when she begins to work out her view of the relationship between the Autobiography and the early letters, 'idealisation' and 'truth' are her central terms, implying that there *is* an unproblematic level of truth in one form of written material. Among the primary sources at the biographer's disposal, one group is bound to hold a 'deeper' truth, and it involves Grosskurth in a hierarchy of evaluations. Not because she sees the family correspondence as uncomplicated, but because she has, nevertheless, identified it as such a locus of truth. From this starting point she rather briskly dispatches what to her seem like unjustified grievances in the Autobiography ('far from being helpless and neglected, [Klein] was a beautiful Jewish princess'), only to follow an impatient remark of her own with the impulse to put Klein back on a pedestal because of her achievement in the culture of psychoanalysis as a whole.[15]

More seriously: even if Grosskurth is right, and Klein's memory of herself as a child and of her mother Libussa is a positive idealisation, it doesn't rule out the possibility that the early letters are themselves a complex form of fiction.[16] Or, looked at differently, it surprises me that a biographer as Kleinian as Grosskurth sets out to be doesn't consider the possibility that Klein precisely *did* make reparation to the (internal) Libussa during her adult life, and that the rather kind portrait Klein gives of her in the Autobiography (a 'gentle and unassuming' mother) is more psychically authentic than Grosskurth allows. That is, Klein would not only be subject to the psychical processes she herself theorises – and here Grosskurth fails to pick up on the rather obvious signs of denial and positive idealisation in the heart-rending correspondence with her married lover, whom Klein continually draws back from upbraiding – but her mental life could itself exemplify the processes of internal movement that such a genuine reparation would suggest.

Other things strike one about the way in which Grosskurth deploys the technical vocabulary of psychoanalysis to write about personalities. One is that it is strangely generalised, another that it then goes in very deep. On the first, and in line with her view of it as a fiction, she sees the Autobiography as the creation of a 'family romance', in which Klein then becomes fully enmeshed. Here the family romance is generalised out from being an (unconscious) fantasy of royal or noble birth, to a looser heuristic device – an unmasking device – for discrepancies between facts and Klein's picture of them. To take one example only: from the evidence presented in the book, it looks to me as though Klein wasn't deluded about her parental background in this rather specific way, but she did, seemingly, 'obliterate' the fact that her uncle provided financial support for the family's purchase of a house in Vienna when she was a little girl. Grosskurth attaches to this (to my mind) rather trivial amnesia the status of an organising fantasy; and such an approach to fantasy becomes a central interpretative device for the book as a whole.[17]

The issue is one of depth, to take up the point suggested above: the depth of a biographer's claim. It comes out even more forcefully in Grosskurth's presentation of the family background, which I find almost wholly unconvincing at the level of interpretation of unconscious motive. In Grosskurth's view, all the family members are unconsciously intent on causing each other harm as much of the time as possible: the family is 'humid, symbiotic', 'riddled with guilt, envy and occasionally explosive rages'.[18] Unless Grosskurth had access to sources other than those given in the book, one can go only by the gap between the letters themselves and the interpretation put on them. Libussa, for example, writes in the egocentric style of a rather controlling mother, but she comes across as mixed in her qualities, not as motivated with the malign intent consistently ascribed to her. There is a possibility,

I think, that Grosskurth *infers* malign intent from the chronic nature of Melanie Klein's depressions, but that is a different matter, and she doesn't address it directly. There are, admittedly, occasions where Grosskurth relies on 'could have felt', 'might have felt' to put unconscious states of mind into words, but there are probably as many definitive pronouncements about the unconscious of the protagonists as there are any other.

Reviewers of the biography are divided on Grosskurth's treatment of the family dynamic; the most perceptive readings of the book's representation of motivation are by the two main Kleinian reviewers, Hanna Segal in the *Sunday Times* and Edna O'Shaughnessy in the *International Review of Psycho-Analysis*, and they are the most critical of Grosskurth's method.[19] O'Shaughnessy, for one, rightly poses the question: how can Grosskurth know that Klein, on a specific occasion in her adult relationship with her sister, unconsciously 'retained the envy of a powerless baby sister'?[20] For despite this extensive reliance on a Kleinian language, psychoanalysis as such is never discussed in a reflective way, or problematised, and it makes for a book in which the deepest level of interpretation is presented as though it were the most self-evident.

In representing Klein as 'a woman with a mission', Grosskurth's approach recalls that of Ronald Clark, whose widely publicised, mainstream biography of Freud was, at least in part, organised around Freud's sense of himself as heroic Conquistador.[21] It may be that when a biographer closes the distance between the individual and his or her professional discipline to the extent that Grosskurth does (and as Clark before her did, I think), the ideas themselves become extensions of the subject. Here the concept of the unconscious itself is personified as a 'seductive lure', and Klein's papers are identified, in the main, with Klein's own inner turbulence, and rather inconsistently related to an existing literature. Sometimes – and especially in the Controversial Discussions – Grosskurth's presentation of the debate over ideas is lucid. Sometimes – and usually on motive and meaning – it is reductive, and here her acuity is mixed.

The interpretation of theoretically innovative work is confined to the immediately familial. Or rather, there is initially the discretion of a meticulous biographer: 'in the absence of documentary evidence, everything about [the death of her son] Hans remains disturbingly shadowy', immediately undercut by a speculative use of part of Klein's classic paper on the psychogenesis of manic-depressive states. Grosskurth reads off from it not just thoughts about Hans's possible suicide (his death having been considered a suicide on occasion), but about Klein's unconscious at the time: 'Such a passage would suggest that Klein in her unconscious might have suspected that Hans could have committed suicide, consciously or unconsciously.'[22] Grosskurth summarises the paper well, but almost wholly without considering what it was that was so intellectually productive within the field about this work on the inner world. It is a strange kind of closure, locating the interpretation of ideas so powerfully at the level of an individual unconscious.

This absence of an evaluation by Grosskurth herself of Klein's intellectual contribution is resolved, at the level of the biography, by the use of interview material, and especially in the last chapters on the post-war world. Here Grosskurth tries to do something with the idea of 'multiple personae' that she mentions at the outset of the book, but it isn't developed, at least not in her own words. Sometimes it is in the recollections of her interviewees, but she usually doesn't comment, or try to gather any of these very disparate threads together. If there are issues of the validity of psychoanalytic work, then they speak only in the voice of an interviewee. Indeed, throughout the book, legitimate issues bearing on the status of the theory make fleeting appearances, but always connected to individuals.

Nor does Grosskurth evoke anything of the quality of speech of her interlocutors – their tone, hesitations, emphases – so that one lacks the sense of a personal encounter.[23] Nor does she seem to know what to do with discrepancies of memory when she talks to Klein's former patients, or when colleagues remember Klein in radically different ways, and in these cases she simply notes the differences. But she does on occasion operate a form of textual splitting. For she has an intermittent tendency to use footnotes when she wants to draw a distinction between fact and fantasy. Footnotes are for refutations of 'fact' mentioned in the text, and may take the form: 'This was sheer fantasy on the part of X.' It isn't clear to me why these could not have been worked into the narrative as part of a stronger authorial voice for the text as a whole.

To my mind, this shifting, discontinuous pattern of idealisation and de-idealisation, now in Grosskurth's voice, now in another's, is what is weakest in the book. Klein calls for a more assured, more *stable* critical presence at the level of the ideas. The calibre of Klein's work – her sharpness of observation, tactical skill, precision of language in her professional correspondence, stamina – is vividly present. The evolution of the French translation of *The Psychoanalysis of Children* is an example: this extract from Klein's correspondence with the French translators of the work clearly shows her mastery of her concepts and her understanding of a linguistic difference that was significant to her:

> I think that the 'inside' is not correctly translated by 'ventre'. In the [German] original I have not chosen the word corresponding to 'belly' or 'ventre' because it does not reproduce the child's feeling that there is something within the mother's body which, although in some places it refers to inner organs, in the phantastic sense does not – it is just an inside.[24]

Grosskurth may have been right to begin her biography of Melanie Klein with the view that, for a large part of her life, the woman and her work were indistinguishable. But she has followed through this view, as I have tried to show, by responding to Klein's papers as though they were effectively *only* autobiographical texts, interpreting them as signifiers of inner, usually unconscious, conflict. Somewhere here is a larger, more general issue about the nature of psychoanalytic theory: its susceptibility to analysis in its own terms, its own language. It was a theme the Kleinian analyst Susan Isaacs took up with disarming honesty in her correspondence with Melanie Klein, which Grosskurth reproduces in the biography. It illustrates the difficulty that existed – and that Isaacs could see existed – in disentangling the substantive issues that divided one group of analysts from another, on the one hand, from issues of 'unresolved transference', or the desire to possess and display knowledge, on the other. Even so, although Grosskurth is in general right to remember that, speaking (clinically) psychoanalytically, 'whether something happened is immaterial; the important thing is that Melanie Klein believed it had', I think it leads her into many kinds of confusion when she is constructing a narrative involving a central character and many subsidiary characters. It involves a kind of speculative relativism of the unconscious. 'Melanie Klein was an embodiment of her own later theories,' Grosskurth writes. 'The world is not an objective reality, but a phantasmagoria peopled with our own fears and desires.' Kleinian theory does not, I think, go so far as to claim that the *world* is not an objective reality; but that subjectivity is a special form of reality, always invested with phantasy. The terms of its theorisation – necessarily involving a concept of the unconscious – may contribute to the construction of a biographical or conceptual narrative, but may well not be appropriate if used as a fundamental interpretative device.

4

Real events revisited

My title refers back to the starting point of Chapter 1, and the sense I have, on looking back to it, of a debate that is 'besieged' by impingements from the outside. Consequently it suggests a perhaps singular notion of the psychoanalytic, and one that needs complexifying. Here, then, I want to begin with a shift to the analytic. In the initial debate Freud's seduction theory was under the microscope, in the wake of a new climate of opinion, of reporting and of debate. Now I want chiefly to look at recent discussions within the psychoanalytic field itself about 'events'. Although these bear on sexual abuse they are not coterminous with it – a point sometimes overlooked – for they inherit a long tradition of theorising trauma. And because thinking about what constitutes trauma implies thinking about sexual abuse in relation *to* the psychoanalytic, it might be more accurate to pose a question about sexual abuse as a special case of the 'traumatic event'. This raises a further point: what if some experiences are actually unassimilable? In this chapter I explore the question using a variety of psychoanalytic maps, interwoven with recent feminist-therapeutic writing on the experience of incest and the question of dissociation.

In Chapter 1 I noted that Jeffrey Masson did not address the issue of how much or how little, at the level of mental structure, depended on the actuality or fantasy of a particular kind of experience. For Masson, only the 'external' event was the 'real'. Thus Masson, I argued, was confusingly identifying 'real memory' solely with 'the event', that is, the external event, observable and describable by others. I want to bring these considerations forward in time. When I look back on Chapter 1 I now see such a stress on the actuality of sexual abuse, and on the existence of psychoanalytic respect for the pathogenic effect of real seduction, that what is left out is the very uncertainty that attaches to these questions clinically; and the question of theorising the processes that may be at work psychically in organising experiences over time. Here the vocabulary of repression, dissociation and the more recent notion of the enigmatic signifier become key terms. We have (depending on one's theoretical starting point) a series of binaries, which could include event/trauma; real/fantasy; real/transference; internal/external; infantile sexuality/adult symbolic. There is both a spatial and a temporal quality to these binaries.

To return to first principles, the classical theory of psychoanalysis tells us that deferred action, 'afterwardsness', following Laplanche's formulation, is what makes an event traumatic.[1] As Laplanche and Pontalis pointed out, Freud distinguished between event and trauma.[2] (Masson, by contrast, fetishises the event itself.) The distinction is seen clearly in 'The Aetiology of Hysteria',[3] the 1896 paper most usually associated with Freud's stress on the external event as causative, and, as we have seen, the paper favoured by Jeffrey Masson and Alice Miller, doubtless because it speaks the language of sexual abuse and sexual assault.

In it Freud invokes Breuer's discovery that the symptoms of hysteria are 'determined by certain experiences of the patient's which have operated in a traumatic fashion and which are being reproduced in his psychical life in the form of mnemic symbols'.[4] In therapy the physician leads the patient's attention back to the scene in and through which the symptom arose and, having located the scene, removes the symptom by bringing about, 'during the reproduction of the traumatic scene', a subsequent correction of the psychical course of events. But the scene has to be suitable to serve as a determinant and has to possess the necessary 'traumatic force'. Analytic work is along 'chains of memory'.[5] No hysterical symptom can arise from a real experience alone: in every case memory of earlier experiences plays a part in causing the symptom. In every case '*we infallibly come to the field of sexual experience*', 'after the chains of memories have converged',[6] and we come to a small number of experiences, for the most part at puberty. Some may be severe traumas – an attempted rape or the involuntary witnessing of sexual acts between parents – but some are trivial; so both 'experiences affecting the subject's own body' and 'visual impressions too and information received through the ears'[7] play a part. Where 'apparently' trivial, Freud says that we must look for yet other determinants.

> And since infantile experiences with a sexual content could after all only exert a psychical effect through their *memory-traces*, would not this view be a welcome amplification of the finding of psycho-analysis which tells us *that hysterical symptoms can only arise with the co-operation of memories*.[8]

What characterises the very early experiences is their uniformity. Interestingly, it is no longer for Freud a question of 'some sense impression or other' but sexual experiences 'affecting the subject's own body'; it is this premature sexual experience which lies at the bottom of every case of hysteria, the *caput Nili* – the source of the Nile – in neuropathology.[9]

Freud himself engages with the likely scepticism about such an assertion. In a prescient engagement with the argument for suggestion so vividly encountered in recent

False Memory Syndrome controversies ('Is it not very possible . . . that the physician forces such scenes upon his docile patients, alleging that they are memories'[10]), he offers a defence on grounds of conviction ('the behaviour of patients while they are reproducing these infantile experiences is in every respect incompatible with the assumption that the scenes are anything else than a reality which is being felt with distress and reproduced with the greatest reluctance'). But in a celebrated footnote added in 1924 he observes that all this is true, 'but it must be remembered that at the time I wrote it I had not yet freed myself from my *overvaluation* of reality and my *low valuation* of phantasy'.[11] Herein lies a long debate.

And yet, and yet. A core structure – of temporalisation – was in place. That structure remains. The suggestion in the paper, ultimately, is that an infantile state of the psychical functions, as of the sexual system, is required for a sexual experience at this time to 'later on, in the form of a memory, produce a pathogenic effect'. Freud himself notices the possible objection that it is memory which is seen to produce such a pathogenic effect, rather than the experience itself. His synthesis introduces the notion of the defensive effort *against* a distressing idea that must be present to form a hysterical symptom, and that this idea must be in an associative connection with an unconscious memory with a sexual content.[12]

By the time of Freud's much later 'Splitting of the Ego in the Process of Defence', which rests on the full elaboration of psychoanalytic theory, it is perception which counts, along with the subsequent words that bind the memory of a perception.[13] But temporalisation is again and always the theme, parental words completing the sequence. Take the following illustration of the process, delineating a conflict between a demand by the instinct and its prohibition by reality. Freud is using 'reality' here to signify the social setting of the family (in Laplanche's words, the relation of kinship[14]) with its unavoidable demands:

> A threat of castration by itself need not produce a great impression. A child will refuse to believe in it, for he cannot easily imagine the possibility of losing such a highly prized part of his body. His earlier sight of the female genitals might have convinced our child of that possibility. But he drew no such conclusion from it . . . it is different if both factors are present together. *In that case the threat revives the memory of the perception which had hitherto been regarded as harmless* and finds in that memory a dreaded confirmation . . . Thenceforward he cannot help believing in the reality of the danger of castration.[15]

In this setting sight is crucial, but cannot act alone. Its significance is retrospective. There is an irreducible concept of the event – a moment of sight rather than of insight – as potentially traumatic only.

Nine years after 'The Aetiology of Hysteria' came *Three Essays on the Theory of Sexuality*, and Freud's reading of children's sexual theories.[16] In a brilliant account of traumatic vision, of 'narratives of anxious sexual investigation', Mandy Merck has argued for the value of reading a work like Andrea Dworkin's *Intercourse* 'as though it were written from a child's viewpoint, or at least from within the youthful understandings of intercourse which erupt – like those of the Wolf Man – in the nightmares of our later lives'.[17] For in the Freudian uncanny, she continues, the classic co-ordinates of the primal scene involve an attack that is silently witnessed by a third party.[18] In this context, in a discussion of the primal scene in Freudian theory and the notion of primitive anxieties about genital penetration – 'the passage into another body' – John Fletcher has pointed out that Freud's account of adult sexuality is of something intrinsically disturbing.[19] It is presented as an attack played out between the parents with the child as observer. It is, then, significant that the originary moment – once the theory of infantile sexuality, with its sexual theories of childhood, is in place – is now taken as being a perception by the child rather than, as before, an act *done to* the child. It is an evolution from the 1896 notion of the tactile. In Lacan's model this primal scene is grasped and interpreted by the child some time later than his original observation of it, by after-revision at a time when he can put it into words.[20]

There seem, then, to be two strands: that of deferred action (which we met at the outset of this chapter); and that of the intrinsically disturbing. They combine at the point when the senses combine with the faculty of speech. Sight is crucial, but words too. Yet there is another lineage: the effect of the traumatic itself. We have the important ingredient that Freud himself links traumatic events with exact repetition: the internal effects remain unaltered. I began by considering the effect of deferred action, but our vocabulary also includes that of the sudden. Here trauma may lead to enactment. For example, in a discussion of a case where a four-year-old girl had witnessed a 'violent quarrel between her parents in which her father had attacked her mother physically and mother had subsequently attempted suicide and been taken to hospital in an ambulance', Ronald Britton inferred, in the child's session the following day, from the way she was using the toy animals, that:

> the traumatic episode temporarily put a stop to the continuity of interchange between her inner and outer life. This glimpse of the effect of recent trauma gives rise to interesting speculation on the sequestrated nature of unassimilated experience in mental life.[21]

Something is locked away, sequestered, Britton argues, forming an alien object in the mind; separate from the normal introjective and projective processes of daily life.[22]

As earlier, I want to pose the question: is there something about certain events which renders them apparently unassimil*able*? Deferred action should play a part, but it is hard to know how. It is as though the experience is reproduced by the body, bypassing the ordinary processes of the mind. Valerie Sinason, in a recent discussion of working with survivors of satanist abuse, speaks of marks on the body, body memory as a substitute for remembering the traumatic event. Physical acting out can be 'a substitute for remembering a traumatic childhood experience' which 'unconsciously aims to reverse that early trauma. The patient is spared the painful memory of the trauma.'[23] And in work with incest survivors, the Women's Therapy Centre has noticed the difficulty that some sexually abused women experience in taking part in brief therapy groups. Again the experience appears to be 'held' in the body. 'Women who have only body or trace memories of their abuse may find that listening to the experiences of others creates a persecutory environment which reinforces the need to sustain their defence of "not remembering".'[24] For other women, significantly, the moment of seeking a group comes when 'their usual way of managing – the "not-remembering" – is breaking down and they are having flashbacks, sensations and memories of the abuse'.[25] This time, we might say that memory starts to break in.

We may wonder, then, whether with patient investigation psychic history can indeed always be reconstituted. It may not be possible. The analyst Judith Trowell, working with an interdisciplinary perspective, has proposed that disavowal, displacement and dissociation are the key defence mechanisms in cases of sexual abuse. She suggests that the 'split-off, denied experience' of abuse forms a kind of 'bubble' – becoming encapsulated, it drops down into the depths of the unconscious, and may have one of at least two effects: learning difficulties and 'becoming cut off from feelings'.

> It is not clear where the knowledge is held. The experience is 'gone' unless and until the bubble surfaces . . .

> many children have no fantasies because the whole area of fantasy is damped down.[26]

Spilling out takes place, however, if the experience is so overwhelming that the defence mechanisms do not work. The sequestered nature of unassimilated experience is again called to mind. Such experience may not turn on repression. Some more radical excision may perhaps be being proposed.

Here the distinction between repression and dissociation is sometimes made. In a succinct and imaginative *Guardian* article, Susie Orbach put it this way: 'Unlike repressed material which is located in the unconscious, and which once there is elaborated on and thought about unconsciously, dissociated material is held in a frozen state, detached, parcelled off in its original form.'[27] In this discussion of 'active forms of "forgetting"', the source is again trauma. Dissociation occurs when people sustain continual or persistent trauma. Her discussion implies a 'separating out', perhaps the kind of excision I was mentioning earlier; repressed material, by contrast, is potentially available to consciousness.

It is interesting to see the different effects this may have clinically. Fiona Gardner suggests that if dissociation is complete – involving both emotions and event – then if abuse is re-enacted in the therapy it may be tempting for the therapist to think the abuse was imagined.[28] But dissociation may of course be of the moment, if it does duty as a present-day coping mechanism when memories are still relatively fresh, as in an Icelandic study reported in the *Journal of Social Work Practice* in 1990. It is indeed striking to see the fluidity – as opposed to the sequestrated – that may be in play (and, incidentally, to notice the very 'benignness' that attaches to this report of a study published a few years before False Memory Syndrome reframed the debate about a lost past).

> In some cases (two Icelandic and three English women) they managed to forget the abuse totally until some incident later on in life suddenly brought it all back to them. 'It all came back to me suddenly three years ago. I was studying abroad at the time and I was reading a newspaper, and saw that there was going to be this conference about incest. It was like a shock, like an electric power going through me or something, when I read this.'[29]

The point is made that this is unusual; one could say that more common is a remembering that the subject is negotiating all the time, trying to minimise.

Let me illustrate, bearing in mind that a single vignette works not as evidence for one or other pole of the empirical but as evidence within a way of thinking, or of 'thinking through'. Milena, a patient on a psychiatric admissions ward, was an East European woman in her late thirties. Both her parents had been in a concentration camp. She had had a professional career until her late twenties, and then lived with her sister in an apartment in her parents' house, at which time she first came into contact with the psychiatric services. The words incest and abuse did not appear in the initial notes; just that Milena felt she was getting sick, and feeling sexual towards her father and that she shrank from that.

There was a gap. Then she was admitted to the hospital after threatening to burn down her parents' house and talking of her own funeral. She refused to eat and now reported a history of incest. Within two days she was delusional and openly talking to herself. She sat on the floor and chanted. In a moment of lucidity she said that she was starting to remember childhood experiences. Then there came a crisis. From my journal:

> Paula in charge last night – warm, joking, laid back and in full control of the unit – Milena walked

> nude in the corridor, and then lay on her bed nude jigging about and pointing to her vagina. 'I scream' and 'Rape' she was saying or chanting. Eyes closed. Paula sent Kate and me to get her clothed; Kate was her usual sharp-mother self when we were getting Milena into clothes. She was moved to a quiet room with constant observation and given medication. Then she moved about on the bed as though having sex or masturbating. We made a group of workers alternatively embarrassed and grimacing. 'She's putting on a show,' said one. It *was* mesmerizing. Paula spoke of a 'trance-like state'.

At a later and quieter stage Milena said that she had had enough of talking about incest. She was familiar with survivors' groups and wanted to put it all behind her. I asked her what made her so sure she had been sexually abused. The gist was that when she became interested in boys, she knew something was *wrong*. (Although not decisive in and of itself, it is worth noting that we also meet this intuitive sense of conviction, simply and plainly put, in Sylvia Fraser's autobiography of incest *My Father's House* in Chapter 6.) Although she had no memory of sexual abuse, she was sure it had happened when she was young, younger than five. What are we seeing? My use of the word 'seeing' is doubtless no coincidence. We were looking at her, and sight continued to play its part. But what to make of her behaviour, of the relationship between a psychotic process and a reported history of sexual abuse? Could her bodily contortions be a reliving of actual incest; might they be some complex, delusional acting-out of an imaginary incestuous encounter? Her 'broken speech' may indeed be evocative of the incomplete relations of the Oedipus complex, in Bernard Burgoyne's words.[30] But the whole sequence illustrates the problem of an uncertain narrative. A number of features struck me: the oscillation between rationality and delusional thinking; the absence of memory, but the conviction based on inference from what happened in the family once she reached adolescence; and the gap between this account of abuse (and of putting it behind her) and Milena's bizarre behaviour on the unit. It suggested a high level of dissociation. One might speculate that she was reliving experiences of sexual abuse in her behaviour, sexual language, display. But, importantly, at these times she was truly out of reach to us.

For in the clinical setting the question of absence – of knowledge, of certainty – asserts itself. Here a poignancy may have to be borne: as a colleague of mine said to me, 'Sometimes the abuse will never be proved and will never again be spoken of. The team may then have to live with the painful fact that they may never know.' The uncertainty is often seen as uncertainty about the child's experience, but my point is that it can be paralleled in the team. The thinking is about trauma: not just about its effects on the subject who is traumatised but on the professionals who work with the subject, the trauma, and their effects on them. What is seen is an intensification not just of transference but of counter-transference. Sebastian Kraemer notices divisions in child abuse teams, 'as if individuals holding opposite opinions could not trust each other any more or look each other in the eye'.[31] The special connection with sight – perhaps the guilt of sight – recurs. Interestingly, a further aspect of the situation of the traumatised child is reproduced in the professional community trying to help. It was 'the gaps in our memories', reports Elisabeth Hadjiisky, in considering the question of the extent of child abuse (not only sexual) which went unrecognised in France, that led her and her colleagues to research the reactions of teachers, doctors and social workers dealing with abused children.[32] They suggested that

> a defensive system arises in the form of a primitive countertransference which is capable of destroying

> those efficient reactions which could be used for the treatment and protection of the endangered child . . . it seems that violence inevitably provokes archaic counter-identifications .[33]

Denial and doubt lead to abstaining; omnipotence leads to acting alone; splitting leads to the desire not to act; banalisation leads to a trivialisation. 'In countertransference terms, this factor corresponds to the abusing parent's inability to change'.[34]

The French work focused on the defences professionals may use, and helps to name some of these. Indeed a welter of reactions is being noted in the clinical literature. For Mary Adams, the enactment was further reproduced in the therapist's own experience of taking a weekly incest survivors' group: 'as in incest, relieved to have survived for another week'.[35] David Mann also speaks of intensification, in a way which suggests it operates for both patient and therapist;[36] while the Women's Therapy Centre notes the pull to avoid memory:

> We have found that the therapist working alone can become overwhelmed and, when their ability to retain their capacity to think is threatened, it becomes extremely difficult to hold the group on course. This is because of the unconscious pull to avoid painful memories and powerful emotions that are but a part of the legacy of incest.[37]

This widening discourse on working with incest, its clinical specificity, its therapeutic demands, represents a striking change from the period evoked so vividly by Brendan MacCarthy in one of the most frequently cited of all psychoanalytic papers on working with incest, 'Are Incest Victims Hated?': 'I am old enough to remember that once upon a time no trainee was allowed to see an incest victim;

when I was a student they were considered untreatable by psychoanalysis as being unable to form a transference.'[38] Although it is in a different register, and concerns a 'freely chosen' incestuous relationship in adult life, I am reminded of Anaïs Nin's writing on incest[39] and the powerful sense of withdrawal – if not removal – from the social that her incestuous relationship with her father offered, indeed required.

> I had promised Father utter secrecy. But one night here in the hotel, when I realized there was *no one* I could tell about my father, I felt suffocated . . . It all stifles me. I need air, I need liberation . . . No one can teach me to enjoy my tragic incest-love, to shed the last chains of guilt.
>
> When I see a letter from Father at the post office, I am stirred – stirred in a nonhuman way . . .[40]

In the words of the 1990 *UCH Textbook of Psychiatry*, actual incest destroys the symbolic function.[41] Winnicott famously put this in a therapeutic context (see Chapter 1, p. 12); this formulation is more purely developmental.

> A normal child playing with the fantasy of marrying his opposite sex parent has to learn that this wish cannot be fulfilled in reality. The fantasy play helps the child prepare for future adulthood. However, the abused boy or girl has *become* the daddy or mummy. Symbolic functioning has been destroyed.[42]

Again, within her very different idiom, Anaïs Nin puts it similarly. Of Henry Miller (with whom she was having a relationship at the same time) she said in her journal: 'He gives me what my Father cannot give me, because my Father is me, and Henry is the *other*.'[43]

To ask questions about the unassimilable, then, is to ask a question about language, or about the absence of speech.

It does not necessarily imply collapsing traditional distinctions between real and imaginary, or real and imagined. Jean Laplanche has reminded us that in *Civilization and Its Discontents* Freud wrote that in mental life, 'nothing which has once been formed can perish',[44] but it does not settle the question of whether some things do not get formed, or get formed in a way which renders their assimilation problematic. And when it comes to repetition: 'It would seem that the only way to deal with an intolerable experience, the memory of which cannot be borne, is to expel it by making someone else experience it instead', as Valerie Sinason has written.[45]

We might make a comparable point. In Torok and Abraham's work on transgenerational haunting (see Chapter 6) there is the notion that what returns to haunt is the unsaid and unsayable of another; more colloquially, the way in which family secrets are not spoken but nevertheless transmitted across the generations. It is a point well captured by Brendan MacCarthy in 'Are Incest Victims Hated?', exploring the dynamics of the situation where incest victims fear that disclosure will provoke a hostile response – disbelief, blame, indifference or outright hostility, for the young women have achieved in actuality what others achieve in fantasy alone: Oedipal triumph.

> The younger the child at the incest encounter the more deeply disturbed by the experience will she be. It relates also to the impact on a very young child of her father's sexual need and her role in containing and managing it at a time of limited understanding. Not only does she replace her mother in the Oedipal configuration and suffer the guilt-ridden consquences of doing so; she is also confronting a regressed, overwhelmingly needy father in search of a primitive reunion with *his* mother's body, so the child also in her passive acquiescence becomes the lost maternal object for father . . . sexual contact between

> father and a daughter aged 3 or 4, especially the first encounter, bears no relation to adult sexuality . . . Incestuousness is a fantasy goal of father since the child was born, if not before . . . [In the confusion of the first encounter] the child will be swamped with sensations, overwhelmed by father's anxiety and need, and there will be zonal confusion, and role confusion, even without the severe perceptual and verbal limitations of the experience.[46]

And where no fantasy appears to be possible. To make the contrast: in the classic account of the relationship between sexuality and fantasy, Laplanche and Pontalis remind us that sexuality,

> disengaged from any natural object, moves into the field *of fantasy* and by that very fact becomes sexuality . . . the taking of food serving, for instance, as a model for fantasies of incorporation. Though modelled on the function, sexuality lies in its difference from the function.[47]

We might want to think about this 'moment when the external object is abandoned' in relation to child sexual abuse: one might speak of an external object precisely being intruded *in*, and link this to the later disturbance of sexuality. The question of deferred action and the potentially traumatic, versus the notion of the inevitably traumatic without the temporalisation that's assumed *by* deferred action: this remains a point of debate.

I want, lastly, to return to Freud, and to a rereading of Freud. In Jean Laplanche's recent work, by contrast, the notion of the 'real event' is not foregrounded. Indeed, the contrast that he draws is between event and scene. There is also a much greater stress on the notion of the 'message', on the enigmatic signifier in *Seduction, Translation, Drives: A Dossier*, and the theoretical priority he gives to 'the other's implantation of sexual messages' in psychic formation.[48] But two questions can still be put: what is the effect on psychic structure of actual seduction; and how is the infantile psychic apparatus established?

In *New Foundations in Psychoanalysis*, Laplanche reconstructs the seduction theory in a way that enables a move from Freud's 'special' theory to a new level, 'no longer restricted to pathology'. Seduction is rather 'accorded its originary value as a central element in becoming human'.[49] At the same time, we feel the resonances – or 'sedimented meanings', to bring in the idea of 'new meanings' – of current debates about seduction, trauma and sexual abuse. In that sense the context for the terms used in these debates – as an ICA leaflet for the panel discussion with Professor Laplanche in 1992 put it, 'debates concerning narratives of sexual and violent trauma' – has been intensified both by recent public discourse about such trauma, and by the recent elaboration of psychodynamic clinical writing on its effects.

Laplanche's continued use of the word 'seduction', whose etymology I noted in Chapter 1, is helpful precisely because it does suggest the unknown, unconscious dimension in abuse by an adult. But how would the theory of primal seduction be *inflected* by sexual assault? The question is prompted by a striking, because simple and succinct, statement about repression: 'After all – and one is slightly ashamed to say so – psychoanalysis with and since Freud has omitted to note that repression and the unconscious exist in the Other before being present in the child.'[50] We need to bear this in mind when thinking about the failure of repression, or the incompleteness of the repression of incestuous impulses in the *Other*, in actual seduction.

Perhaps processes of implantation in the infant, though necessarily more violent, would be no less enigmatic – for, as I have cited from the clinical literature, the abusive father's desire may be for reunion with his lost mother; but processes of translation may be more precarious. The question bears on a topic discussed in the earlier *Life and Death in Psychoanalysis*: the derivation of psychoanalytic entities. Laplanche reminds us in *Life and Death* that trauma is a very old concept, 'present at the origins of medicosurgical thought'.[51] The trauma, at source, is a wound, conceived of as a piercing of the surface of the body. Although the concept of psychical trauma evolved, through processes of displacement, from that of physical, 'so clear a separation between what is purely somatic and what is purely psychical in the trauma has never been sustained in the Freudian tradition'.[52]

It will be important to map how this model differentiates 'types of implantation' and their structural consequences.[53] For the burgeoning clinical accounts of working with sexually abused patients highlight a particular form of temporalisation. In this tradition, too, there is Christopher Bollas's suggestion, in 'The Trauma of Incest', of a topographical reversal: the father becomes an object that seeks the child's body for his purposes, reverses the direction of the child's sexual desire. The effect is to

> sponsor a selective deletion [from the psyche] of subsequent representations. Mental processes such as condensation and displacement, which are vital factors in the child's formation of symbols and expression of unconscious life through play, are denuded.[54]

Incest also constitutes an attack on dreaming: 'If he is the object of the child's desire, then he is meant to be inside the dream space, not in the outside actual world.'[55] All this takes me back to the crucial notion of 'piercing', for Bollas is suggesting that actual seduction destroys a certain kind of psychic formation. Laplanche's own focus on the somatic and psychic valencies of 'the traumatic' may be of use to us here.

Laplanche attaches importance to the passivity of the infant, contrasting it with the activity of the other:

> The mechanisms that I say are primal are the ones where the other implants . . . that is the primal passivity of the subject towards something that is implanted into him. Afterwards, there is a transformation into an active temporalization and that is the mechanism of afterwardsness, but the primal mechanisms are to be understood as coming from the other.[56]

The transmission and causality are not linear; the adult is 'unaware of most of what he means' and the child has only 'inadequate and imperfect ways to configure or theorize about what is communicated to him'. But how does this reshaping take place? Repression is central; indeed Laplanche refers to it as 'the break, the profound reshaping, which occurs between the two'. Is there some receptivity within the infant? What characterises the reshaping? The account of the infant *faced* with the enigma of the adult world is persuasive, but the mechanism not entirely clear. Here there is, incidentally, an analogy with an issue that has been raised, in the Kleinian arena, about the mechanism of projective identification. How *does* the psyche of one act on the psyche of another? And mentioning Klein leads to another, contrasting, issue bearing on passivity: the question of infantile fantasy. In Laplanche: 'the adult knows more than the infant',[57] albeit that knowledge is unconscious. If we take the sadistic, infantile model of parental sexuality – of tearing and destroying, battles, slaughters – to be found in early Klein,[58] we can see Klein's model as being in the tradition of one of Freud's infantile sexual theories, in which the child interprets the act of love as an act of violence. But a further dimension to this contrast can be drawn. In Klein there is not only a sadistic model of parental sexuality, but a very *active* model of infantile mental life – a flooding, a swamping with internal stimuli and fantastic imagery. The infant is – crucially – *already* saturated with sexuality. The infant, as I suggested in Chapter 2, is in part the pivot of its own psychic formation. Laplanche's reservations are expressed in a critique of both Freud and Klein:

> The Other – in particular the parental Other – is barely present at all, and then only as an abstract protagonist of a scene or a support for projections; this is the case with Freud, but also, and to an even greater extent with, for example, Klein.[59]

It brings me back to my starting point. All told, the theorised relationship between inner and outer structures of fantasy and causation continues to be problematic. When traumatic vision has become a cycle of projection and reprojection, a real event has been revisited, but this time as part of a largely interior trajectory. The balance and distinction – in act and fantasy – between subject and other perhaps remains hard to locate. The interrelation of perception, traumatic action and temporalisation may need further mapping.

5

Fantasy, memory, trauma: psychoanalytic reflections on biography and False Memory Syndrome

My title is doubtless hubristic. I want to say something about memory; there will be a certain amount about trauma; least, overtly, about fantasy. My question is this: how do we probe unconscious experience? I am framing the beginning of this chapter under that heading, because I am talking both about biography as a mode of work and writing, and about False Memory Syndrome (FMS) as a site of controversy and difficulty in clinical settings. What links both topics is memory: or, to put it another way, temporalisation. In biographical work temporalisation occupies a wide field: all the subject's experience could be held under the term; and within that, memory is central. In false memory as a clinical issue, on the other hand, we are concerned explicitly and chiefly with the temporalisation of *trauma*.

I want to pose a group of questions. Do we need to oppose the concept of false memory? If it is taken for granted in certain forms of writing – as I want to show that it is – why has it become such an explosive issue in the theorisation of sexual abuse? I want to create a space for thinking about it. I shall be using biographical material illustratively, to pave the way to False Memory Syndrome as a clinical issue.

The repression of memory

I have for some time wanted to find a place for a particularly haunting observation in Philip Rieff's *Freud: The Mind of the Moralist*; it seems very appropriate here, given the topic, even though the era in which it was written is a different one. It is America at the heyday of Freud's influence on the culture, as Rieff himself points out.

> Freud plunges us into an incredible world: fantastic realities beneath reasonable appearances; worlds composed of absurd conjunctions – *events that never happened and yet control those that do* [my italics] – cure coming through a stranger who aims to know another more intimately than his intimates have ever known him; thoughts that wander in an overdetermined way. Consider alone the absurdity, and yet the demonstrated inevitability, of that faith the patient develops in his analyst – there you have a hint of the profound and true absurdity of psychoanalysis.[1]

This notion of 'events that never happened and yet control those that do' is my leitmotif in this chapter. It connotes classical psychoanalysis, but I think it is relevant in the climate we are now in in relation to FMS. In condensed form, one could borrow Rieff's phrase and apply it to the phenomenon that FMS points to: the initiation of legal proceedings, in the United States particularly, on the basis of recovered memories; but where a crucial issue is: are these recovered memories of 'real events'?

Psychoanalytically, FMS presents us with a paradox: most of the evidence so far is from America, and most of the forms of therapy in which memories of abuse have been recovered are not the psychoanalytic therapies, but therapies in which suggestion is seen as playing much more of a part. Yet the notion of repressed memory has become central in the debate, and the validity of psychoanalytic thought is right back on the agenda. We could say that the question of repression of memory has come back into the cultural mainstream. Let me stress that in this debate at the moment the stakes *are* very high, because criminal proceedings are involved; it is statute-of-limitations changes which have enabled lawsuits to be brought; and which have brought a *conceptual* issue into the domain of public policy.

So if I look back at what Freud did say about memory, and make some glancing comments on the idiom of Freud's writing, I am most struck by two features of the Freudian view of memory: on the one hand, its benevolence, which is very different, as I want to show, from the status of memory in the current debates around false memory; and, on the other hand, its liberating character. Neither facet strikes me as unique to Freud, but as characteristic of a particular climate of thinking about the self.

David Krell's absorbing textual study of memory from Aristotle to Derrida and Heidegger offers the notion that we long for memory; we strive to remember but frequently we are not able to remember. In writing about Freud's work in the 1890s he makes the point that

> one of its earliest and most enduring traits was the significance of memory [for psychoanalysis] . . . *Studies on Hysteria* established memory as both the mainspring of the hysteric mechanism and the principal tool of the therapy . . . memory is responsible for the formation of symptoms in the first place.[2]

Krell's point, which would also be mine, continues:

> Freud's talking cure rests on the confidence that there is something in the patient which, in spite of all resistance, wants to express itself and to know . . . Freud encourages the analyst to have faith in the ultimate fidelity – and also the benevolence – of memory.[3]

We see this notion of benevolence in Freud's confident dismissal, in 'Remembering, Repeating and Working Through', that suggestion is at work;[4] and the relaxed way in which Freud will write about there being more than one version of a scene; indeed the continuous stress on 'experience' as a kind of overarching term which does not make distinctions between the truth and falsity of an event, but locates memory in the sphere of experience as the cardinal principle of psychic life. To illustrate, I shall take just one example from the Rat Man: Freud's discussion of whether a particular scene took place. It concerns a misdeed in early childhood, which contains within it a sexual misadventure, for which the child was punished:

> [I]t will help to put us on the right track in interpreting it, if we recognize that more than one version of the scene (each often differing greatly from the other) may be detected in the patient's unconscious fantasies. Childhood memories are only consolidated at a later period, usually at the age of puberty . . . and involve a complicated process of remodelling, analogous in every way to the process by which a nation constructs legends about its early history.[5]

The analogy with the historical reminds us that case histories – as forms of writing – belong within a historical as well as a psychical genre. But we might also identify this way of thinking about memory as an organisation of psychic transcendence. The anthropologist Michael Fischer, for example, writing on the post-modern arts of memory, links Freud with a longer cultural tradition:

> Only through memory, honed by constant exercise and effort, could one purge the sins of past lives, purify the soul, ascend and escape from oblivious repetitions.[6]

Fischer goes on to point out that, as Walter Benjamin and Freud in differing ways pointed out, language itself

> contains sedimented layers of emotionally resonant metaphors, knowledge and association . . . much of the contemporary philosophical mood . . . is to enquire into what is hidden in language, what is deferred by signs . . . repressed, implicit or mediated . . . these are a modern version of the Pythagorean arts of memory: retrospection to gain a vision for the future. In so becoming, the searches also turn out to be powerful critiques of several contemporary rhetorics of domination.[7]

Very impressionistically, I see a parallel with the *daughters'* trajectory in FMS accusations: what seems to be in play is a tremendously powerful contest, which one could frame in terms of a rhetoric of domination. The point about language could also be taken a step further. If one looks at the situation of women who go into therapy, say, without memory, and who recover memory through therapy – leaving aside whether it is through suggestion or through some unprofessional conduct by the therapist – they are in fact achieving a rhetoric of their own which was not available to them before. There *was* no language – language repressed or mediated; there was instead an apparent excision of memory.

One could also look at it a different way round and make a different point: for Freud is also saying that nothing escapes registration.[8] If nothing escapes registration, then in principle all experience can be recovered. In the late paper 'Constructions in Analysis', Freud looks at 'the psychical object whose early history the analyst is seeking to recover': here we are regularly met by a situation which with

> the archaeological object occurs only in such rare

> circumstances as those of Pompeii or of the tomb of Tutankhamun. All of the essentials are preserved; even things that seem completely forgotten are present somehow and somewhere, and have merely been buried and made inaccessible to the subject. Indeed, it may, as we know, be doubted whether any psychical structure can really be the victim of total destruction.[9]

Memory and biography

The fascination that we feel with Freud's case histories – and which the analogy with archaeology illustrates – is, in part, the fascination that we have with the layering of memory. This brings me to biography, and then to the memories that we are concerned with in False Memory Syndrome.

What makes the biographical form generally popular? asks the textual critic Carolyn Steedman.

> The confirmation that biography offers, that life stories can be told, that the inchoate experience of living and feeling can be marshalled into a chronology . . . and that central and unified subjects reach the conclusion of a life, and come into possession of their own story; the way in which biography partakes of the historical romance . . . the hope that that which is gone, that which is irretrievably lost, which is past time, can be brought back, and conjured before the eyes as it really was, and that it can be possessed.[10]

Steedman leads us on to another area: that of the family romance, most ingeniously deployed in her study of working-class autobiographical writing. Steedman excavated and edited a working-class autobiography from the 1920s.

> I discovered what I knew I would discover: that Kathleen Woodward was born in relatively genteel Peckham, not in abandoned Bermondsey, that Jipping Street [also the title of the book] was the landscape of her imagination, an invented way of making the writing of a 19th century childhood possible . . . she wrote what I would call a psychic reconstruction of working class childhood, rather than a historical account of one.[11]

It is interesting to think about biographical study in the light of the present topic. All biographers – it is a truism to say this – must negotiate discrepancies of memory. It is also a commonplace to observe that biography constructs fiction. But biographers vary in how knowing they are in this area. We see this in a variety of ways. In Chapters 3 and 7 I look at this more closely. Anticipating a point I make in Chapter 7, I am suggesting that a 'bleak depression' which Anne Sexton, for example, fell into in her thirties was produced within Sexton's own reworking of her past work, a way of looking back at a period of her life from which she felt distant but which she was still in the grip of; just as Kathleen Woodward reworked her past in a family romance about her own origins. It is the deceptiveness of hindsight that is in play.

And that, too, is found in autobiography. Let me take the work of the literary critic Allon White, who died young not long ago and a collection of whose autobiographical and literary writings has recently been published. Looking through the index, under the heading 'memory', I found a sub-entry that reads 'False memory, of sister's death'. It is a knowing account, a psychoanalytic account; knowing because it is written from within a false memory – of his sister's death by drowning.

> This memory, etched into my mind with the clarity of total recall, is false. I was not in the garden at the time

> when she wandered off. According to my mother, I was elsewhere, playing with a friend in his garden. I couldn't have seen her go. It was impossible. I was not there.[12]

False Memory Syndrome

If it is commonly accepted that our memories are uncertain and can be revised, I want to ask why are we so shaken by the issue of false memory in the therapeutic domain? One of the reasons may be because it touches on an issue which has *already* produced division, is *already* saturated with anxiety: sexual abuse, with its attendant denials and denunciations. If we were to accept that events can be repressed[13] – and not only the affect associated with them – then recovery of memory in therapy is in line with Freud's view that nothing escapes registration. But 'FMS' – shorthand for the group of ideas that are now constellated around False Memory Syndrome – argues that such is not the case: rather that suggestion is at work. And here, evidence *for* repression of memory *is* surely crucial. A few years ago, for example, I started hearing, anecdotally, of people going into psychoanalytic therapy 'wanting to remember something'; it implies that something is felt to be there but buried. The contrast with memory and the Holocaust is instructive.

As has been widely noticed in the case of the Holocaust, the event is remembered; we are not talking about repression of the event itself. Even so, recent work in the States by the literary critic Shoshana Felman and the psychiatrist Dori Laub, working together in a centre for videotaping and memory work based at Yale University, amplifies the point.[14] They have found that Holocaust survivors have needed to 'tell their story' in order to survive; and there has to be a phase of *joint* acceptance of the Holocaust reality.[15] By contrast, in what comes under the heading of 'false memory' in the domain of sexual abuse, not only is there frequently a lack of any clear evidence of a traumatic impingement, what we actually see is *dis*unity. We do not see that joint acceptance of a shared reality. We see a most distressing excision. The memory is not validated, but violently disconfirmed.

In False Memory Syndrome, then, the event is in dispute. What is the character of this dispute? Those who argue from an FMS position are at pains to point to the existence of child sexual abuse, to distinguish false memory from the prevalence of actual sexual abuse. Their position is that recovery therapists work against the grain of accepted research data on memory. I quote Richard Gardner, in *Issues in Child Abuse Accusations*, on recovery therapists:

> They do not believe that our mind can play tricks on us . . . that memory is reworked, reconstructed and integrated with other memories, each of which is distorted and changed over time . . . They believe that if an individual has a memory of a childhood sexual experience, it must be true.

Gardner does raise an important point about memory of the Holocaust: that survivors were not in a state of total repression of their experience.

> I am certain that [Holocaust] survivors would not be found to have developed a multiple personality disorder, nor would they *suddenly* exhibit the signs and symptoms of a posttraumatic stress disorder 30 to 40 years after their release. And this would be true of other people who were subjected to other forms of prolonged childhood trauma, such as chronic physical illness, physical abuse, wars, earthquakes and ongoing emotional abuse. In short, if we are to believe these victims and their therapists, we have to consider childhood sexual traumas to be such a special kind

> of experience that a whole series of well-accepted psychological principles are inapplicable.[16]

Or, in the words of two of Gardner's colleagues:

> Most people experiencing trauma do not develop amnesia for the trauma. Case studies on the reactions of people to *documented* severe trauma [the examples that they give are of fires, aeroplane crashes and car accidents] show many symptoms but total amnesia for the event is not mentioned as a common response. Research with children who have experienced documented trauma indicates that children over the ages of three or four do not develop amnesia for the trauma. All the children had full verbal recall or extensive spot memories, although the memories may have been inaccurate or fragmented. Although they may have denied parts of the aftermath and the effect on them, they did not deny the event.[17]

The clear contrast *is* with documented trauma. It is the notorious privacy of the family which has made it very difficult for certain forms of sexual trauma to be known and spoken about. By the same token, now that sexual abuse has come out of the privacy of the family, there is still a frequent lack of an evidential basis for it and it continues to be, and will presumably continue to be, an uncertain event.

I want now to ask the question: is there anything we can say psychoanalytically about the families where this is at stake? I think there is, and that we need to think about it in the round. It will have become clear by now that I think false memories do exist – indeed I do not see how we could think psychodynamically without not just the 'weaker' notion of incomplete memory but the stronger notion of false memory. False memory (at least in the character of a fantasy) is around us, at the most innocent level in the family romance, and at a more ambiguous level in the reconstructions of what I would think of as 'ordinary' memory in 'ordinary' psychotherapy. So I suspect it is also important to look at FMS not just in its own context, but as having a contribution to make to our debates. It inverts the family romance, by offering a family of exquisitely ignoble birth – the abusing family. It invalidates experience, but here – and this is a point I want to stress – the invalidation is mutual. Daughters invalidate fathers, and fathers invalidate daughters. The symmetry that has been shown to be therapeutic in work with Holocaust survivors is profoundly absent.

I want to come back now to the point that I began with about the benevolence of memory in Freud – for the memories of abuse, in False Memory Syndrome, are, as I have said, expulsive and disruptive. We would have to ask the question: why can they not be contained therapeutically? What *is* this longing for confirmation, for reclamation? If the patient 'longs to recover memory', to paraphrase David Krell, we might speculate that this is because health depends upon it.[18] My point here is that if nothing has escaped registration, the registration itself was outside the body boundary of the individual, and might need to be reclaimed. Within and across the generations memory has leaked. Interestingly, the most telling metaphors in this field often concern not people, but buildings: the 'crypt' in Maria Torok and Nicolas Abraham's work on transgenerational transmission, and the 'house' in Sylvia Fraser's extraordinary autobiography of incest, *My Father's House*, which I discuss in the next chapter.

We also need to note that FMS concerns *adult* children. The legal process around child cases may be simpler for us to think about, because of the number of cases where the judge has ruled that the account of experience that a child has offered has been so graphic that there is a high level of probability that sexual abuse has taken place.[19] This poses a question about the immediacy of memory: the closeness in time to an experience perhaps guaranteeing that sense of the experience. It brings us to the heart of questions of temporalisation, and the heart of trauma. How *do* we guarantee the validity of an adult's experience? We need to think about it carefully. I do not think that FMS just represents a backlash, or an inevitable reaction against a progressive truth-telling in the public arena (although there has undoubtedly been such truth-telling).

But, by the same token, if we were to say false memory could not exist, we would be creating a kind of sequestered space, for we know that patients in therapy come to have a modified sense of what the lived experience if not the actuality of their childhood or their family was. We do, I think, have to ask whether that sense could play them false, or at least slip and slide.[20] So I am not in principle perturbed by 'retractions'; they seem to me to be the inevitable consequence of changes of mind seen in the discursive framework of legal proceedings. The sense that 'it didn't happen after all' forms a legitimate part of what we could call a renarrativising of the self in ordinary, everyday life.[21] We also have to recognise, as I said earlier, that the confirmation for the women in therapy is disconfirming for others; it is the violence that I am pointing to at the familial level.[22] I am reminded, by contrast, of the ethnographer's claim: 'It remains the case that the ethnographer's translation/representation of a particular culture is inevitably a textual construct, that as representation it cannot normally be contested by the people to whom it is attributed.'[23] In situations of 'false memory' we know that that is not so.

In conclusion

We have moved a long way from the tenet that it does not really matter whether something actually took place or not. (Remember, after all, the powerful line of Freud about the psychical object as Pompeii or the tomb of Tutankhamun: simultaneously the most valuable, the most priceless and, paradoxically, the most concrete.) It seems to me that both sides in this debate are returning to old sources. Alice Miller and Jeffrey Masson originally returned to the Freud of 1896. Psychodynamically there is renewed interest not just in Ferenczi, but in the work of Freud's predecessor Pierre Janet on traumatic memory and the conceptual trends that have evolved from it.[24] We may also need to complexify our thinking about memory in the light of the very exigent demands on theory and practice made by sexual trauma. Ultimately what is interesting about our present situation is the suggestion that certain forms of bodily and psychic trauma insist on external confirmation. Here I come back to Jacqueline Rose's 'Afterword' to the collection of Allon White's writings; the question she posed is, I think, relevant clinically: whether memory destroys or saves.[25] We are very used, psychodynamically, to memory as restorative – and I hope that the quotations from Freud have shown that – but in the situation we find ourselves in now, memory has had an expulsive effect – whether that memory is true or false.

6

'Reclaimed once more by the realities of life': hysteria and the location of memory

> Just as the first dream represented her turning away from the man she loved to her father – that is to say, her flight from life into disease – so the second dream announced that she was about to tear herself free from her father and had been reclaimed once more by the realities of life.[1]

The quotation that forms the first part of my title is taken from the closing words of Freud's 'Dora', poignant and aggressive on Freud's part as they have always struck me as being. I also find them deeply evocative, at the level of psychic life. How much does life claim us; how much are we claimed by our past, by memories of our past? This chapter is organised around the paradoxical role that memory can play: it can make free – like life, be an agent for reclamation – while in its inaccessibility it can haunt. We seek ways of theorising both the remembered and the unremembered, and ways of thinking about what it is that memories are memories of.

Here one possibility might be that memories that can be held within the psyche are of a different order of experience from those that are projected out, expelled. It is this theme

– the location of memory – that I explore here, considering differences between 'classical' hysteria (in Freud's work) and 'hysteria today'. I want to pose a group of questions: what happens to the memories – to use Freud's terms, the reminiscences – from which the hysteric suffers? Classically they are 'abreacted' in speech. But if they are not abreacted, might they become located in another: a person, or perhaps a place that represents psychic space? Because we cannot separate our thinking from a more recent psychoanalytic and therapeutic language, it is clear that I'm hinting at wider questions – broadly, under the heading of splitting and projection – and at a larger number of disorders than the hysterias. But my focus here remains the hysterical as denoting questions about the body and its registration of the sexual, whether experienced or fantasied.

I shall look briefly at Freud's early case material, in the transition from the traumatic theory of hysteria to the theory of infantile sexuality, to remind us what's in play, or represented as being in play, in the hysteric's body; and then at some French analytic writing at the time of another 'Hysteria Today' panel, in the 1970s, which argues for the limits of speech in understanding the hysterias. I shall continue the exploration of memory and its disturbances by means of two contemporary writings: one example from the literature of incest survivors, unavoidably relevant to the vexed topic of Freud's move away from the traumatic theory of hysteria, and one theme within Terry Johnson's play *Hysteria*: Jessica's mimicry of her mother's symptoms. The play stages, actually and symbolically, the paradox I began with: that memory may be too burdensome for the subject, even as it is supposed to make free.

What form does memory take in *Studies on Hysteria*? In the 'Preliminary Communication' Breuer and Freud say that external events determine the pathology of hysteria to an extent far greater than is known and recognised;

they add that the patient is genuinely unable to recollect the precipitating cause (the event) of the symptoms of hysteria.[2] Here we find the familiar notion of the psychical trauma, and the stress on memory as pivotal; but memory that lies in wait before it pounces. Here the memory is located *inside* the subject, with the resonance of the 'foreign body' creating a subtle ambiguity about location: psyche, body?

> the causal relation between the determining psychical trauma and the hysterical phenomenon is not of a kind implying that the trauma merely acts like an *agent provocateur* in releasing the symptom . . . the psychical trauma – more precisely the memory of the trauma – acts like a foreign body which long after its entry must continue to be regarded as an agent that is still at work.[3]

That passage forms the preamble to the celebrated statement: that hysterics suffer mainly from reminiscences. One may also wonder what significance Freud wants us to attach to his different usages of 'memory' and 'reminiscence', at least as they come to us in the Strachey translation. For he is quite precise: in the main he writes of memory (*die Erinnerung*); but in key instances he writes of reminiscences (*Reminiszenzen*).[4] With the English terms the *Shorter Oxford Dictionary* has difficulty in distinguishing the two, and if one were to follow the distinction that it does make (with memory as a faculty; and reminiscence as the process of remembering, or the act of recovering knowledge), then Freud's usages may be idiosyncratic: for Breuer and Freud are adamant that however vivid, the hysterics' memories are not at their disposal.

But if memory is not at their disposal, it can still be called up. The textual critic David Krell has proposed a relationship between symptoms, memory and reminiscence which reminds us of the centrality of speech to the *Studies on Hysteria*. Reminiscences are '*unknown* memories', he suggests, 'as though memories do not have to be remembered in order *to be*'.[5] The essence of psychotherapy, he continues, is the countermanding of somatic conversion:

> if unremembered reminiscences yield the somatic symptom, then reminiscences remembered dissolve it . . . The spoken word – much more than a sign signifying a signified – reasserts its rights in the domain of the symbolic: symptoms or 'symbols of remembrance' are disbanded and the reminiscences behind them reappropriated as memories proper. *The latter, no longer dissociated, are brought home*. They can now be corrected by means of a kind of dialogue with one another, in which each remembrance understands itself as a perspective, as one associated with others. (my italics)[6]

Krell's reading seems to me supported by Breuer and Freud's own. Of the curative effect of their psychotherapy, they say: 'It brings to an end the operative force of the idea which was not abreacted in the first instance, by allowing its strangulated affect to find a way out through speech.'[7]

We find a successful example of the claim in the case of Lucy R., the young governess who suffered from rhinitis and was tormented with subjective sensations of smell. The treatment brings to light the 'experience in which these smells, which had now become subjective, had been objective'. There had actually been a burnt pudding, burnt at the same time as a letter arrived for Lucy which caused her great pain and presaged a loss; as Freud says, 'the sensation of smell that was associated with this trauma persisted as its symbol'.[8] What the treatment then leads to is an opening out of the governess's love for her employer, and her memory of a scene which crushed her hopes. Now in this classical account of abreaction the memories simply lose their force, as the denouement shows:

> Lucy visited me once more. I could not help asking her what had happened to make her so happy . . . 'Are you still in love with your employer?' 'Yes, I certainly am, but that makes no difference. After all, I can have thoughts and feelings to myself.'[9]

This ending has pointed up the double role of memory in the theory: 'unknown' memory forms the symptom; and memory released constitutes the therapy.

The sexuality that lies at the heart of the *Studies on Hysteria* is, in the main, that of young women, women at the start of their adult life (and I do say 'in the main', since *Studies on Hysteria* is also the work in which the traumatic effect of the seduction of children is stressed). We find the constrained eroticism of the governess who pines, or the adolescent girl at the sickbed. It is with 'Dora' that we move into the realm of infantile sexuality; where, as Freud says in the case, the symptom signifies the representation – or the realisation – of a phantasy with a sexual content.[10] It has also been widely acknowledged that disturbances of memory lie at the heart of the Dora case. In the special issue of the literary journal *Diacritics* on the case some ten years ago, Collins et al. remarked on 'the [striking] parallel, unnoticed by Freud, between the . . . characteristics of his presentation and what he perceived to be characteristic of the neurotic's discourse in analysis – reticence, amnesia, paramnesia, and alteration of chronology'.[11] Freud has his own way of saying this: hysterics cannot produce 'an ordered history of their life in so far as it coincides with the history of their illness'.[12] And thus, to paraphrase, it is the analyst's task to help the patient articulate her history – the memory of her history, one might add – within a coherent and continuous discursive flow.

But what a history, and what a flow; what we find in

'Dora', to a quite extraordinary extent, is Freud's speech. 'When I told Dora,' for example, 'that I could not avoid supposing that her affection for her father must at a very early moment have amounted to her being completely in love with him, she of course gave me her usual reply: "I don't remember that".'[13] I cannot address the extensive commentary that exists on this, and for my purposes it is not relevant to locate it in gender terms,[14] or to express dismay at Freud's control of the narrative. My point is rather to note that Dora does not gain access to her reminiscences; 'classically', she does not abreact them. That could be seen as the therapeutic puzzle; theoretically, the case remains fascinating about the hysterical symptom, the registration of the sexual. What happens to the memories? They are incompletely repressed.

The ensuing displacement, in the Dora case, operates as a circuit *within* the body boundary. I'll give three examples. There is firstly the infamous episode of Dora's sexual revulsion from Herr K., with its upward displacement, in which Dora feels the pressure of Herr K.'s erection on her body: it is revolting to her, is dismissed from her memory and repressed, but the incompleteness of the repression shows in an irritation of her throat. We next see the 'body economy' of displacement in the analysis of the first dream. Dora's sexuality, Freud tells us, veers round from an inclination to masturbation to an inclination to anxiety, after hearing adults making love, that lies behind her asthma. As he says: 'She had preserved in her memory the event which had occasioned the first onset of the symptom.'[15] We have a third instance of displacement within the body when Freud takes up Dora's dragging foot, her 'false step'. The neurosis, he says, has an utterance of its own and is a displacement from a guiltier reading, concealed in her memory behind the innocent one (a fall): it represents a phantasy of childbirth. It is Dora's body which reveals, inadvertently, her past (and in contrast with the *Studies*, a past of phantasy).

Freud's notion of 'utterance' can also act as a reminder of his passion for the therapeutic effect of speech. But what of the very limits of speech? A series of discussions in the French analytic literature of the 1970s is illuminating here, for by this time hysteria has been retheorised within the psychosomatic domain.[16] Let me take, for example, a commentary by Christian David. David is concerned with the limits of the symbolic, derived from the very limit that is implied by the fact that 'conversion itself implies a partial failure of psychic working out: the conversion symptom, from the fact that it engages the body, imposes a limit on mental working out, all the more a limit to the full inscription of the dynamics of the conflict in the linguistic apparatus':[17]

> There are elements of psychic life, such as certain aspects of the dream life of Dora, which 'offer a current which is not navigable', to pick up an apt Freudian metaphor, a current which no removal of amnesia, no working through of relationship or transference can ever render for us as it is . . . If there is . . . in each of us this internal hysteria, immanent in the psyche, is it not . . . because of inescapable limits in the definition of ourselves in and by language? Always in us, both in spite of and because of our hysteria, an element of the undefined subsists, *of the unspoken; of the unknown, perhaps a radical unthinkable*; something in the heart of the unconscious to which Freud could only give the name of the id. (my italics)[18]

'Unspoken, unknown, radical unthinkable'. What to make, then, some twenty years after this was written, of our current literature of incest survivors? In a different register (and, in the context of a discussion of Freud and hysteria, a significantly overdetermined register), the words could almost perfectly describe the cultural location of incest until the last fifteen years or so. I'm not arguing, I should stress, for a return to the traumatic theory of hysteria in moving to a discussion of a particular form of writing. But Freud's move from the traumatic theory of hysteria to the theory of infantile sexuality is retrospectively haunted by the question of sexual abuse and its implications for theory in general; and, as I'm suggesting, for how we think about and theorise both the remembered and the unremembered in particular. Here there is, as we know, a great desire, one could say a psychic imperative, to recover and then articulate experience in language; one is reminded, to come back to the 'Preliminary Communication', of Freud's concern with strangulated affect. It links my concern with the written with Freud's own concern with the possibilities – or, as I might put it, the conditions – of utterance. In a situation where the body boundary has been pierced (and we owe to Laplanche and Pontalis the stress on the origin of the concept of 'trauma' as lying in the medical term for the piercing of the surface of the body),[19] it seems to me that memory may be dispersed – violently expelled – rather than abreacted, because it is in a form that cannot be abreacted. Where does it go; where is it located? What needs to happen when it is found again?

With Freud when there is a crisis of knowledge there is displacement, and in the hysterias, classically, a displacement from one part of the body to another. Let us take, by contrast, the example of incest survivor Sylvia Fraser's 'house that knew': symbolically memory has been 'displaced' from the person to the family house, the 'place' that I hinted at earlier. In her memoir, *My Father's House*,[20] we find a very different notion of the location of knowledge from that of Freud in both the *Studies on Hysteria* and 'Dora'. And there are other important differences, for Fraser is not a diagnosed hysteric (though she talks of hysteria rising up in her); and she is creating her own narrative (with her own choices of literary and typographic devices), after memory has returned. Yet the key is again dreamlife, but this time dreams which lead to a building and then to a person. For most of her memory is more clearly located symbolically – the point I want to stress – in her father's house. As she writes in her 'Author's Note':

> The story I have told . . . is autobiographical. As a result of amnesia, much of it was unknown to me until three years ago. For clarity, I have used italics to indicate thoughts, feelings and experiences pieced together from recently recovered memories, and to indicate dreams.[21]

A word about Sylvia Fraser's story. At the age of seven, during her father's sexual relationship with her, she acquired another self and memories and experiences separate from her own. 'Since I didn't know what or whom I truly feared, I feared the house we shared, which by guilty association became the house that knew.'[22] The breaking up of her amnesia begins with depression after twelve years of marriage. She writes a book which depicts incest, without knowing why. Believing that the psyche struggles to reveal itself,[23] she allows her dreams to lead her to the truth; a dream of the cellar of another house gives her insight into her father's affair with her aunt. 'Now that my father's house has given up its secrets it has become an old friend.'[24] One is reminded of David Krell, writing that in therapy reminiscences can be reappropriated as memories proper; no longer dissociated, they can be brought home. I'd add that here, 'home' is the survivor's psyche, the house having been a container for the seemingly unthinkable, though not, permanently, the unrepresentable.

We find ourselves here, I suggest, in a variation on the territory charted by Nicolas Abraham and Maria Torok in their work on transmission of symptoms and the creation of crypts: pockets of encapsulated memory. Abraham and Torok initially argued – in a larger retheorisation that takes its distance from the Oedipal in psychoanalysis – that psychic development is in certain cases constituted by specific influences outside the individual's immediate or lived experience; the maternal unconscious, say, can be communicated without ever having been spoken and resides as a silent presence within the child: the phantom.[25] Further, symptoms occur when a shameful and therefore unspeakable experience must be barred from consciousness or kept secret. This is transgenerational haunting:

> Should the child have parents 'with secrets' . . . he will receive from them a gap in the unconscious, an unknown, unrecognized knowledge . . . The buried speech of the parent becomes a dead gap, without a burial place, in the child. This unknown phantom comes back from the unconscious to haunt and leads to phobias, madness and obsessions. Its effect can persist through several generations and determine the fate of an entire family line.[26]

The phantom differs from the return of the repressed: what returns to haunt is the 'unsaid' and 'unsayable' of *another*.[27] Fraser's disturbance of memory was based not solely on a parental trauma passed on to her, for she had been, unknown to her conscious self, participating in her father's scenario. But we could say there were paternal secrets; there was a gap; and there was no resting place within her. This brings me back to Christian David's point about a necessary failure of language within the interior of the psyche, and to an amplification of it. If one extends the reach of the psychic, one possibility is that the gap is filled up in the next generation, a 'coming home' of memory. Let me approach this from a contemporary dramatic vantage point. It too comes under the heading of 'Hysteria Today' – Terry Johnson's play *Hysteria*, which dramatises the conflict between Freud and 'women' by bringing to

Freud's London home the daughter of one of his hysterical patients.[28]

One critic commented at the time the play was first put on at the Royal Court Theatre in London in autumn 1993, that 'the whole is a mixture of fantasy, formal debate and British farce',[29] but it does, nevertheless, through its formal structure, offer a contemporary catharsis for the audience. Let us note, too, an observation of Didier Anzieu's about drama and catharsis in relation to Freud's intellectual development in the 1890s, the period of the transition from the traumatic theory of hysteria to the theory of infantile sexuality and the Oedipus complex. It gives us a motif within a motif.

> [T]he notion of cathartic effect . . . is doubly Freudian because it regards psychical conflict as a personal drama similar to that presented by the novelist or playwright, and its treatment as a liberation . . . It was very like Freud to derive scientific notions from Ancient Greek tragedy.[30]

Anzieu, describing Aristotle's notion of catharsis as purification or deliverance, reminds us that 'tragedy effects through pity and fear the proper catharsis, or purgation of emotions'.[31] I use this quote intentionally, for I think Jessica, in the play, herself seeks purification and deliverance: on her own behalf, and on her mother's.

Jessica, albeit ambiguously, displays the symptoms that her mother had suffered from – retching, pawing, rubbing movements; she appears to have been bequeathed them. I say ambiguously because the audience does not know until the end of the first act that Jessica is the daughter of Freud's patient Rebecca and that Rebecca killed herself; and does not know until the end of the second act that Jessica too will report a history of sexual abuse at the hands of the same man, her mother's father. Are we to think that Jessica is displaying her own symptoms? I tend to think not; the point is downplayed in the action, and the affective power of the drama derives from the relentlessness with which Jessica lives the body-speech of her mother while reading from her mother's diary.

Freud, in writing about mimicry in the hysteric, pointed to the way in which the patient's symptoms mimicked an element in her (own) past, and thereby offered a route to that past. We find one example in Anna O.'s loss of the capacity of speech:

> She tried to pray but could find no words; at length she succeeded in repeating a children's prayer in English. When subsequently a severe and highly complicated hysteria developed, she could only speak, write and understand English, while her native language remained unintelligible to her for eighteen months.[32]

In the character of Jessica, by contrast, one might want to say that the symptom has been transferred across the generations. Jessica inhabits, literally and symbolically, her mother('s) tongue. Hysterical mimicry has been relocated.

Those who have seen the play will have seen the precise re-creation of the mother's symptoms, although the word re-creation may still be too weak. What is in play is perhaps something more reminiscent of incorporation, following the distinction that Abraham and Torok drew between incorporation and introjection. But a special form of incorporation: one taken on by the next generation.

> Grief that cannot be expressed builds a secret vault within the subject. In this crypt reposes – alive, reconstituted from the memories of words, images and feelings – the objective counterpart of the loss, as a complete person with his own topography, as well as the traumatic incidents – real or imagined – that had made introjection impossible. In this way a

whole unconscious fantasy world is created, where a separate and secret life is led.[33]

Jessica, her mother and Freud are both in and not-in the situation that Abraham and Torok describe. Abraham and Torok speak of the parents having secrets: in the play the 'secret' is actually located in the mother's diary so it is not erased; yet it is a form of buried speech. The 'unsayable of the other' is actually represented as the unsayable within a relationship; and the unsayable can easily turn into the unbearable. Take the following exchange between Freud and Jessica, at the very end of the play:

Freud: The young may speak what the old cannot bear to utter.
Jessica: Because I can articulate these things does not mean I am able to bear them.[34]

To conclude. I want to return to the point at which I began, with Freud's last words about Dora. 'Reclaimed by the realities of life' implies the cathartic effect of the second dream – Dora's deliverance, her being able to tear herself away from a regressive identification, a regressive structure. But what of Rebecca, Freud's fictional patient? Jessica believes that when 'Freud' sees only a fantasy structure, he fails to set her mother free. The question she leaves the audience with is in principle this: were Jessica's mother's memories not articulated but projected out, expelled? Was she therefore still claimed by her past? And were her memories not then handed on to the next generation, to Jessica's body?

We come back again to the body. In Jean Laplanche's report of the panel discussion in 1974 on 'Hysteria Today', we find a thought-provoking commentary on the problematic of conversion:

It is our understanding of the body, more than

> our understanding of hysteria, which has changed. The body now appears to us as the locus for a communication which is potential, implicit, veiled and fixed.[35]

In speaking of attacks or crises, Laplanche continues, one is referring to 'what the French language designates by the simple word *scène*'. It indicates an action which unfolds according to a certain scenario; the place where the action is carried out; and a demonstration aimed at violently moving the partner. I want to suggest that the action which unfolds in Johnson's *Hysteria* is Jessica's mother's history; the place where it is carried out is Jessica's body; and the action is addressed to 'Freud', whom Jessica wishes so deeply to move. But it is we, the audience, who hold a complex memory of the original debates on hysteria as well as their dramatic representation today.

7

'Tied together, body to body': Anne Sexton, Linda Gray Sexton

'It is the culture,' Jerome Bruner has written, 'that provides the formulae for the construction of lives. And one of the principal instruments by which the culture does so is through its narrative forms, its genres, its modes of "packaging" forms of life.'[1] In this chapter I look at two such modes: the biographical and the autobiographical. Here they carry an additional layer of reference, for they depict not only a mother–daughter dyad, but one marked by illness. Diane Middlebrook's justly celebrated biography of the American poet Anne Sexton,[2] who committed suicide in 1974 at the age of forty-five, cannot but pose a set of questions about our time, our era, with its preoccupations with both mothering and therapy.

The book's jacket explicitly links the poet's achievement with her mental disorder – 'hers had been an important new voice in American poetry; "madness" and its cultural meanings were central in her work'. Madness is central in the biography too. The book, published in 1991, construes a world *within* therapy, *of* therapy, in the context of a life lived on the edge of madness. It is, in a sense, part of Sexton's 'truth' that her madness be depicted openly: as Middlebrook rightly points out, of the period by which Sexton had won major prizes, 'Many of Sexton's readers identified with her mental illness'.[3] So what does the book look like, feel like in the hand? To adopt Roland Barthes's distinction between the 'work' and the 'text',[4] I want to allow the book as text to be larger than its tangible form, and to represent a way of approaching, of thinking psychic life; and to link it with a second text: Anne Sexton's daughter's autobiography, published four years after Middlebrook's biography.[5]

As the biography vividly demonstrates, Anne Sexton's creativity found expression in a musical performance group, 'Anne Sexton and Her Kind'. But just as biography poses and explores a set of questions about identification, so too does autobiography, and Linda Gray Sexton's memoir, published when its author was forty-one and already a published novelist, asks a more frightened, turbulent question about the sense of inheritance, of the 'handing-on' of trauma, and about her mother's legacy. Torok and Abraham's notion of the 'unsayable of the other', which implies unconscious transmission of trauma, is not at stake here. The sense of repetition is of something all-too-recognised, and something to be consciously resisted. 'Was I turning into her? I wondered with a flat sort of horror. Had I become "Her kind"?' She continues defiantly, if sadly: '. . . I would not *be* her'.[6] Her autobiography charts the slow achievement of a voice of her own; as she puts it, of daring to speak in her own name – an achievement hard-won, and born of the slow relinquishing of her mother, paradoxically through owning experience in her own way. 'Only when I was able to acknowledge what had happened to me could I begin to dig a grave for those events.'[7] Biography and autobiography have perhaps rarely been in such close dialogue – indeed Linda Gray Sexton's book extends and amplifies Middlebrook's Sexton, with its inevitable overlaps of narration, the accounts of a given event varying slightly from one participant to the other. *Searching for Mercy Street* also raises questions about the difficulty a daughter had in experiencing the boundary of her own body as her own, as she slowly found words with which to symbolise a differentiation of herself from her mother's history, celebrity and ultimately her body. It is the texture of that dialogue which this chapter considers.

When we turn to *Anne Sexton: A Biography*, we find, on the face of it, the mirror image of Phyllis Grosskurth's framework, with its deep speculation about Melanie Klein's unconscious. In Middlebrook the clinical setting is available and made overt, in a reversal of the traditional opaqueness of psychotherapy. As the Institute of Contemporary Arts described it in a leaflet announcing a discussion with the author on publication of the book:

> At the time of her suicide in 1974, Anne Sexton was renowned for her 'confessional poetry'. In her highly controversial biography, Diane Wood Middlebrook has used the recollections of Sexton's therapist, based on recordings of their sessions, to fill in the lapses and caesuras of her life – thus interweaving public and private confession.

In this interweaving of clinical and biographical narrative there is a fascinating switch, by which that which is usually most private, hidden, sequestered (the psychiatric relationship) is the book's framing device, its foreword by Sexton's principal psychiatrist, Dr Martin Orne. It begins with his memory of his first meeting with her. Thus the book includes as a structuring element of the narrative not just a consideration of the subject's inner world, but the apparently direct access *to* that world of Anne Sexton's account of herself to her psychiatrist, and of his response to her. (In Martin Orne's words in the foreword: 'Whereas the therapist usually holds all the cards, the patient now could know more about what was happening in treatment than the therapist did.')[8] The apparently most neutral access is to be found in a transcript of one of the sessions that appears as an appendix to the book; I am reiterating the 'apparently' because of the difficulty any 'writing of madness' will encounter in reproducing the obscured messages within the overt speech of the patient.[9] We know the words, but can we know what is being said?[10] In some way the question replicates the dynamics of the oral history interview, but here there is the added dimension of a clinical transference.

The presentation of Sexton as deeply disturbed is one of the central features of the book. Anne Sexton dreaded being alone with her babies and feared she would kill them. She made innumerable suicide attempts and suffered from alcoholism. And yet, as Middlebrook so sensitively says,

> She was sick, and she needed treatment. Yet something not merely pathological is struggling to get a hearing in these pages: an irrepressible wish for an authentic social presence that was not wife, lover or mother. Sexton was beginning, tentatively, to release her 'terrible energy' not only in symptoms but in writing.[11]

She had been in treatment with Dr Orne for a year then, and it was he who suggested she write poetry. Not surprising, then, that the wish to write the therapy would be there; and to account for the fact that despite psychotherapy, and the help it gave, Sexton stayed sick. And, despite staying sick, that an 'I' emerged who could write. In Middlebrook's words, considering her famous 'signature poem' 'Her Kind': 'Through the use of an undifferentiated but double "I", the poem sets up a single persona identified with madness, but separated from it through insight.'[12] But Sexton herself doubted the authenticity of her poetic self, seeing the 'I' in poetry as a con;[13] what then of the 'I' of therapy?

The relationship to clinical material in the biography, it seems to me, is a relationship at two levels. One level consists in the amplification of mood that the sessional material offers.

> [The engagement] occurred when Anne was seventeen, but shortly thereafter, in their senior year, Jack broke off the relationship. In the heartbroken phase that followed, Anne wrote her first poems (*'bleak, depressed, horrific poems' at that, she scoffed later*).[14] (my italics)

'She scoffed later' refers to a therapy session in 1961, some seventeen years later. The phrase 'bleak, depressed, horrific' stems, it seems to me, from the self-hatred of the woman of her thirties, rewriting her past work. Neither reading obliterates the other. Indeed Middlebrook has said that the tapes did not provide her with new information but rather with confirmatory material. The one exception to this is the sessions in which Sexton was in a trance: in the biography her narratives when in trance are treated as 'not reports of actual events but explanatory fictions summoned by the power of transference to evoke sexual feelings and fantasies' (and we see Sexton slipping away from Orne's attempt to work in the transference, when he suggests the possibility that she may have sexual feelings about him).[15] The trances, then, are the point of uncertainty or disruption within the therapeutic narrative (as there are points of uncertainty in any clinical narrative); and, perhaps too, of the biographical narrative. They also enable Middlebrook to adopt a helpfully provisional stance in relation to her subject, as in her suggestion that Sexton 'may have been very dissociated when she made sexual use of Linda'.[16]

The second level is constituted by Middlebrook's recognition of the very deceptiveness of hindsight, and the delicate relationship between Sexton's writerly preoccupations at any one time and her memories of her childhood. After all, it was partly because of her 'problems with her memory' that Dr Orne suggested taping in the first place.[17] Middlebrook is herself judicious about the reliability of Sexton's memory of a possibly incestuous relationship with her father: 'the veracity of the incest narrative cannot be established historically, but that does not mean that it didn't, in a profound and lasting sense, "happen"'.[18] And perhaps because of this recognition, the psychodynamic focus of the book (the explicit reference to Freud's work; the playing out of unconscious conflict or screen memory; the question of whether Sexton was herself sexually abused) is rather to be found in Middlebrook's own commentary on her subject. It is commentary with a very light touch – particularly in relation to Sexton's daughters as they became adolescent.

Middlebrook has handled her sources with exceptional skill and sensitivity. The controversy that the book aroused, on both sides of the Atlantic, was over whether Dr Orne's decision to release the audiotapes of the therapy sessions could be justified. The professional consensus was, broadly, that it could not.[19] Dr Jeremy Lazarus, chairman of the ethics committee of the American Psychiatric Association, said only the patient could give permission for publication: 'What the family wants does not matter a whit.'[20] 'That may be true in psychiatry,' commented W.J. Weatherby, 'but not in biography', and therein lies one of the key conflicts over who should (or could) authorise an audience for Sexton's psychic life.[21] Dr Orne's stated basis for releasing the tapes was to honour the spirit of Sexton, and to help others:

> Although I had many misgivings about discussing any aspects of the therapy, which extended over eight years, I also realized that Anne herself would have wanted to share this process – so that other patients and therapists might learn from it . . . It is in the spirit of helping others that I also offer here a view of what I believe contributed to Anne's untimely death.[22]

The disclosure issue is inflected by the changes in legislation in recent years which have given patients and their relatives access to medical and psychiatric records;[23] a shift illustrated by Anne Sexton's son-in-law in a letter to the *New York Times* defending Dr Orne's decision.[24] John Freund argued that Sexton had revealed so much of her own life in her poetry, as well as allowing Linda Gray to 'use her best judgment' as literary executor with those sessional records that had not been designated as never to be published, that 'it would have been a betrayal by Linda not to allow the tapes to be used in the biography'. This formal right of access complexifies the situation, and, as Robert Stoller observed in an impassioned meditation on writing up cases, 'Who owns the tapes of interviews? – patient or doctor?' Stoller regarded many of the problems raised in writing as insoluble, and it is a reminder that the legislative and the psychic are not co-terminous.[25]

Biographers entered the debate before the biography was published, freely acknowledging the 'wish to know'. Jean Strouse, who was denied access to William James's psychiatric records for her biography of Alice James, recognised the frustration that this entailed, but still felt that 'for current patients to know that somebody could even look at such private confidential information could be devastating. Of course all biographers want to know everything, but it is still morally extremely complicated.'[26] I share this view, and believe that Dr Orne should not have released the tapes.[27] But the question about the clinical in biographical work is also a question about the status of the clinical *per se* and of writing (or speaking) from within the clinical. What kind of truth do we think it confers? What is being privileged when the clinical is foregrounded? Sexton herself wrote, in a letter to Dr Orne, of 'the big cheat' of transference.[28] Anne-Marie Sandler, in a discussion on biography with Richard Holmes at the Institute of Psycho-Analysis in 1990, made the point that the analyst gets a very selected text, in which a great deal has been forgotten, falsified.[29] And although Sexton was not in analysis with Dr Orne, she was bringing to her long therapeutic relationship with him all the passions and griefs and (in the words of the ICA leaflet) caesuras of her life to be filled in by him, or by the him she imagined a male other could be.

But to go back to Orne's confidence in what Sexton would have wanted. Much has been made of Sexton's lack of a sense of privacy. Can one be so sure that this justifies full disclosure, or indeed that we know what it is that is being disclosed? What, at source, is this genre, of clinical notes 'or, in the case of the Sexton tapes, transcriptions of sessions: what genre?'[30] Robert Stoller has mapped the issue of 'writing', 'writing up' and 'writing with' in a paper exploring the disruptive or benign effects of writing up cases. Let us set aside the specificity of Sexton's case: a suicide, an ending (which, after all, enabled Sexton's executors to make the decisions on access), the therapist's considered view that his patient would have wanted the material made public; and look more widely at the dynamics of this kind of writing.

In 'Patients' Responses to Their Own Case Reports', Stoller noted a professional silence on the topic: it is 'a problem pretty much untouched in our literature – that our version of the clinical moment is the official one'. It is his starting point for a discussion of his practice of writing collaboratively with his non-analytic patients, for publication.

> The two patients with whom I did this work during treatment both felt it was powerfully helpful. Can we trust their opinion? Will their enthusiasm persist after treatment ends? In later years? The jolt of insight is a rare occurrence in insight treatments. Should that jolt come from seeing oneself written about?
>
> We must cut to the bone on the nature of our evidence. Can we know what was happening in the

> office as doctor and patient talked? Can the analyst, the patient, a third party? How are the reports on the encounter related to the event being described? . . . how can I share with you the original event in an analysis?[31]

Stoller's questioning offers a thought-provoking counter to one of Middlebrook's comments on Sexton: 'she was floundering in self-disgust and confusion – a condition that eludes representation but is well registered in the doctor's notes'.[32] The comment suggests, perhaps too confidently, that the scholar – like the analyst – can 'know' what took place, or complete another's experience, thus securing a narrative. Here I think we need the enigmatic and yet subversive import of John Forrester's observation that psychoanalysis is a conversation taking place in the absence of the real.[33] 'Even the analyst is absent when addressed in the transferential mode of the second person.'[34] It is an interesting point of reference back to Sexton's own sense of the 'big cheat' of transference, her capacity to problematise the therapeutic relationship; and her comparable puzzle about the 'I' of poetry, its status as con.

The point is arresting in relation to the project of the biography. There is a sense in which the seamless interweaving of the sessional material – and to say that the book reads like a dream may be no coincidence – produces the ambience *of* everyday life within the consulting room. There is no sense, in the main, of a different discourse, a different *order* of things, at odds with the 'constructed eloquence' that a biography confers.[35] Yet is that not the paradox at the heart of Middlebrook's writing, and indeed in the notion of the transference? Transference implies a layering of emotion, the source of which is initially obscured, and calling for deconstruction over time; the rhetorical mode of a biography inclines towards synchronic coherence. I would want to suggest that the analytic dialogue is, and always remains, a 'different order of things' from the everyday. The prose form of a biography, in which the audiotapes are presented, ostensibly, as another branch of the data – as opposed to a different order of reality, of experience, cut across and swathed in disturbances of memory and emotion – may obscure that necessary gap.[36]

The question would then be (if one could resolve the ethical question): *would* there be a way of representing the relationship between everyday life and the analytic space in prose, in a biography; and one organised, as Diane Middlebrook's is, around the linear time of narrative?

Linda Gray Sexton's *Searching for Mercy Street: My Journey Back to My Mother, Anne Sexton* is also a retrospective prose narrative,[37] but written in part in a considered yet urgent present tense, a tense of discovery: 'As I sit here today at my word processor, I can see both what was and what is yet before me. I become my own character: my life, this book.'[38] I am reminded of John Berger's felicitous comments on tense, for his remarks on 'I am' can be applied to Linda Gray Sexton's 'I become':

> The present tense of the verb *to be* refers only to the present: but nevertheless with the first person singular in front of it, it absorbs the past which is inseparable from it. 'I am' includes all that has made me so. It is more than a statement of immediate fact: it is already biographical.[39]

As in Middlebrook's biography, *Searching*'s chosen frame is mental illness, with its still-vivid demands – 'Mother's mental illness, which lived among us like a fifth person'. But identification and its vicissitudes provide the narrative energy of the memoir. Is she like her mother? How can she make herself as unlike as possible? Is she like a mother, or is she like a mental illness? The book charts a fervent, at times disrupted, search for health, but more often escape from what the book jacket calls Anne Sexton's 'toxic embrace'. For Linda Sexton was rarely angry as a child, but became angrier as her own therapy proceeded, and as she got further away in time from her mother's death in 1974. Time thus had the power both to release her and to claw her in. In recording this angry search for health, the memoir raises a point about identity.

Rosalind Delmar once observed that the central, organising 'I' of the feminist autobiographical novel (of which Agnes Smedley's *Daughter of Earth* is a noted example) finds its identity in its opposition to the 'he' of the world outside the novel;[40] here 'mother' is the opposite term. In Linda Sexton's memoir a sense of likeness is opposed most severely. I am suggesting that it is *because* she feels linked bodily to her mother, and that necessarily disturbs identification. Similarly, where the 'I' of autobiography is often a self-affirming I, confidently assumed,[41] in Linda Sexton's case we find initially the virtual absence of a subject, and then, gradually, a determination to replace the clamorous 'I' of her mother with her own, independent 'I'. For although she had co-operated fully with Diane Middlebrook, she had not anticipated the revival of grief and mourning which the book's publication would stir up. It is indeed striking that Middlebrook's biography seems to have acted as a toxic object for Sexton's daughter, exerting the powerful effect of the mother once more. And perhaps not surprising, as it exposed to the light of day not just Anne Sexton's sexual use of Linda, but Anne Sexton's rage towards the daughter who she claimed she had 'never loved'.

How to counter such rage? 'Perhaps what I needed to do was to write about the issue directly,' Linda Sexton writes.[42] The memoir is presented as a confession; the jacket tell us that it has taken the author twenty years to address these words to her mother. It is a paean to writing as therapy, as integration of self, though its shifting between present and past tenses is suggestive of a troubling eternity of certain psychic states. Significantly, those described in the present tense are usually associated with incest, and 'incest' appears as both fact and interpretation: it both states its presence in the Sexton family and acts as an interpretative device.[43] Incest both explains why something is as it is, and why the author's life doesn't work as it should. This use of tense is in fact a repetition, as Linda Gray Sexton tells us that when she was working on a novel at the same time as Diane Middlebrook was working on the biography,

> an odd phenomenon occurred and continued to recur whenever I was creating the scenes of incest in the book: . . . I began to type, quite unconsciously, in the first-person voice of the daughter and in the present tense as well – even though the rest of the book was crafted in the third person, using the past tense.[44]

It felt compelling and she left it intact. It formed the prelude to her gaining access, in therapy, to new memories of her mother's sexual relationship with her.

From the outset, then, *Searching* depicts, in its author's words, 'motherhood as a dangerous state of being'. There is the desperation to grow up and away from Anne Sexton; the minutiae of emergency American psychiatry, in a darkly evocative account of admissions wards and their regulations; the atmosphere of secrecy, well drawn, that pervaded the family's efforts at maintaining a suburban Boston front. We met it first in Middlebrook's account; here it carries the more aggressive, fight-for-life quality of a key protagonist. And where the trances in Anne Sexton's therapy, in Middlebrook, work as an explanatory fiction, their meaning for Linda Gray Sexton was of palpable loss or the onset of such loss.

> [D]epression could and did flood her during the

> [Christmas] season, especially after her parents died, and some years she would sit twirling her hair, trance-like, at the kitchen table, dragging herself through the season. Then the rituals became painful symbols of all she had once possessed and all she had lost at their passing.[45]

Absence and loss – of a mother – run through the text. Because she allowed no distance between them, Anne Sexton could not be a mother to Linda. But at times the absence of distance did not feel merely symbolic to the daughter: Linda describes her mother masturbating on her body in bed.[46] Here the openness of meaning or memory that a biographer is able to rely on may not be available to the autobiographer. Linda Gray Sexton is author and subject of her own text – she can write only of what is most real to her, and true for her. Ultimately, then, it is having sex which takes her from her mother 'with a finality no psychiatrist could have managed'. The body, again; this time, in an act that separates. Yet, throughout it all was her mother's commanding stage presence and the telling observation, over a reading at Harvard College, that 'we were tied together, body to body'.[47] Once again there is the ebb and flow of identification: now subverted by an utter sense of physical identity, now strengthened by some act of independence.

When it came to Anne Sexton's death, Linda Sexton's account of her mother's suicide amplifies the short, dramatic statement of it in Middlebrook. There may have been a reason for this: 'how cathartic . . . to experience each time the shock of her death through my own words'.[48] More words. On reading her mother's papers, she was presented with a seemingly unanswerable question: 'How should a daughter feel on learning her mother wanted to kill her? As a child I had learned to split off feeling.' But the news that audiotapes of her mother's therapy would become available brought old feelings troublingly close to home:

> I could not begin to imagine the pain contained in over three hundred hours of such tapes. But then it occurred to me: Diane would be the buffer; Diane would listen and transcribe.[49]

'When she interviewed me for the first time, I cried and released into Diane's care all the ambivalence I felt at having been my mother's daughter. I was anxious to give it away – and naive enough to believe I could.' Interestingly, in this situation of proximity to another's listening – Middlebrook and the tapes – Linda Gray Sexton seems to have gained access, in her own therapy, to a new and this time tormenting memory. And here the sequence of pronouns became crucially important to her – witness her beleaguered reversal of her psychiatrist's probing of her sexual involvement with her mother: '*She* had been fooling around with *me*',[50] most definitely not the other way round. Responsibility had to be in its proper place, psychically and syntactically. By the time Middlebrook's biography was published, however, Linda Gray was beside herself with distress, and it is striking that the cultural stir the biography created coincided with her becoming suicidally depressed. It was the writing of *Searching* that gave her an identity, and indeed makes identification, or nearness, almost benign: 'It no longer seems a crime to admit, I have been her kind.'[51]

On reflection, though, what *did* Linda Gray Sexton have to distinguish herself from her mother? To claim her independent 'I'? It is painful to see the arduous establishment of the merest sense of existing in Linda Sexton's memoir. From a sense of not existing at all, with no vocabulary for an existence, and no sense of choosing between possible vocabularies, the daughter was able to secure a frame for her life. Such a process belongs in a very different tradition from that exemplified, for instance, in J.-B. Pontalis's autobiography *Love of Beginnings*: 'One shouldn't write *one* autobiography but ten of them or a hundred because, while we have only one life, we have innumerable ways of recounting that life (to ourselves).'[52] At the outset Linda Sexton seems to have felt she had only another's life to recount. So we could suggest that Linda Sexton's memoir creates itself by *resisting* the invitation to be drawn into another's life (her mother's life) – or asking the reader not to be thus drawn in.[53]

To whom, then, is the appeal addressed? It is in part to herself. But only in part. Here the question of *how* that sense of existing is created is important. It is via the reading public, as well as via therapy. It is the reader who is addressed, who is invited to witness Linda Gray Sexton's resistance to a malign identification. The memoir sets up and reinforces the paradox that Linda Sexton herself feels revulsion from knowledge yet insists on the reader's exposure to it, a paradox resolved in the book's closing chapters where the author is making her peace with her mother's creativity, and the notion that the 'only way to transcend hurt is to tell it all, honestly'.[54] Is this a betrayal? And if so, of whom? Linda Gray was herself preoccupied with this when she wondered if she should release the 300 hours of therapy tapes that Dr Orne had in his possession. In therapy she had gone over and over her decision to release the tapes and had concluded it had been because they would 'illuminate the roots of the poetry'. It was her second experience of such a situation. When she first listened to the small batch of therapy tapes found among her mother's papers she had wanted to burn them but decided that they were part of her mother's gift to the world and that her mother had invaded her own privacy long before; so she decided on a restricted collection at the Harry Ransom Humanities Research Center in the University of Texas at Austin.

When something becomes public, then, is betrayal inherently in play? Richard Holmes, for example, has suggested that the biographer makes a life his own (like a friendship) and the public's (like a betrayal).[55] But the 'public' is constituted in different ways at different times. Susan Cheever's cover endorsement for *Searching* tells us that 'any mother and any daughter' will recognise themselves in this account, thus establishing the Sexton family as emblematic. And perhaps so, at least as emblematic of a certain way of reading the culture. For it does sometimes seem as if child abuse has become 'the' signifier of our time (as in a study of Virginia Woolf by Louise de Salvo, which took Woolf to be a representative of the abused child of the twentieth century, the bearer of the culture, *tout court*).[56] To borrow a phrase from an earlier discussion of women's autobiography, Linda Gray Sexton presents a 'story of damage and neglect', but this time on a scale which led at least one of her reviewers to lament the absence of stories of domestic life in the USA in which incest and child abuse did *not* take place.[57]

At source, however, Linda Sexton's memoir explores different forms of talk. What it is to talk; when memory is 'tugging' (in her words); when she coolly tells one of her mother's companions that no good would come of talk, as 'no one would feel better'. Linda Gray Sexton's memoir, saturated with anxiety and rage about her mother's mothering, takes as part of its project the affirmation of a sense of self as mother that allows for boundaries and difference. It is the sense of a boundary achieved that enables her to draw a line under her experience as a daughter. For ultimately, when we ask questions about 'truth', we draw a distinction between biographical (or actual) and narrative (or psychic) truth.[58] The achievement of a narrative does not imply that there can be only one actual truth. There are different ways of reading a narrative truth and considering the action of the past on the present. Knowledge remains deceptive, after all, and there may be no going back to a solid or real knowledge of origins. Does something the child speaks of directly symbolise the mother, or does it stand for something that the child distinguishes from the mother?[59] In the case of Anne Sexton and Linda Gray Sexton that debate was played out over ownership of the body, the subject's and the other's. It was only, I am suggesting, when Linda Sexton believed that her body now belonged to her that she was able to draw on the power of words to compose her own narrative. The process may have been more primitive still: perhaps it was only then that she knew that the possibility of narrative might be available to her.

8

Unveiling and obscuring in the image of abuse

Debates on 'real events', 'fantasies', memory and the influence of the past take place in part in the context of the sea change in cultural and political life created, at least in the UK, by the events in Cleveland. It is now a truism to observe that we are surrounded by intensified representations of sexual abuse, and to observe that sexual abuse has a visibility and a profile which largely date from the events in Cleveland. We see this in charity and police advertising, in investigative journalism, in discussions of the eroticised in art photography of small children, in the sexual abuse storylines of TV soaps like *EastEnders* and *Brookside*. And what might make my starting point less of a truism and perhaps more vivid would be to take, at random, some indications of that sea change. It is associated not just with a quantity of images, but with the sense of a truth-value in 'showing', or sight, and the close association of truth with vision.[1] This idea is particularly relevant to the question of child abuse, with its location as a 'reality' to which many have been 'blind', as a writer like Alice Miller has been so powerfully effective in conveying.

Here, then, are three moments in the space of twenty-four hours in December 1994, reported in the first person to conjure up the subjective sensation of bombardment by images and sound. I watched a BBC TV documentary in the 'Forbidden Britain' series, this one on memories of abuse, in which elderly women talked movingly and with restraint about experiences as small children for which they had no vocabulary. The next day I picked up some sugar packets in a café near Oxford Circus, and noticed that each of them advertised an NSPCC sugarthon, and carried a message: '£15 could help pay for a counselling session for an abused child', '£15 could help ensure abused children have the protection that is theirs by right'. Then I bought the *Evening Standard* and read about a new London Transport advertising campaign which would cover entire buses with ads: 'Next month the capital will get a taste of things to come with a "consciousness raising" display in which 750 double-deckers will carry posters on the theme of child abuse.'[2]

This proliferation of representations – from the miniature of a sugar packet to the larger-than-life vista of a fleet of buses acting as town crier – is striking. The difficult but important question in it all is not so much what has brought this about, but rather: is it to be straightforwardly read as a sign of cultural advance, of society at last taking on board the real conditions of children's lives? What kind of sign is it? Is child abuse representable? If so, in what way? What 'drops out' in these representations? In this chapter I am suggesting that the representations are simultaneously an unveiling or truth-telling and an obscuring or displacement, an attempt at an account of a reality which, while destructive in and of itself, is in important ways evanescent and perhaps unrepresentable.

Yet its representation is now ubiquitous. It coexists with an almost limitless set of other representations, is framed by those other representations, and its reception is inevitably determined by a pre-existing mode of looking. To explore these images is to pose a question about the relationship between representation and 'reality'. For the very term 'sexual abuse' has come to cover over the inarticulacy and inchoateness of an experience which may have made no sense at the time. It is that wordless confusion which lies at the heart of the destructiveness of the experience.

There have recently been high-profile media campaigns by children's charities, of which the most notable has been that of the NSPCC. Indeed the recent crop of ads for the charities working with disadvantaged or abused children has been made possible by the deregulation of the charity sector under Margaret Thatcher. The increase in awareness of child sexual abuse coincides with this deregulation, which persuaded charities of the need for marketing solutions to their problems.[3] Andrew Cooper, writing from a social work perspective, has argued that professionals have been faced with a dilemma: 'how far child protection professionals can set the agenda in terms which both enable their view to compete effectively in the marketplace of public images, and respect the complex, uncertain experiences of abused children and adults and those who work with them'.[4] At the same time large agencies saw that big money was to be made from the charities; agencies had 'responded to their saturated markets by trying to create and construct new ones'.[5] So it might be thought that a mutual fit could be found: two sets of needs, one strategy. But even if ads do not offer 'false' ideals, or obscure the real structure of society, as Judith Williamson's *Decoding Advertisements*[6] suggested they did (it is clear that the charity ads aim to make a point, an announcement, about the 'real structure' of society) the abused-child ads are still located in a contradictory space: one associated with purchases, with material and cultural aspiration – that is, with fantasies about the self and its choices.

More broadly, the charities' own history is being reasserted too, for we are also witnessing the anniversaries of important charities. Blake Morrison's profile of Dr Barnardo's betrays one of our most powerful cultural assumptions at the moment: that it is better to know about the truth – whether one is the progeny of incest or not – than to repress it (in his words, 'than to live among lies and secrets'). As Morrison reports, 'it is a principle of modern childcare . . . that children who have been adopted or fostered or placed in local authority care need to know about their past, not repress it'.[7] It stands for the 'announcement' end of a spectrum of meanings that I am suggesting is in place. Yet Nick Hedges's experience of photographing for Shelter in the late 1970s points up some of these difficulties. 'By presenting to the public the "real" world of bad housing I thought that the truth of these observations would effect a change in their attitudes.'[8] He found they did not.

What kind of announcement is this? The ads are often found in city spaces, and here the notion of the urban uncanny is relevant. As James Donald writes:

> The disquieting slippage between a place where we should feel at home and the sense that it is, at some level, definitively unhomely provided the starting point for Freud's idea that the uncanny, the *unheimlich*, is rooted in the familiar, the *heimlich* . . . This uncanny city is not out there in the streets. It defines the architecture of our apparently most secret selves: an already social space.[9]

Child sexual abuse (as opposed to paedophilia) is associated with the family. And so the dark space of the city, epitomised in the anomie of the Underground, provides the setting for many of the charity ads. But the ads present the spectator with a dilemma, for they are 'read' within a transitory environment – the journey to work, the night out – associated with escape into fantasy.

And there is a further layer to the contradictory location of these images. As Victor Burgin has reminded us, fantasies of seduction are frequently represented in ads generally.[10] In the abused-child ads the transgressive, the socially disruptive is represented. Thus they embody a contradiction. They take a visual form associated with the representation of a 'primal fantasy' – being seduced into a purchase, or a desire – while at the same time they 'tell the story' of a desire transgressed which has caused harm. And since, further, the erotic is latent in all acts of looking, advertising images of sexually abused children thus carry a multiplicity of messages, and evoke a multiplicity of responses, perhaps a replication of the eroticised look of the abusing adult.

These largely black and white ads ostensibly portray a reality, and they are in competition with colour and with pleasure. According to Sean Brierley, the most used adjectives in advertising are 'free', 'new', 'better', 'safe', 'clean', 'delicious', 'full', 'rich'.[11] There is, then, a welter of convention associated with the form and content of print ads within which charity advertising occupies a liminal, edgy space. These ads are in an understandably paradoxical relation to the seduction fantasy associated with advertising – for in them not much is obscured or made symbolic.[12] As Brierley tells us, creatives in advertising want to create the feeling of a 'magical world of the brand, to lift it above the world of everyday practices; more than real', a feeling that can tap into the popular pre-conscious of common knowledge (holidays, etc.).[13] But in the abused-child ads something naked – I use the word deliberately – is on display; something that is associated with a traumatic past, rather than something delicious and rich or safe and clean (see Figure 1). It is this personal past which is conjured up by means of the caption.[14]

The anchorage of the caption in the sexual abuse ads is never surreal, but is usually explicit and unadorned. Thus in the NSPCC's 'A Cry for Children' campaign in 1995, one of the Underground posters was titled 'Alexandra's story', and captioned: 'Child abuse isn't just about sexual assault and physical brutality, but can have less obvious effects which can be just as devastating, like neglect and

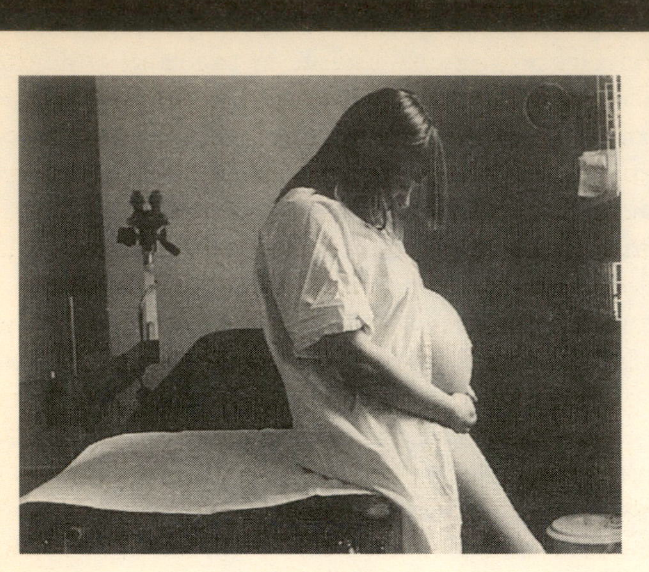

We both have the same Father.

This is Sally's story.

'My mum died when I was twelve. One night when I had a bad dream my dad said I could sleep in his bed.

To start with he just cuddled me, but then he started doing other things. I wanted him to stop but he wouldn't. I hated it, it really hurt. He said it meant he loved me.

The next day when I was leaving for school he said I mustn't tell anyone about what happened. After that he wanted me to sleep with him every night. He called it our little secret.

Later, when my periods stopped my dad kept me off school. He told them that I was ill.

Sometimes I can feel the baby moving inside me, it feels horrible.'

Luckily Sally's school reported her absence and now she's getting all the support she needs.

Of course, there's more to her abuse than becoming pregnant.

She'll need long term counselling to tackle the emotional damage, such as feelings of guilt and an inability to form relationships.

In fact, all forms of abuse can cause emotional harm. Not just the more obvious forms involving sexual assault and physical brutality.

For example, withdrawal of any signs of affection, ignoring children, constantly criticizing or shouting at them can lead to emotional scars which last a lifetime.

Sometimes, children can even be driven to commit suicide.

Because of all this, the NSPCC has launched a campaign called 'A Cry for Children'. It's a cry to everyone to think about the way they behave towards children.

To listen to them, talk to them and treat them with respect.

And to recognise the impact that any form of cruelty can have on a child. Please answer the cry.

If you, or someone you know is suffering from abuse, please call the NSPCC Child Protection Helpline on 0800 800 500 any time, day or night.

Or if, after reading this, you would find more information helpful, please call us on 0171 825 2775.

NSPCC

A cry for children.

TO PROTECT THE INDIVIDUAL'S IDENTITY A MODEL HAS BEEN USED. BASED ON A CASE HISTORY. REGISTERED CHARITY NO. 216401. STORE CODE 0451.

Figure 1

emotional cruelty'. It is a most direct mode of address. And to the idea that people bring their own history, desires and knowledge to texts (with ads as texts), we might respond that in a certain sense in the case of child sexual abuse they do not; rather they bring the desire *not* to know, as has been shown consistently in clinical work in the area. It implies a problematic relationship to knowledge, for some of the most effective print ads do by contrast stimulate the desire to know; often precisely because they are almost exclusively image based within the setting of recognised if elusive landscapes, but lack the anchorage of the caption.[15]

It might be argued that the notion of defamiliarisation offers a way out of the impasse that the abused-child ads present: it is the very visual surprise that reveals the 'truth' of society;[16] the unveiling that can be achieved by the visual. And this is, in some senses, what the charity ads seem to be seeking. The device of defamiliarisation is of special relevance to text-based ads, for it gives a sense of deviating from 'ordinary language', of disrupting our habitual perception of the world, enabling us to 'see' things afresh (see Figure 2). Thus the YMCA's fundraising print ad 'At 15, Emily stopped having sex with a man she didn't love anymore' (Figure 3) is dominated by its bold sans-serif headline, white reversed out of black, which is read against an angled family snap which shows us that the man she didn't love any more is in fact her father (a middle-aged man with his arm protectively round a pubescent girl, both smiling to the camera but the girl edging just slightly away from him). In much smaller print the ad informs us that 'At 16 she was sleeping in doorways. Over 40% of Britain's homeless young women were sexually abused in childhood.' The eye is drawn inexorably down from the headline to the image, and then to the detailed text, which encourages the reader to send money 'and help restart some lives that stopped a long time ago'. Another from the YMCA, 'Some people just see garbage' (Figure 4), is more confrontational, its mode of address more provocative.

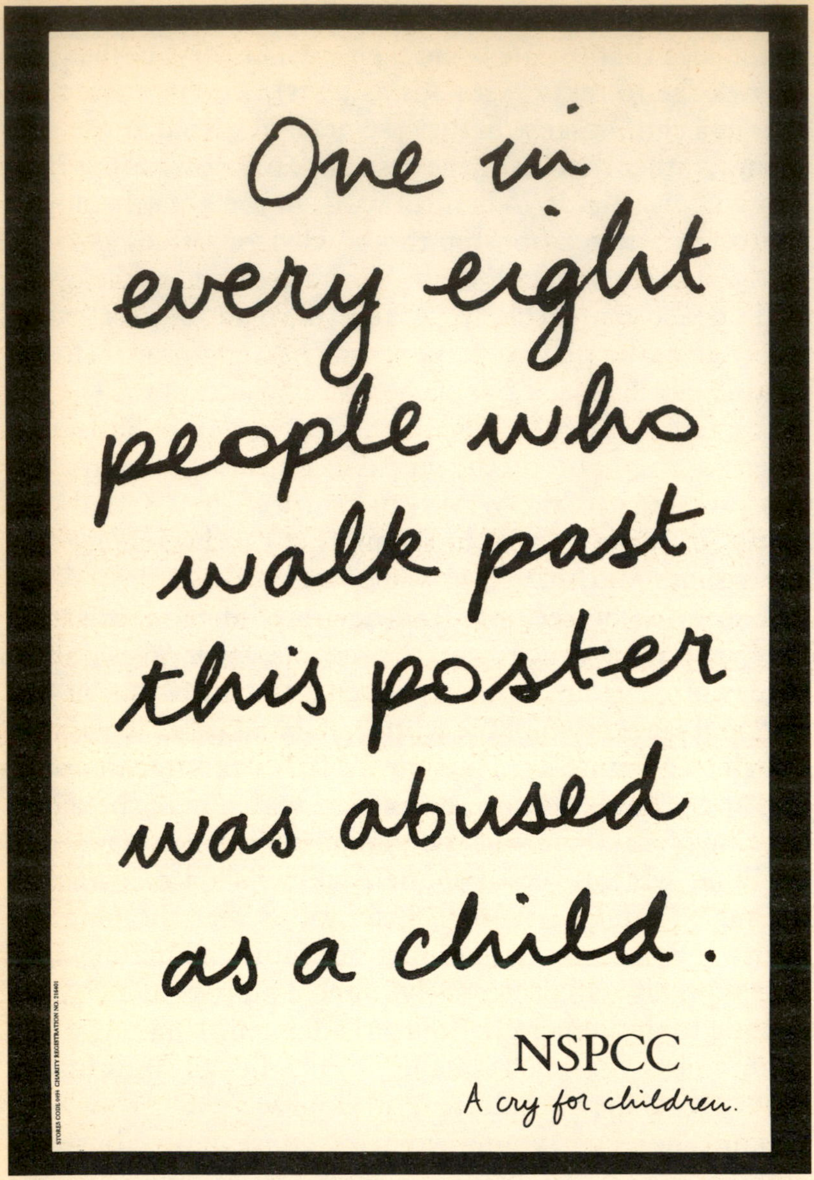

One in
every eight
people who
walk past
this poster
was abused
as a child.

NSPCC
A cry for children.

Figure 2

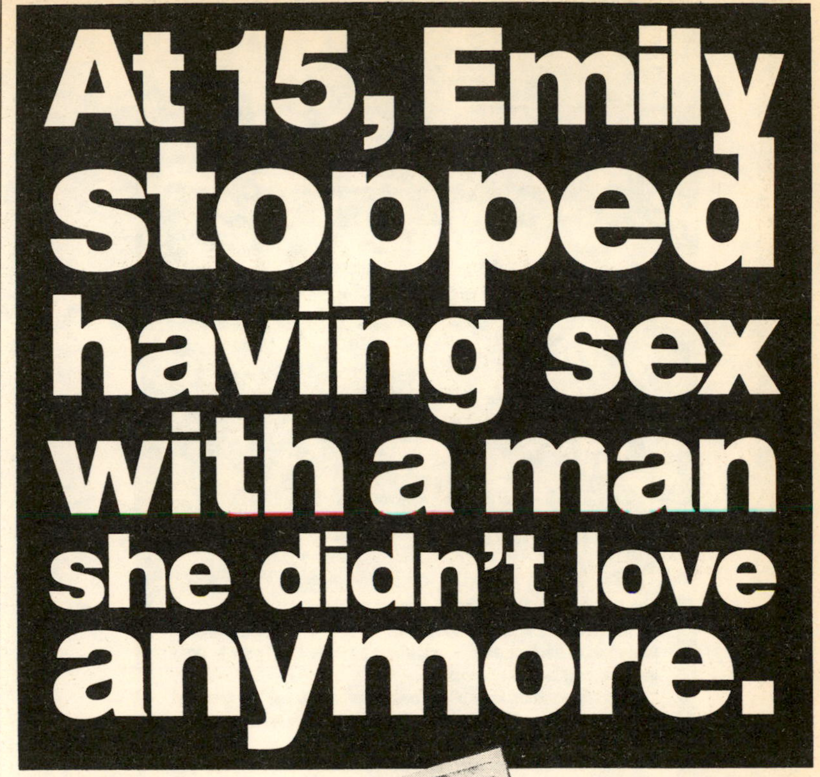

At 15, Emily
stopped
having sex
with a man
she didn't love
anymore.

At 16 she was sleeping in doorways.

Over 40% of Britain's homeless young women were sexually abused in childhood.

Most carry the scars for the rest of their lives. The streets are often preferable to the horrors they face at home. And so, many move to the cities in an attempt to start again.

But there they join the thousands of other youngsters, homeless as a result of poverty, broken homes or unemployment.

The YMCA movement is Britain's largest charitable provider of accomodation and training for young people. We are there to respond before a problem becomes a crisis. And to catch vulnerable youngsters before they get hurt. But we can only help if you help.

Through 200 local associations, all over the country, your money can give comfort to those most in need. You can prevent homelessness and unemployment. You can provide rooms, expert counselling, training and a future.

Lasting care instead of short term relief.

All these youngsters ever wanted is what we all take for granted. Safety and the sort of love that asks for nothing back.

So please, if you really want to help, do this. Send them your love in the form of a cheque and help restart some lives that stopped a long time ago.

I want to help. Please find enclosed my cheque for £10 ☐ £20 ☐ £50 ☐ other £______

Name(Mr/Mrs/Miss)

Address

Postcode

Send your donation directly to your local YMCA or to:
John Naylor, National Secretary, National Council of YMCAs, 640 Forest Road, Freepost, London E17 3BR

BI1

MEETING THE NEEDS OF YOUNG PEOPLE SINCE 1844

The YMCA is a Christian charity committed to helping young people, particularly at times of need, regardless of gender, race, ability or faith

Figure 3

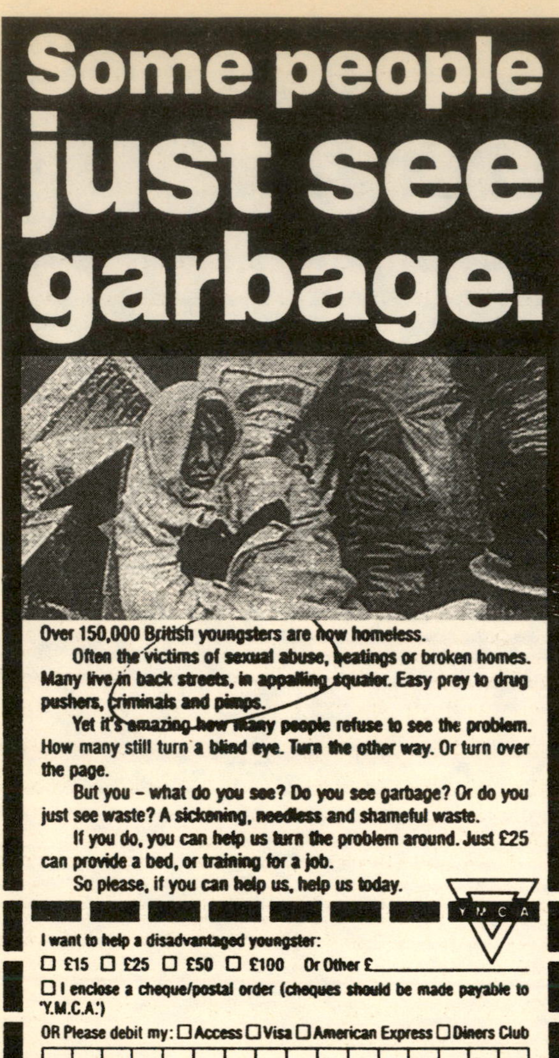
Some people just see garbage.
Over 150,000 British youngsters are now homeless.
Often the victims of sexual abuse, beatings or broken homes. Many live in back streets, in appalling squalor. Easy prey to drug pushers, criminals and pimps.
Yet it's amazing how many people refuse to see the problem. How many still turn a blind eye. Turn the other way. Or turn over the page.
But you – what do you see? Do you see garbage? Or do you just see waste? A sickening, needless and shameful waste.
If you do, you can help us turn the problem around. Just £25 can provide a bed, or training for a job.
So please, if you can help us, help us today.
YMCA
I want to help a disadvantaged youngster:
£15 £25 £50 £100 Or Other £
I enclose a cheque/postal order (cheques should be made payable to 'Y.M.C.A.')
OR Please debit my: Access Visa American Express Diners Club
Card Expiry Date:
Name (Mr/Mrs/Miss/Ms):
Address:
Postcode
Signature
Date
IS/A
Please enclose your donation in an envelope, and send to:
John Naylor, YMCA National Council, FREEPOST, London E17 3BR.
YMCA
GIVING TODAY'S YOUNG PEOPLE A BETTER TOMORROW.

Figure 4

The heavily cropped image is of the pavement level of a street; we see bin liners and part of a hooded, grim-faced young person. Again a fundraiser about homelessness, the small print informs us that the young homeless are 'often the victims of sexual abuse, beatings or broken homes'.[17]

These children's faces are usually solemn and to camera. The images are designed to shock. In the NSPCC's 'A Cry for Children' campaign, the images are mainly in the tradition of art and documentary photography (which, in its graininess, has been increasingly used for television commercials for mineral water, fragrance, upmarket clothing – items for the body, items to be worn on the body). This use of black and white for both documentation of abuse and the aspirational imagery of consumption is striking: desire (and the family, as in the Calvin Klein 'Eternity' series) is signalled in the use of black and white, but so is the perversion of desire. 'Desire and the body'/'perversion of bodily desire' is the binary involved. For just as colour is intricately coded in established advertising practice, the use of black and white in both types of advertising illustrates the point that black represents both the sophisticated and mysterious, and the sinister.

There is a less dramatic group of ads, in what may seem a more euphemistic approach than the 'defamiliarising' of the YMCA ads. It relies on the reader's pre-existing understanding of what is being said. In fact it is only apparently a euphemism; it offers merely a more subdued, shadowy image. The caption is discreet (see Figure 5). The Children's Society ran 'Send £15. Before someone else offers her more' widely at the end of 1994; the word 'sexual' does not appear, but the phrase 'working the streets' does: the image depicts a young teenager walking down a darkened street while a man on his own, a little behind her, is ambiguously in her orbit. What will become of her?[18] 'Innocence can be traded for the price of a meal. Once it's gone, it can never be bought back,' the copy continues.

Send £15.

Before someone else offers her more.

Today, she's lonely and walking the streets. Tomorrow she could be working them.

When you're cold and hungry, innocence can be traded in for the price of a meal. Once it's gone, it can never be bought back.

Research recently carried out for The Children's Society found that, before they reach 16, more than 10,000 of today's children will repeatedly run away and find themselves facing the same dangers.

There's no shortage of people ready to exploit kids who are new to the streets. There is a shortage of people they can trust.

The streetworkers from The Children's Society are invaluable. They offer advice, counselling and refuge when needed. But, most importantly, they listen.

Your donations are vital if we are to keep the streetworkers on the streets. And to help get more young people off them.

Please send whatever you can now. Stop another childhood ending overnight.

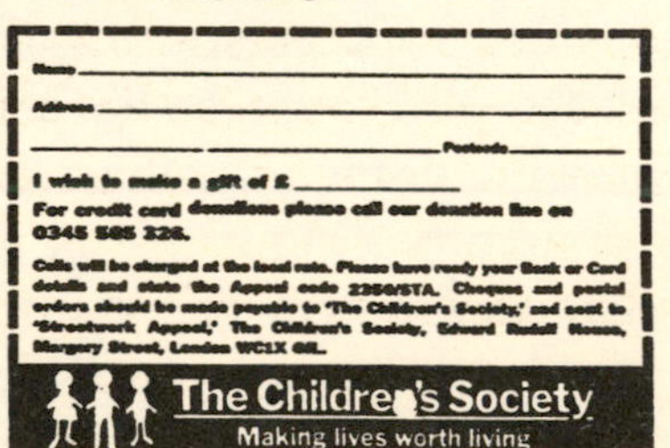

I wish to make a gift of £
The Childre's Society
Making lives worth living

INCOME FROM THIS APPEAL WILL BE PUT INTO A CENTRAL FUND AND USED WHERE THE NEED IS GREATEST. REGISTERED CHARITY NUMBER 221124.
A VOLUNTARY SOCIETY OF THE CHURCH OF ENGLAND AND THE CHURCH IN WALES.

Figure 5

In the idea of innocence that can be lost it may be no coincidence that what's at stake is sexual exploitation (prostitution) rather than familial sexual abuse, the former being a traditionally recognised social problem. But what, even so, do all these images share? They *wish* to offer a depiction of loss – usually of the permanent loss of innocence (or we read them thus). Can they do this? They also wish to inspire action: while they aim to represent a lost personal past they display a past (like museum ads); but unlike museum images, which invite looking at a past, these are an invitation to act upon it, and act fast. This notion of lost innocence – of loss, more widely – brings to mind a remark by Barthes in *Camera Lucida*, written in the wake of his mother's death.[19] John Tagg reads Barthes as asserting a realist position, taking the photograph as authentication, of a reality one can no longer touch. Tagg reads this in the context of the loss of Barthes's mother;[20] here we have a poignant exploration of the way in which a powerful image can stand in for a past that is slipping away from the subject. Yet within the realism there may also lie a contradiction, for Barthes speaks of the photograph's totality of image:

> this very special image gives itself out as complete . . . the photographic image is full, crammed: no room, nothing can be added to it.[21]

The contradiction I am pointing to is not one which Barthes was addressing. Sexual abuse as a subjective experience is often described as being far from a totality, far from being full – more of an evacuation of the inside of the personality, and so often of the evacuation of meaning. This is the displacement at work. It acts to deny the unbearable.

Barthes's 'punctum' denoted the way in which a particular photograph pricks you, seeks you, pierces you, wounds you; the punctum also stood for the piercing lost reality Barthes wanted to experience.[22] This notion of a punctum uncannily echoes the very etymology of the 'traumatic' as a wound on the surface of the body that I looked at in Chapter 4. Charity advertising images strive to do the same: to evoke a lost reality. But Tagg says that photography cannot do this, it produces a new and specific reality: here, we could say it would be that of the abused child. I suggest that the images of the sexually abused child work at this level: in their unadorned brutality they give to the viewer *one* part of the experience that is being depicted: piercing and wounding; but not perhaps the emptiness that is so often its aftermath.

Whereas the charity advertising is designed to stimulate giving, the documentary explosion and the sexual abuse storyline of *Brookside* offer a more mobile set of identifications for the viewer. Documentary sequences make use of the passage of time (the real time of viewing) to achieve emotional impact through silence or sound, through the juxtaposition of images, and through the subject's own speech. Here the unspeakable may be not only the distress of the experience but a psychic dimension which may be too embarrassing or too undignified to put into words, though yet a dimension which the subject may be able to signal. One of the most telling moments in the BBC TV programme I mentioned (p. 110), for example, came when an elderly woman described how she 'couldn't always match her husband's virility' and he thought she was tiring of him. She said 'it was not him, it was me – because of certain experiences. And in all honour I felt I should tell him. Then he was *more* considerate and never again referred to it.'[23] It seemed that for this woman it was her husband's silence, as much as her own announcement, which was healing.

'Forbidden Britain' introduced the possibility of silence rather than speech as therapeutic. There *is* a voice. But there is also a capacity, through the intercutting of old documentary footage, to *evoke* a wordless atmosphere of betrayal, to portray childhood as a felt state of innocence, delicately intercutting between old footage – often of parts of the bodies, usually girls' lower limbs, mainly playing, with children's songs, old blocks of flats – and women talking to camera. An environment is gradually established, displayed. Narrative makes this effect possible; still photography cannot achieve it in the same way.

Roland Barthes himself draws this contrast, in *Camera Lucida*, speaking of the photograph's totality of image, and here I give the earlier quotation in full:

> this very special image gives itself out as complete . . . the photographic image is full, crammed: no room, nothing can be added to it. In the cinema, whose raw material is photographic, the image does not, however, have this completeness (which is fortunate for the cinema) . . . in the cinema, no doubt, there is always a photographic referent, but this referent shifts, it does not make a claim in favor of its reality, it does not protest its former existence.[24]

Let's consider these shifting referents. Drama shares with documentary the scope for representing the dynamics of situations, including repetition and, more ambiguously and problematically, denial. *Brookside* is not the first soap to run a sexual abuse storyline (*EastEnders* did this early in 1991), but in 1995 *Brookside*'s fictional Jordache family became part of a wider cultural and political debate about incest and wife-battering and their effects. Television in general occupies a structurally different position from the urban uncanny: it is more defiantly associated with the tamed and the everyday, as Barthes put it, and as a backdrop to the everyday.[25] All the more interesting, therefore, that the line between fiction and reality, representation and actuality, became blurred with the *Brookside* murder trial.

The storyline turned on a battered wife, Mandy Jordache,

who murdered her husband with the help of her sexually abused daughter Beth. The younger daughter, Rachel, did not know of the murder (which they kept secret for two years, having buried Trevor Jordache under the patio in the back garden of their Liverpool home). When Rachel found out that her father had been killed she was devastated and claimed he had never touched her, though Mandy told the police (in a fragmentary, faltering way), in a reference to his sexual abuse of her younger daughter, that it was when 'he did . . . *that* . . . to Rachel that I had to kill him – I just found the knife in my hand.' The story was thus staging all the elements of a contested narrative.

At the time of the murder verdict in May 1995, Suzanne Moore wrote in the *Guardian* – presciently, as it turned out – that the Jordache trial had touched a nerve in a way that the real-life plight of the convicted killer Sara Thornton had not.[26] That view was echoed on *Newsnight* two months later on the release on appeal of ex-prostitute Emma Humphreys, who had killed her boyfriend, and whose murder conviction was reduced to manslaughter.[27] The programme noted that 'it took a fictional case' to bring the issue of cumulative abuse as provocation to public attention, saying that the case had 'galvanised opinion in a way that real-life cases failed to do', and showed clips from the courtroom scenes in the *Brookside* trial. Only ten days later the Cardiff court freed an eighteen-year-old girl who had 'suffered enough' and had stabbed her grandfather, by whom she had been sexually abused since the age of three. There were said to be 'very strong similarities' with the *Brookside* case.[28] Indeed the trial, whose impending cliffhanger verdict was reported almost nightly in the *Evening Standard*, so caught the imagination of the viewing public[29] that the *TV Times* mimicked the standard device of the tabloids, the phone-in poll, and with a typographical presentation that came straight from the *Sun*, asked viewers to ring to say whether they thought Mandy and Beth Jordache should go to jail or not. An ensuing press release stated that 6,500 people had phoned in and 'a resounding 96%' thought that Mandy and Beth should go free.

But Mandy and Beth did not. The verdict provoked unprecedented protest at Mersey Television, which makes *Brookside*. Phil Redmond, *Brookside*'s creator and executive producer, 'enter[ed] the dock to face his viewers' in a 'Right to Reply' special a few days after the verdict was announced.[30] His jury comprised women who worked in refuges as well as campaigners and women involved in legal reform. 'What message have you sent to the youngsters who watch your show?' he was asked in tones of angry complaint. And it was interesting that his defence was at the level of the real. He told the women that 'we were taking legal advice right up to the moment of shooting. We put all the papers in front of a High Court judge to ask for the most probable and credible verdict.' He also stated at the time of the protests over the verdict, that 'there is something disturbing about the capacity of a television story to provoke a debate which seems entirely to have passed by politicians and other pundits who remain so Westminster-focused that they often appear no longer to notice the really big questions facing people on a daily basis.' It was 'as if' a real-life event (down to the pen and ink illustrations in *TV Quick*, replicating the no-photographs rule in trial reporting in Britain), though Redmond himself traced *Brookside*'s impact back to the lineage of Dickens:

> Ever since Dickens sealed the fate of Little Nell, serialised fiction has demonstrated a remarkable capacity to reach out to enormous audiences. Brookside – in its own way – demonstrated . . . the cumulative power of a story told serially – in this case over a period of two years.[31]

As in a real-life event, then, structures of denial and

repression may be seen at work. I want to consider the ways in which they are represented, and to ask how successful these representations are. The dramatic structure had offered the television audience a perspective on Rachel's initial denial, and in the main the script followed the *silences* of everyday talk, the unspeakable dimension. But there was, at a crucial moment of contestation, an insistence on naming, as shown in exchanges between the father and the older daughter, Beth. The dialogue consistently alternated, then, between the explicit and the unvocalised.[32] It was the trial, in the unenthusiastic words of the *Guardian* TV critic 'a drama of reiteration',[33] which brought home the tension of 'lying vs. denial'. Meanwhile, both *TV Quick* and *TV Times* were speaking of blocking out the memory and of repression, and quoting academic psychologists on the trauma that leads to repression: 'Having blocked out the nightmare memory of her own rape by her dad, Rachel is still bitter over the murder and won't forgive her mother.'[34] After the trial, however, the focus sharpened, while the different characters carried one or other 'pole' of a psychic state. The psychic structures that are usually associated with individual life (in the psychoanalytic sense) were allocated to different members of the Close, or to the (real-life) media commentary on the family and their predicament.[35]

Knowledge is of course frequently fractured and its dissemination in the networks that soaps portray frequently fractured and partial also. My suggestion is that the 'split' in *Brookside* is of a different kind from the traditional (where the audience knows something that only one character knows – often the paternity of one of the fictional characters – while the rest of the fictional network are ignorant of it). Here the character herself may or may not know something of her own past. In a fictional setting, the debates associated with repressed memory were being staged.[36]

* * *

So, to return to the question of whether child abuse is representable, we might ask not just what the representations look like, but what we are aiming to represent, and with what objectives: to raise money, to help the victims, to enlighten the public, to sustain a never-ending soap narrative, and so on. I said at the outset that there may be something unrepresentable, a territory more familiar from the coverage of social atrocities and thus on a very different scale from the intimately familial. In a discussion of psychosis and its theorisation Mark Cousins has posed the question of 'what it would be to represent the unrepresentable', suggesting that one could perhaps make representations of that which is adjacent to madness, and giving as an example the Jewish Museum in Berlin ('not a representation of the void, but something that hollows us out in our adjacency').[37] So let me end by taking as an example, from the field I am considering, the front cover of a recent publisher's catalogue (see Figure 6). The image on its own is of a tentatively geometric 'shape', fragmentary, conjuring up (if anything) the sense of an 'edge'. It becomes a surprisingly arresting and evocative image. Why? Because it is linked to the words: 'Child abuse. Books from Sage'. In everyday terms I might say that this is because it elicits thoughts and feelings about an experience that may be too chaotic and formless to be representable, and in that sense may be closer *to* that experience.

But an image will always be in principle a message without a code.[38] If we take away the words we have an abstract image with the hint of a border, an edge. If we add words (the anchorage function of 'Child abuse' in the title, distinguishing it from the publisher's other subject areas) we might start to think that what is being evoked is something to do with a precipice, or perhaps something adjacent to a void, a particular kind of psychic state. At the same time, as John Tagg wrote, 'what

Child
Sexual
Abuse
Books from SAGE
SAGE Publications, 6 Bonhill Street, London EC2A 4PU

Figure 6

exceeds representation, however, cannot, by definition, be articulated'.[39] It is an ambiguity with which I want to close.

Notes

Introduction

1 Roland Barthes (1979) *A Lover's Discourse: Fragments*, Harmondsworth: Penguin, 1990, p. 73.
2 Janice R. and Stephen R. MacKinnon (1988) *Agnes Smedley: The Life and Times of an American Radical*, London: Virago, p. 97.
3 Agnes Smedley (1943) *Battle Hymn of China*, London: Gollancz. Reissued as *China Correspondent*, London: Pandora, 1984, p. 19. See also Rosalind Delmar, letter to *Spare Rib*, 26, September 1974, for Agnes Smedley's involvement in psychoanalysis.
4 Barthes, *A Lover's Discourse*, pp. 41–4.
5 In the work of Maria Abraham and Nicolas Torok; see especially Chapter 6. The general issue of 'transgenerational transmission' was the theme of the sixth annual research conference of the International Psychoanalytical Association, London, March 1996.
6 See Chris Jenks (ed.) (1995) *Visual Culture*, London: Routledge; Parveen Adams (1995) *The Emptiness of the Image: Psychoanalysis and Sexual Differences*, London: Routledge.
7 As in Freud's celebrated example of the 'conditions of loving'. See Sigmund Freud (1910) 'A Special Type of Choice of Object Made by Men (Contributions to the Psychology of Love I)', in *On Sexuality (Pelican Freud*

Library, Vol. 7), Harmondsworth: Penguin, 1977, pp. 227–42. For a 'classical' account of the topic, see Charles Brenner (1955) *An Elementary Textbook of Psychoanalysis*, New York: International Universities Press. See also Jean Laplanche and J.-B. Pontalis (1973) *The Language of Psychoanalysis*, London: Hogarth Press and the Institute of Psycho-Analysis, and R.D. Hinshelwood (1989) *A Dictionary of Kleinian Thought*, London: Free Association Books, 2nd, revised edn 1991. Meir Perlow (1995) *Understanding Mental Objects*, London: Routledge, provides a taxonomy of concepts indissolubly linked to questions of fantasy.

8 See, for example, Mandy Merck (1987) 'The Critical Cult of *Dora*', in *Perversions: Deviant Readings*, London: Virago, 1993, pp. 33–44; and for the real 'Dora', Ida Bauer, see Maria Ramas (1980) 'Freud's Dora, Dora's Hysteria', in Charles Bernheimer and Claire Kahane (eds) (1985) *In Dora's Case: Freud, Hysteria, Feminism*, London: Virago, pp. 149–80. See also Jacqueline Rose (1993) '"Where Does the Misery Come From?" – Psychoanalysis, Feminism and the Event', in *Why War? – Psychoanalysis, Politics, and the Return to Melanie Klein*, Oxford: Basil Blackwell, pp. 89–109, and pp. 233–5.

9 Eleanore Armstrong-Perlman (1993) 'The Zealots and the Blind', paper presented at Psychoanalytic Forum conference, 'Contemporary Psychoanalysis, Contemporary Sexualities', London, July. See also The Bridge (1991) *Sukina: An Evaluation Report of the Circumstances Leading to her Death*, London: The Bridge Child Care Consultancy Service, and The Bridge (1995) *Paul: Death through Neglect*, London: The Bridge Child Care Consultancy Service.

10 Quoted in Ruth S. Kempe and Henry C. Kempe (1984) *Child Abuse*, London: Fontana, p. 9.

11 Cf. Julie Browne (1996) 'Unasked Questions or Unheard Answers? Policy Development in Child Sexual Abuse', *British Journal of Social Work*, 26, pp. 37–52.

12 In the Sexual Offences Act 1956. See *Halsbury's Statutes of England and Wales* (1994) *Fourth Edition, Volume*

12, *1994 Reissue, Criminal Law*. London: Butterworth, pp. 247–8.

13 Cf. Department of Health (1995) *Child Protection: Messages from Research*, London: HMSO, pp. 75–7.

14 *Working Together Under the Children Act 1989* (1991), revised version. London: Department of Health.

15 Andrew Cooper, personal communication, 1995. See *Messages from Research* (1995) London: Home Office, for the current data on prevalence.

16 Bridget Pilkington and John Kremer (1995) 'A Review of the Epidemiological Research on Child Sexual Abuse: Clinical Samples', *Child Abuse Review*, 4, pp. 191–205.

17 Cleo van Velsen (1995) Review of Elaine Westerlund, *Women's Sexuality after Childhood Incest, British Journal of Psychiatry*, 166, 2, pp. 270–1.

18 Bridge Report, *Sukina*, p. 2.

19 *Guardian*, 14 June 1995.

20 Suzanne Moore (1995) 'For the Good of the Kids – and Us', *Guardian*, 15 June.

21 Juliet Mitchell (1974) 'Conclusion' in *Psychoanalysis and Feminism*, Harmondsworth: Penguin, 1975, pp. 364–98. I discuss this issue in Ann Scott (1994) 'Childhood and the Forbidden', paper to Freud Museum conference, 'Psychoanalysis and Feminism: 20 Years On'. See also Beatrix Campbell (1988) *Unofficial Secrets. Child Sexual Abuse: The Cleveland Case*, London: Virago, esp. pp. 2–3.

22 In Mark Cousins and Parveen Adams (1995) 'The Truth on Assault', *October*, 71 (Winter), p. 101.

23 See, for example, Darian Leader (1994) 'Lacan and Phantasy', lecture to THERIP in lecture series, 'Dialogues between Klein and Lacan', London, October.

24 Eric Laurent (1992) 'Phantasy in Klein and Lacan', lecture to THERIP in lecture series, 'Phantasy', London, April.

25 Quoted ibid.

26 Malcolm Bowie (1991) *Lacan*, London: Fontana Modern Masters, pp. 103, 180.

27 Ibid., p. 94

28 Aisling Campbell (1995) in 'Post-traumatic Stress Disorder and Accidents – A Psychoanalytic Perspective', paper

presented to Greenwich Consortium conference on Post-Traumatic Stress Disorder, October, was commenting on the evolution of the classification of mental disorders, from DSM-III (American Psychiatric Association (1984) *Diagnostic and Statistical Manual of Mental Disorders (Third Edition)*, Washington, DC: American Psychiatric Association) to DSM-IV (American Psychiatric Association (1994) *Diagnostic and Statistical Manual of Mental Disorders (Fourth Edition)*, Washington, DC: American Psychiatric Association).

29 Ibid., p. 6.

30 Quoted in Jacques-Alain Miller (ed.) (1988) *The Seminar of Jacques Lacan, Book 1, Freud's Papers on Technique, 1953–1954*, trans. John Forrester, Cambridge: Cambridge University Press, p. 48.

31 Roger Kennedy (1996) 'Bearing the Unbearable – Working with the Abused Mind', *Psychoanalytic Psychotherapy*, 10, pp. 145–6.

32 Masud Khan (1963) 'The Concept of Cumulative Trauma', in *The Privacy of the Self*, London: Hogarth Press and the Institute of Psycho-Analysis, p. 46.

33 Kennedy, 'Bearing the Unbearable', p. 146.

34 Ibid., p. 148.

35 Jean Laplanche (1995) 'Seduction, Persecution, Revelation', *International Journal of Psycho-Analysis*, 76, pp. 663–82.

36 Ibid., p. 665.

37 Cf. Jessica Benjamin (1993) 'Sameness and Difference: Like Subjects and Love Objects', paper presented to Psychoanalytic Forum conference on 'Contemporary Psychoanalysis, Contemporary Sexualities', London, July.

38 Carolyn Steedman (1992) *History and Autobiography*, London: Rivers Oram, p. 124.

39 Quoted in Phyllis Grosskurth (1986) *Melanie Klein: Her World and Her Work*, London: Hodder & Stoughton, pp. 447–8. See also note 14, p. 146 below.

40 Cf. also Neville Symington's remark that he thought he had 'truly become' an analyst when a patient, 'after quite a long analysis, said to me that he had not heard me say anything which he could not have heard in his local pub';

see his review of Bruno Bettelheim, *Freud and Man's Soul*, *Guardian*, July 1993.

41 Andrew Cooper (1995) 'Child Abuse' ('Britain in a Moral Panic: Part 4'), *Community Care*, 3–9 August (pull-out supplement), p. vii. See also Allan Levy (ed.) (1989) *Focus on Child Abuse: Medical, Legal and Social Work Perspectives*, London: Hawksmere, pp. 26–8.

42 Initially in a panel presentation (panel: 'Victims of Power') at the British Institute for Integrative Therapy conference on 'Therapy and Power', London, July 1993.

43 David Krell (1991) *Of Memory, Reminiscence and Writing: On the Verge*, New Haven, CT and London: Yale University Press, p. 110.

44 See Chapter 5, pp. 67–8.

45 Cf. Linda Grant (1993) 'A Past Imperfect', *Guardian*, 24 May.

46 Panel discussion at the Institute of Contemporary Arts, London, 1993, to launch Mandy Merck's *Perversions: Deviant Readings*. For Freud's concept of a 'switch-word' or verbal bridge, see Freud 'Fragment of a Case of Hysteria', pp. 65, 84, 94.

47 Murray Cox, 'Dynamic Psychotherapy with Sex-offenders', in Ismond Rosen (ed.) (1970) *Sexual Deviation*, Oxford: Oxford University Press, p. 335. In legal terms, the woman's or girl's consent has no bearing on the offence.

48 There is now an extensive commentary on False (Recovered) Memory Syndrome. See, for example, Marie Maguire (1995) 'False Memories of Sexual Abuse', in *Men, Women, Passion and Power: Gender Issues in Psychotherapy*, London: Routledge, pp. 153–71; *British Journal of Psychotherapy* (1996) 'Recovered Memories of Sexual Abuse' (special section), 12, 3, pp. 342–71; Valerie Sinason (ed.) (forthcoming), *Memory in Dispute*, London: Karnac.

49 Peter Fonagy (1994) 'A Psychoanalytic Understanding of Memory and Reconstruction', *British Psychological Society Psychotherapy Section Newsletter*, 16 (December), p. 14.

50 Ibid., p. 18.

51 Deirdre Sutton-Smith (ed.) (n.d.) *The Women's Therapy Centre. Groups for Incest Survivors – A Handbook Based*

on Practice at The Women's Therapy Centre, London: Women's Therapy Centre.

52 In a radio discussion, 'Vice or Virtue' (chair: Mark Lawson) BBC Radio 4, 31 July 1995.

53 In *She*, May 1995, p. 199.

54 See *Journal of Traumatic Stress* (1995) Special Issue: Research on Traumatic Memory, 8, 4, and the discussion of it by John Morton (1996) 'The Dilemma of Validation', *British Journal of Psychotherapy*, 12, 3, pp. 367–71.

55 Cf. Estela Welldon (1995) 'Female Perversion and Hysteria', *British Journal of Psychotherapy*, 11, 3, pp. 406–14.

56 André Green (1995) 'Affects versus Representations: Or Affects as Representations?', paper presented at BJP/Freud Museum conference, 'How Do We Think About Feelings?', London, May. Summary published in *British Journal of Psychotherapy* (1996) 12, 2, pp. 208–11.

57 Barthes, *A Lover's Discourse*, p. 167.

58 See, for example, Kurt M. Bachman and Jeannette Bossi (1993) 'Mother–son Incest as a Defence against Psychosis', *British Journal of Medical Psychology*, 66, pp. 239–48; Abby Adams-Silvan and Mark Silvan (1994) 'Paradise Lost: A Case of Hysteria Illustrating a Specific Dynamic of Seduction Trauma', *International Journal of Psycho-Analysis*, 75, pp. 499–510; Jane Milton (1994) 'Abuser and Abused: Perverse Solutions Following Childhood Abuse', *Psychoanalytic Psychotherapy*, 8, pp. 243–55.

59 John Pitts, in discussion of a letter in *The Big Issue*, 1991 ('My father forced me to have sexual intercourse with him first when I was 10') (Personal communication, 1995).

60 Presentation to conference on 'Psychoanalytic Seductions', Institute of Contemporary Arts, London, March 1994.

61 Extracts from Sylvia Fraser's (1989) *My Father's House* (London: Virago) have been used in a British Medical Association doctor's guide (1990) to understanding incest and child abuse.

62 See Chapter 7, p. 106.

63 Cf. Judith Butler (1990) *Gender Trouble: Feminism and the Subversion of Identity*, London: Routledge, pp. 60–1.

64 Susan Cheever, cover puff for Linda Gray Sexton (1994)

Searching for Mercy Street: My Journey Back to My Mother, Anne Sexton, Boston: Little, Brown.

65 Adams, *Emptiness of the Image*, pp. 137, 114.

66 Ibid., p. 2.

67 In a discussion of Catharine MacKinnon's recent work on pornography. See Cousins and Adams, 'The Truth on Assault', p. 93.

68 Christopher Cordess comments on the 'concrete primitive psychological link between the lower half of our bodies and subterranean sites', in Valerie Sinason's discussion of public architecture in urban areas and its psychic effects, 'Designed for Inconvenience', *Guardian*, 25 September 1993.

69 Adams, *Emptiness of the Image*, pp. 2, 114. Although images are involved in both settings, the 'emptiness of the experience' is, I believe, a mirror image of the 'emptying out of meaning' of which Parveen Adams writes, for the latter has a positive valency.

70 Cooper, 'Child Abuse', p. vii.

1 *Feminism and the seductiveness of the 'real event'*

1 Letter of Sigmund Freud to Wilhelm Fliess, 21 September 1897, quoted in Ronald Clark (1980) *Freud: The Man and the Cause*, London: Jonathan Cape and Weidenfeld & Nicolson, p. 161.

2 Janet Malcolm (1983) 'Annals of Scholarship – Trouble in the Archives – 1', *New Yorker*, 5 December, pp. 59–152. 'Trouble in the Archives – 2', *New Yorker*, 12 December, pp. 60–119; Janet Malcolm (1980) *Psychoanalysis: The Impossible Profession*, London: Pan Books, 1982.

3 Janet Malcolm (1984) *In the Freud Archives*, London: Flamingo, 1986.

4 J.M. Masson (1984) *The Assault on Truth: Freud's Suppression of the Seduction Theory*; with new Preface and Afterword, Harmondsworth: Penguin, 1985.

5 J.M. Masson (1984) 'The Persecution and Expulsion of Jeffrey Masson as Performed by the Freudian Establishment and Reported by Janet Malcolm of the *New Yorker*', *Mother Jones*, 9, 10 (December), p. 36. See also Deirdre

English (1984) 'The Masson–Malcolm Dispute', *Mother Jones*, 9, 10 (December), p. 6.

6 Masson, Preface to 1985 edition of *The Assault on Truth*, p. xvii.

7 See Masson, 'The Persecution and Expulsion', pp. 34–47.

8 See Masson, *The Assault on Truth* (1985), p. xix, and 'The Persecution and Expulsion', p. 36.

9 Michael Parsons (1986) 'Suddenly Finding It Really Matters', *International Journal of Psycho-Analysis*, 67, p. 476.

10 Sigmund Freud, Lecture 23 in *Introductory Lectures on Psychoanalysis* (1916), Pelican Freud Library, Vol. 1, Harmondsworth: Penguin, 1974, p. 418.

11 Masson, *The Assault on Truth* (1985), p. 133.

12 Marianne Krull (1979) *Freud and his Father*, London: Hutchinson, 1986.

13 Ronald Fraser (1984) *In Search of a Past: The Manor House, Amnersfield, 1933–1945*, London: Verso Books.

14 Ibid., pp. 106–7.

15 Malcolm, *In the Freud Archives*, p. 14.

16 Alice Miller (1979) *The Drama of the Gifted Child and the Search for the True Self*, London: Faber & Faber, 1983; Alice Miller (1980) *For Your Own Good: The Roots of Violence in Child-Rearing*, London: Virago, 1987; Alice Miller (1981) *Thou Shalt Not Be Aware: Society's Betrayal of the Child*, London: Pluto, 1986. Alice Miller reissued a retitled version of the first book in 1987 as *The Drama of Being a Child and the Search for the True Self*, London: Virago. See my review of *For Your Own Good* and the revised edition of *The Drama of Being a Child*, in *City Limits*, 21–28 May 1987.

17 Sigmund Freud (1896) 'The Aetiology of Hysteria', in James Strachey (ed.), *The Standard Edition of the Complete Psychological Works of Sigmund Freud*, 24 vols, London: Hogarth Press and the Institute of Psycho-Analysis, 1953–73, Vol. 3, pp. 189–224.

18 See, for example, Charles Hanly (1986) Review of Masson, *The Assault on Truth* and Malcolm, *In the Freud Archives*, *International Journal of Psycho-Analysis*, 67, 517–19; and Zvi Lothane (1987) 'Love, Seduction and Trauma',

Psychoanalytic Review, 74, pp. 83–105. For the general cultural debate on Masson's work and its likely influence, see Walter Kendrick (1984) 'Not Just Another Oedipal Drama: The Unsinkable Sigmund Freud' (review of Masson, *The Assault on Truth*, Malcolm, *In the Freud Archives* and other new work on Freud), *Voice Literary Supplement*, June, pp. 12–16, and George Steiner (1984) 'The Fantasies of Freud' (review of Masson, *The Assault on Truth*), *Sunday Times*, 27 May. See also Charles Rycroft's review (note 29).

19 See, for example, R.P. Merendino (1985) 'On Epistemological Functions of Clinical Reports', *International Review of Psycho-Analysis*, 12, pp. 327–35; Scott Wetzler (1985) 'The Historical Truth of Psychoanalytic Reconstructions', *International Review of Psycho-Analysis*, 12, pp. 187–97; and *International Journal of Psycho-Analysis*, 67 (1986) 'Panel on identification in the perversions' (contributions by J.A. Arlow, p. 247; Harold Blum, p. 274); Kinston and Cohen, p. 347; Alan B. Zients, pp. 78–81).

20 See the wide-ranging discussion with John Bowlby about these issues in John Bowlby, Karl Figlio and Robert M. Young (1986) 'An Interview with John Bowlby on the Origins and Reception of his Work', *Free Associations*, 6, pp. 36–64.

21 Anna Freud (1968) 'Indications and Contraindications for Child Analysis', in *Problems of Psychoanalytic Training, Diagnosis, and the Technique of Therapy*, London: Hogarth Press and the Institute of Psycho-Analysis, 1974, p. 122.

22 Charles Hanly (1986) 'Lear and His Daughters', *International Review of Psycho-Analysis*, 13, p. 216.

23 See Hanly, Review of Masson and Malcolm, p. 518.

24 D.W. Winnicott (1961) 'Varieties of Psychotherapy', in *Home is Where We Start From: Essays by a Psychoanalyst*, Harmondsworth: Penguin, 1986, pp. 109–10.

25 See also Moustapha Safouan (1983) *Jacques Lacan et la question de la formation des analystes*, Paris: Editions du Seuil, p. 64.

26 Glen O. Gabbard (1986) 'The Treatment of the "Special"

Patient in a Psychoanalytic Hospital', *International Review of Psycho-Analysis*, 13, pp. 341–2.

27 Brendan MacCarthy (1985) University College London Freud Memorial Lecture.

28 Jean Laplanche and J.-B. Pontalis (1968) 'Fantasy and the Origins of Sexuality', *International Journal of Psycho-Analysis*, 49, pp. 1–18.

29 Charles Rycroft (1984) 'A Case of Hysteria' (review of Masson, *The Assault on Truth*), *New York Review of Books*, 12 April, pp. 3–6. See also T.G. Ashplant (1987) 'Fantasy, Narrative, Event: Psychoanalysis and History', *History Workshop*, 23 (Spring), pp. 166–73.

30 Roger Dorey (1986) 'The Relationship of Mastery', *International Review of Psycho-Analysis*, 13, p. 326.

31 Laplanche and Pontalis, 'Fantasy', pp. 3–4.

32 Lothane, 'Love, Seduction and Trauma'.

33 Masson, 'The Persecution and Expulsion', p. 36.

34 Elizabeth Ward (1984) *Father–Daughter Rape*, London: The Women's Press.

35 Ibid., p. 101.

36 Jane Gallop (1982) *Feminism and Psychoanalysis: The Daughter's Seduction*, Basingstoke: Macmillan, p. 56.

37 Rosalind Coward (1982) 'Erin Pizzey Adrift in a Misogynist Society', *The Guardian*, 2 November.

38 See Judith Ennew (1986) *The Sexual Exploitation of Children*, Cambridge: Polity Press, *passim*.

39 In Ward, *Father–Daughter Rape*, p. 57.

40 Malcolm, *In the Freud Archives*, pp. 55–6.

2 *Melanie Klein and the questions of feminism*

1 Jacques-Alain Miller (ed.) (1988) *The Seminar of Jacques Lacan, Book 1, Freud's Papers on Technique, 1953–1954*, trans. John Forrester, Cambridge: Cambridge University Press, p.68; see also pp. 80–8.

2 For early examples of these discussions, see Elena Lieven (1976) 'Patriarchy and Psychoanalysis', in Feminist Anthology Collective (ed.), *No Turning Back: Writings from the Women's Liberation Movement* 1975–80, London: The

Women's Press, 1981, pp. 246–54; RSJ Subgroup (1978) 'Marxism, Feminism and Psychoanalysis', *Radical Science Journal*, 6/7, pp. 107–17. For a materialist perspective on the turn to psychoanalysis see Elizabeth Wilson (1981) 'Psychoanalysis: Psychic Law and Order?', *Feminist Review*, 8, pp. 63–78; with a response from Janet Sayers (1983) 'Psychoanalysis and Personal Politics: A Response to Elizabeth Wilson', *Feminist Review*, 10, pp. 91–5. The feminist object-relations work of the Women's Therapy Centre in London (cf. Luise Eichenbaum and Susie Orbach 1982, *Outside In . . . Inside Out. Women's Psychology: A Feminist Psychoanalytic Approach*, Harmondsworth: Penguin) had been critiqued in *m/f*. Cf. 'Letter from The Women's Therapy Centre' (1979) *m/f* 3.

For the problematics of difference, see Michèle Barrett (1987) 'The Concept of Difference', *Feminist Review*, 26, pp. 29–41; and Mandy Merck (1987) 'Difference and Its Discontents', *Screen*, 28, pp. 2–10.

3 Juliet Mitchell (1974) *Psychoanalysis and Feminism*, London: Allen Lane. See also the booklet *Papers from the Patriarchy Conference*, London, 1976. For a later perspective on the feminist engagement with psychoanalysis, see Angela McRobbie (1988) 'An Interview with Juliet Mitchell', *New Left Review*, 170, pp. 80–91.

4 Dorothy Dinnerstein (1976) *The Mermaid and the Minotaur: Sexual Arrangements and Human Malaise*, New York: Harper & Row.

5 Nancy Chodorow (1978) *The Reproduction of Mothering: Psychoanalysis and the Sociology of Gender*, Berkeley, CA: University of California Press. See also Deborah Luepnitz (1990) 'Psychoanalysis and/or Feminism' (review of Nancy Chodorow, *Feminism and Psychoanalytic Theory*, 1990), *Women's Review of Books*, May, pp. 17–18.

6 Cf. Sheila Ernst and Marie Maguire (eds) (1987) *Living with the Sphinx: Papers from The Women's Therapy Centre*, London: The Women's Press.

7 For instance, in the culture generally, Phyllis Grosskurth (1986) *Melanie Klein: Her World and Her Work*, London: Hodder & Stoughton; Juliet Mitchell (ed.) (1986) *The*

Selected Melanie Klein, Harmondsworth: Penguin; Nicholas Wright's play *Mrs Klein* at the National Theatre, London, 1988; Margaret Walters (1988) 'The Infant Who Survives', Programme notes for Nicholas Wright, *Mrs Klein*, National Theatre, London, 1988. In women's publishing, Virago's paperback editions of Melanie Klein's complete writings, 1988, 1989. From the clinical and 'left-Kleinian' fields respectively, R.D. Hinshelwood (1989) *A Dictionary of Kleinian Thought*, London: Free Association Books, 2nd revised edn, 1991, and Barry Richards (ed.) (1989) *Crises of the Self: Further Essays on Psychoanalysis and Politics*, London: Free Association Books. Another dimension of this trend is shown in the fact that Janet Sayers (1989) 'Melanie Klein and Mothering – A Feminist Perspective' is a publication in a psychoanalytic journal (*International Review of Psycho-Analysis*, 16, pp. 363–76).

8 Perry Anderson (1968) 'Components of the National Culture', *New Left Review*, 56; reprinted in Alexander Cockburn and Robin Blackburn (eds) (1969) *Student Power: Problems, Diagnosis, Action*, Harmondsworth: Penguin, pp. 214–84; Anderson's work is discussed by Jacqueline Rose (1986) in *Sexuality in the Field of Vision*, London: Verso, pp. 6–8. For the different location of psychoanalysis in France at this time, see Maud Mannoni (1970) 'Psychoanalysis and the May Revolution', in Charles Posner (ed.), *Reflections on the Revolution in France: 1968*, Harmondsworth: Penguin, pp. 215–24.

9 Mitchell, 'Introduction', in *Selected Melanie Klein*, pp. 9–32; Vivien Bar (1987) 'Change in Women', in Ernst and Maguire, *Living with the Sphinx*, pp. 213–58.

10 My use of 'created' here is not intended to displace Klein's view of splitting as a distortion of a reality that becomes modified over time. See, for example, Roger Money-Kyrle (1982) *Man's Picture of His World*, London: Duckworth, for an explication of Klein's view of reality in relation to contemporary philosophical trends.

11 Miller, *Seminar of Jacques Lacan*, p. 54.

12 'World' is used here in the Kleinian sense of 'external world'; cf. Roger Money-Kyrle (1978) 'Melanie Klein and

Her Contribution to Psychoanalysis', in Donald Meltzer (ed.) *The Collected Papers of Roger Money-Kyrle*, Strath Tay, Perthshire: Roland Harris Educational Trust, pp. 408–14. See Jean Laplanche (1989) *New Foundations for Psychoanalysis*, Oxford: Blackwell, for a discussion of the variety of ways in which psychoanalysis has conceptualised 'objective', 'external' and 'objectivity'.

13 See Michael Rustin (1982) 'A Socialist Consideration of Kleinian Psychoanalysis', *New Left Review*, 131, pp. 71–96; and Michael Rustin (1988) 'Shifting Paradigms in Psychoanalysis since the 1940s', *History Workshop*, 26 (special feature on 'Psychoanalysis and History'), pp. 133–42.

14 Cf. Karen Horney (1967) *Feminine Psychology*, New York: W.W. Norton, and the discussion of Horney's feminism in Susan Quinn (1987) *A Mind of Her Own: The Life of Karen Horney*, London: Macmillan.

15 Melanie Klein (1963) 'On the Sense of Loneliness', in *Envy and Gratitude and Other Works 1946–1963*, London: Hogarth Press and the Institute of Psycho-Analysis, 1975, pp. 300–13. Quotes pp. 302, 304.

16 Melanie Klein (1927) 'Criminal Tendencies in Normal Children', in *Love, Guilt and Reparation and Other Works 1921–1945*, London: Hogarth Press and the Institute of Psycho-Analysis, 1975, pp. 170–85. Quote p. 173.

17 See, for example, Stephen Robinson (1984) 'The Parent to the Child', in Barry Richards (ed.) *Capitalism and Infancy: Essays on Psychoanalysis and Politics*, London: Free Association Books, pp. 177–80; and Barry Richards' 'Introduction', ibid. p. 17.

18 Hanna Segal does not accept this latter objection to Klein's work, stressing that it is not entailed in Klein's notion of the maternal or parental environment. See her conversation with Jonathan Miller in 'Kleinian Analysis: Dialogue with Hanna Segal', in Jonathan Miller (ed.) (1983) *States of Mind: Conversations with Psychological Investigators*, London: BBC Books, pp. 260–3, in which she indicates that the way in which an infant is related to crucially affects the outcome of its infantile conflicts.

19 Michèle Barrett and Mary McIntosh (1982) *The Anti-Social Family*, London: Verso.
20 See the discussion of Michael Rustin's 'A Socialist Consideration', ibid. pp. 127–8. See also Rustin, 'A Socialist Consideration', pp. 78, 83–4, 86–7.
21 Melanie Klein (1957) 'Envy and Gratitude', in *Envy and Gratitude and Other Works*, pp. 176–235.
22 See Mitchell, *Selected Melanie Klein*, p. 27.
23 Juliet Mitchell (1984) *Women: The Longest Revolution. Essays in Feminism*, London: Virago, p. 310.
24 See Laplanche, *New Foundations, passim.*
25 In *Feminist Review*, 14 (1983), pp. 5–21. Reprinted in Rose, *Sexuality*, pp. 83–103, with a note on debates since 1983, p. 83.
26 Klein, 'Criminal Tendencies', p. 173.

3 *Unconscious explanations*

1 Quoted in F. Robert Rodman (ed.) (1987) *The Spontaneous Gesture: Selected Letters of D.W. Winnicott*, Cambridge, MA and London: Harvard University Press, p. 145.
2 Quoted in Phyllis Grosskurth (1986) *Melanie Klein: Her World and Her Work*, London: Hodder & Stoughton, p. 237.
3 Melanie Klein (1932) *The Psycho-Analysis of Children*, London: Hogarth Press and the Institute of Psycho-Analysis, 1975.
4 Technically, an interpretation is wild if 'the repressed content is simply imparted to the patient with no heed paid to the resistances and to the transference' (Jean Laplanche and J.-B. Pontalis, 1973, *The Language of Psychoanalysis*, London: Hogarth Press and the Institute of Psycho-Analysis, p. 480). In the case of a biography, the 'patient' is now the subject of the narrative, but it is to the *reader* that the interpretation is imparted, and the reader is thus positioned quite differently from the subject: almost, to borrow a Lacanian epithet, as 'the one supposed to know'. See also Robert M. Young (1988) 'Biography: The Basic Discipline for the Human Sciences',

Free Associations, 11, pp. 122–3, for the tendency to wild analysis in Grosskurth's *Klein*.

5 These issues are considered at length in Jacqueline Rose's (unpublished) discussion of *History Workshop*'s special feature on 'Psychoanalysis and History', Institute of Contemporary Arts panel, London, 1988.

6 Grosskurth, *Klein*, pp. 31.

7 Since this review was published, the New Library of Psychoanalysis has published the Controversial Discussions. See Pearl King and Riccardo Steiner (eds) (1991) *The Freud–Klein Controversies in the British Psycho-Analytical Society, 1941–45*, London: Routledge.

8 See, for example, the links Klein made between Richard's absorption in the events of the war, and the vicissitudes of his relationship with his parents: 'The increasing sympathy with the attacked enemy [U-boats bombed by British aeroplanes], which was shown in the material of that day, as well as of the previous ones, is noteworthy . . . It has repeatedly appeared in the material that Richard had become aware of his hostility and that the German aeroplanes and ships came to *represent* the hated and hostile parents' (*Narrative of a Child Analysis*, London: Hogarth Press and the Institute of Psycho-Analysis, 1961, pp. 267–8, my italics). The interweaving of inner experience and events in the public domain is lucidly described by Ronald Fraser in conversation with History Workshop about *In Search of a Past* (London: Verso, 1984; see also Chapter 1, p. 7 ff., for Fraser's sense of the subjective past), and includes an echo of Klein's preoccupation, this time from the analysand's side: 'My analyst also once ascribed the chaos I had felt as a two-year-old in Germany to the chaos which Hitler's rise to power involved. It appealed to me immediately – but later it didn't feel right. Something else, more intimate, was at work there' (from review discussion, 'In Search of the Past: A Dialogue with Ronald Fraser', *History Workshop*, 20, Autumn 1985, p. 184).

9 A variety of views are held as to whether or not Klein's views of the mind are compatible with Freud's conceptions of its structure and developmental sequences.

Klein herself saw her work as an extension of Freud's. A clear account of Klein as giving a new emphasis to the organisation of the self, but one not conflicting with Freud's metapsychology, is to be found in Donald Meltzer's discussion with Adrian Stokes, 'Painting and the Inner World', in Lawrence Gowing (ed.) (1978) *The Critical Writings of Adrian Stokes*, Vol. 3, London: Thames & Hudson, p. 220.

10 Cf. Ronald Fraser: 'There is no doubt in my mind that the oral history interview and the psychoanalytic session are two different discourses and should not be confused. When we interview, [we are left with a] subjective description of events in which we cannot know what part fantasy – and I use the word here in its psychoanalytic, not its common, usage – is playing' (quoted in review discussion, 'In Search of the Past,' p. 184).

11 Grosskurth, *Klein*, pp. 124, 133, 155, 171.

12 Ibid., p. 79.

13 Ibid., p. 272.

14 R.D. Laing, interviewed by Grosskurth (*Klein*, pp. 447–8), raises a related theme in describing Klein as a 'natural empirical phenomenologist'. In believing that Klein's concept of reparation 'should be put into a larger context of reconciliation, contrition, remorse, repentance, sorrow for one's evil thoughts and actions', he implies that a relationship could be found between some of the mental states and unconscious impulses Klein put into words, and states of mind for which ordinary language already existed.

15 Grosskurth, *Klein*, p. 10.

16 Cf. Rosalind Delmar's observation of an 'awareness that we are all, to ourselves, fictional characters', in her 'Afterword' to Agnes Smedley's *Daughter of Earth*, New York, 1929; reissued London: Virago, 1977, p. 271.

17 See Carolyn Steedman (1986) *Landscape for a Good Woman: A Story of Two Lives*, London: Virago, pp. 5, 74–7, on 'interpretative devices' as they work in the culture, including psychoanalytic evidence and its problems.

18 Grosskurth, *Klein*, pp. 18, 20.

19 Hanna Segal, review of Grosskurth, *Klein*, *Sunday Times*, 22 June 1986. Edna O'Shaughnessy (1987) review of Grosskurth, *Klein*, *International Review of Psycho-Analysis*, 14, pp. 132–6.
20 O'Shaughnessy, review of Grosskurth, p. 133.
21 Ronald W. Clark (1980) *Freud: The Man and the Cause*, London: Jonathan Cape and Weidenfeld & Nicolson, pp. 4, 18, 29. Ernest Jones uses the same material, but more temperately, in *The Life and Work of Sigmund Freud*, Harmondsworth: Penguin, 1967, p. 83.
22 Grosskurth, *Klein*, p. 218.
23 Cf. 'Editorial: Oral History', *History Workshop*, 8 (Autumn 1979), pp. i–ii; and Alessandro Portelli (1981) 'The Peculiarities of Oral History', *History Workshop*, 12 (Autumn), esp. pp. 97–8.
24 Melanie Klein, letter of 19 September 1952 to Jean-Baptiste and Françoise Boulanger, quoted in Grosskurth, *Klein*, p. 390.

4 *Real events revisited*

1 See Jean Laplanche (1989) *New Foundations for Psychoanalysis*, Oxford: Blackwell, *passim*; Jean Laplanche (1992) 'Notes on Afterwardsness', in John Fletcher and Martin Stanton (eds) *Jean Laplanche: Seduction, Translation, Drives*, London: Institute of Contemporary Arts, pp. 217–23. See also Jean Laplanche and J.-B. Pontalis (1973) *The Language of Psycho-Analysis*, London: Hogarth Press and the Institute of Psycho-Analysis, pp. 111–14.
2 Jean Laplanche and J.-B. Pontalis (1968) 'Phantasy and the Origins of Sexuality', *International Journal of Psycho-Analysis*, 49, pp. 1–18.
3 In James Strachey (ed.), *The Standard Edition of the Complete Psychological Works of Sigmund Freud*, 24 vols, London: Hogarth Press and the Institute of Psycho-Analysis, 1953–73, Vol. 3, pp. 189–224.
4 Ibid., p. 193.
5 Ibid., pp. 193, 197.
6 Ibid., pp. 199, 200, italic in original.

7 Ibid., p. 201.
8 Ibid., p. 202, italic in original.
9 Ibid., p. 203.
10 Ibid., p. 204.
11 Ibid., italic in original.
12 Ibid., p. 213.
13 In Strachey, *Standard Edition*, Vol. 23, pp. 271–8.
14 Jean Laplanche (1992) 'Interpretation between Determinism and Hermeneutics: A Restatement of the Problem', *International Journal of Psycho-Analysis*, 73, p. 439.
15 Freud, 'Splitting of the Ego in the Process of Defence', *Pelican Freud Library*, Vol. 11, Harmondsworth: Penguin, 1974, pp. 462–3, my emphasis.
16 In Strachey, *Standard Edition*, Vol. 7, pp. 123–245.
17 Mandy Merck (1988) 'The Fatal Attraction of *Intercourse*', in *Perversions: Deviant Readings*, London: Virago, 1993, p. 199.
18 Ibid., pp. 205, 208.
19 John Fletcher, in a presentation at the Freud Forum, London, 9 March 1992, was drawing out the rewriting of the Freudian primal scene in the Kleinian primal scene, whereby the aggressive is relocated from the parents to the child.
20 Bice Benvenuto and Roger Kennedy (1986) *The Works of Jacques Lacan: An Introduction*, London: Free Association Books, p. 149.
21 Ronald Britton (1994) 'The Blindness of the Seeing Eye: Inverse Symmetry as a Defense against Reality', *Psychoanalytic Inquiry*, 14, pp. 368–9.
22 In discussion of this point in Ronald Britton's paper, when given as a lecture to THERIP in London in 1991, a link was made with Laplanche's concept of the 'psychotic enclave' as denoting the traumatically non-assimilable.
23 Quoted in Rob Hale and Valerie Sinason, 'Internal and External Reality: Establishing Parameters', in Valerie Sinason (ed.) (1994) *Treating Survivors of Satanist Abuse*, London: Routledge, p. 277.
24 In Deirdre Sutton-Smith (ed.) (n.d.) *The Women's Therapy Centre: Groups for Incest Survivors – A Handbook Based*

on Practice at The Women's Therapy Centre, London: Women's Therapy Centre, p. 8.

25 Ibid., p. 7.

26 Quoted in Judith Trowell (1991) 'Phantasy in Child Sexual Abuse', unpublished lecture to THERIP, London. See also Judith Trowell (in press) 'Working with Child Sexual Abuse in Girls', in Joan Raphael-Leff and Rosine Perelberg (eds) *Female Experience*, London: Routledge; Judith Trowell (in press) 'The Psychodynamics of Incest', in Cleo van Velsen and Estela Welldon (eds), *Forensic Psychotherapy: A Handbook*, London: Jessica Kingsley Publishers.

27 Susie Orbach (1995) 'When It's All About Self, Self, Self', *Guardian*, 13 May.

28 Fiona Gardner (1990) 'Psychotherapy with Adult Survivors of Child Sexual Abuse', *British Journal of Psychotherapy*, 6, pp. 285–94.

29 Gudrun Jonsdottir (1990) 'Surviving Incest: Feminist Theory and Practice', *Journal of Social Work Practice*, 4, 3/4, p. 63.

30 See Bernard Burgoyne (1990) 'Commentary by a Lacanian Psychoanalyst', in 'Clinical Commentary X', *British Journal of Psychotherapy*, 6, p. 481.

31 Sebastian Kraemer (1988) 'Splitting and Stupidity in Child Sexual Abuse', *Psychoanalytic Psychotherapy*, 3, p. 251.

32 Elisabeth Hadjiisky (1987) 'On First Contact with Child Abuse and Neglect', *Journal of Social Work Practice*, 3, 1, pp. 31–7.

33 Ibid., p. 32.

34 Ibid., p. 35.

35 Mary Adams (1990) 'The Couple and the Group: Co-Therapy with Incest Survivors', *British Journal of Psychotherapy*, 7, p. 32.

36 David Mann (1989) 'Incest: The Father and the Male Therapist', *British Journal of Psychotherapy*, 6, pp. 143–53.

37 Sutton-Smith, *The Women's Therapy Centre*, p. 31.

38 Brendan MacCarthy (1988) 'Are Incest Victims Hated?', *Psychoanalytic Psychotherapy*, 3, p. 118.

39 Anaïs Nin (1994) *Incest*, Harmondsworth: Penguin, is a

posthumous collection from Nin's diaries. Framing the collection in a contemporary idiom, the cover blurb says that 'the material in *Incest* was considered too explosive to include when the journals were originally published'. Twenty years separate the two.

40 Ibid., pp. 217, 223.
41 See Heinz Wolff, Anthony Bateman and David Sturgeon (eds) (1990) *UCH Textbook of Psychiatry*, London: Duckworth, 'Child Sexual Abuse', pp. 541–53.
42 Ibid., p. 55.
43 Nin, *Incest*, p. 217.
44 Laplanche, 'Interpretation', p. 436.
45 Quoted in Wolff, Bateman and Sturgeon (eds), *UCH Textbook*, p. 551.
46 MacCarthy, 'Are Incest Victims Hated?', p. 115.
47 Laplanche and Pontalis, 'Fantasy', p. 16, emphasis added.
48 Fletcher and Stanton, *Jean Laplanche*, p. 5.
49 Laplanche, *New Foundations*, pp. 129, 168.
50 Ibid., pp. 122–3.
51 Jean Laplanche (1979) *Life and Death in Psychoanalysis*, Baltimore, MD: Johns Hopkins University Press.
52 Ibid.
53 Cf. Jean Laplanche, 'Implantation, Intromission' (1990), in *La Révolution Copernicienne inachevée: travaux 1967–1992*, Paris: Aubier, 1992, which develops this theme, considering that the effect of violent implantation is to block (psychic) translation. See also John Fletcher (1994) 'Is the Superego a Psychotic Enclave? Problems in the Theory of Psychosis', paper presented at University of Warwick, July 1994.
54 Christopher Bollas (1989) 'The Trauma of Incest', in *Forces of Destiny: Psychoanalysis and Human Idiom*, London: Free Association Books, pp. 174–5.
55 Ibid., p. 175.
56 Quoted in Fletcher and Stanton, p. 67.
57 Cf. Fletcher and Stanton, pp. 21–5.
58 See, for example, Melanie Klein (1923), 'The Role of

the School in the Libidinal Development of the Child', in *Love, Guilt and Reparation and Other Works 1921–1945*, London: Hogarth Press and the Institute of Psycho-Analysis, 1975, pp. 71–2.

59 Laplanche, 'Interpretation', p. 441.

5 *Fantasy, memory, trauma: psychoanalytic reflections on biography and False Memory Syndrome*

1 Philip Rieff (1959) 'Preface to the First Edition', in *Freud: The Mind of the Moralist*, 3rd edn, Chicago: University of Chicago Press, 1979, p. xii.
2 David Krell (1991) 'Wax Magic', in *Of Memory, Reminiscence and Writing: On the Verge*, New Haven, CT and London: Yale University Press, pp. 107, 108.
3 Ibid., p. 110.
4 Sigmund Freud (1914) 'Remembering, Repeating and Working-Through', in James Strachey (ed.), *The Standard Edition of the Complete Psychological Works of Sigmund Freud*, 24 vols, 1953–73, London: Hogarth Press and the Institute of Psycho-Analysis, Vol. 12, pp. 145–56.
5 Sigmund Freud (1909) 'Notes upon a Case of Obsessional Neurosis', in Strachey, *Standard Edition*, Vol. 10, p. 224.
6 Michael Fischer (1986) 'Ethnicity and the Post-Modern Arts of Memory', in James Clifford and George Marcus (eds) *Writing Culture: The Poetics and Politics of Ethnography*, Berkeley, CA: University of California Press, p. 198.
7 Ibid.
8 Cf. note 44, p. 150 above.
9 Sigmund Freud (1937) 'Constructions in Analysis', in Strachey, *Standard Edition*, Vol. 23, p. 260.
10 Carolyn Steedman (1992) *Past Tenses: Essays on Writing, Autobiography and History*, London: Rivers Oram, p. 21.
11 Ibid., p. 42.

12 Allon White (1993) *Carnival, Hysteria and Writing*, Oxford: Oxford University Press, pp. 40, 42.
13 I gave this lecture some eighteen months before the British Psychological Society's working party on recovered memory, chaired by John Morton, concluded, among other things, that amnesia for traumatic events was a possibility; see John Morton et al. (1995) *Recovered Memories*, Leicester: British Psychological Society. Cf. also B. Andrews et al. (1995) 'The Recovery of Memories in Clinical Practice: Experiences and Beliefs of British Psychological Society Practitioners', *The Psychologist*, 8, pp. 209–14.
14 Shoshana Felman and Dori Laub (1992) *Testimony: Crises of Witnessing in Literature, Psychoanalysis, and History*, New York and London: Routledge.
15 The Association for Psychoanalytic Psychotherapy's 'Conference on Satanic Abuse' had taken place in London on 4 December 1993, the day before this lecture, and had also dwelt on 'joint acceptance of the reality of abuse'. See Valerie Sinason (ed.) (1994) *Treating Survivors of Satanist Abuse*, London: Routledge, and Valerie Sinason (1995) 'Foreword' to Lawrence Wright, *Remembering Satan*, London: Serpent's Tail. In this chapter I do not debate the reliability of reports of satanist abuse; for a useful example of investigative reporting, see Catherine Bennett (1994) 'The Satanic Verses', *Guardian Weekend*, 10 September, pp. 13–20.
16 Richard Gardner (1992) 'Belated Realization of Child Sex Abuse by an Adult', in *Issues in Child Abuse Accusations*, 4, 4, pp. 184, 195.
17 Hollida Wakefield and Ralph Underwager (1992) 'Uncovering Memories of Alleged Sexual Abuse: The Therapists Who Do It', in *Issues in Child Abuse Accusations*, 4, 4, p. 200.
18 David Krell, 'Wax Magic', p. 80.
19 Hon. Mr Justice Waterhouse (1989) 'Allegations of Child Abuse – the Court's Approach', in Allan Levy (ed.) (1989) *Focus on Child Abuse: Medical, Legal and Social Work Perspectives*, London: Hawksmere, p. 12.
20 It could of course be argued that the damage caused by

trauma is augmented over time – Freud makes a point of this kind in 'The Splitting of the Ego and the Process of Defence': the apparently trivial trigger in adult life unleashes a trauma which has been held in an unmodified form. See Sigmund Freud, 'The Splitting of the Ego in the Process of Defence', in Strachey, *Standard Edition*, Vol. 23, pp. 271–8.

21 I am referring here only to those cases in which a daughter's change of mind was achieved without pressure, or a reconciliation between family members took place before full legal proceedings were underway.

22 I develop these ideas in my 'Trauma, Skin: Memory, Speech', in Valerie Sinason (ed.) (forthcoming) *Memory in Dispute*, London: Karnac.

23 See (eds) Clifford and Marcus, *Writing Culture*, p. 163.

24 Cf. B.A. van der Kolk and Onno van der Hart (1991) 'The Intrusive Past: The Flexibility of Memory and the Engraving of Trauma', *American Imago*, 48, pp. 425–54.

25 Jacqueline Rose (1993) 'Afterword' to Allon White, *Carnival, Hysteria, and Writing*, p. 179.

6 *'Reclaimed once more by the realities of life': hysteria and the location of memory*

1 Sigmund Freud (1905) 'Fragment of a Case of Hysteria: "Dora"', in James Strachey (ed.) *The Standard Edition of the Complete Psychological Works of Sigmund Freud*, 24 vols, 1953–73, London: Hogarth Press and the Institute of Psycho-Analysis, Vol. 7, p. 122.

2 Josef Breuer and Sigmund Freud (1893) 'On the Psychical Mechanism of Hysterical Phenomena: Preliminary Communication', in J. Breuer and S. Freud (1893–5) *Studies on Hysteria*, in Strachey, *Standard Edition*, Vol. 2, p. 1.

3 Ibid., pp. 3–4.

4 Josef Breuer and Sigmund Freud (1970) *Studien über Hysterie*, Frankfurt am Main: Fischer Taschenbuch Verlag, pp. 9–11. The English translations are those of the *Standard Edition*.

5 David Krell (1991) 'Wax Magic', in *Of Memory, Reminiscence and Writing: On the Verge*, New Haven, CT and London: Yale University Press, p. 109.
6 Ibid.
7 Breuer and Freud, *Studies on Hysteria*, p. 20.
8 Ibid., p. 107.
9 Ibid., p. 122.
10 Freud, 'Fragment of a Case', p. 58.
11 Jerré Collins et al. (1983) 'Questioning the Unconscious: The Dora Archive', in *Diacritics*, 13, 1: *A Fine Romance: Freud and Dora*, p. 37.
12 Cited ibid.
13 Freud, 'Fragment of a Case', p. 61.
14 See Charles Bernheimer and Claire Kahane (eds) (1985) *In Dora's Case: Freud, Hysteria, Feminism*, London: Virago (especially Mandy Merck's chapter, 'The Critical Cult of *Dora*').
15 Freud, 'Fragment of a Case', pp. 106–9.
16 See Didier Anzieu (1974) 'A Discussion of the Paper by Gisela Pankow on "The Body Image in Psychosis"', *International Journal of Psycho-Analysis*, 55, pp. 415–16; Christian David (1974) 'A Discussion of the Paper by René Major on "The Revolution of Hysteria"', *International Journal of Psycho-Analysis*, 55, pp. 393–5; René Major (1974) 'The Revolution of Hysteria', *International Journal of Psycho-Analysis*, 55, pp. 385–95; Gisela Pankow (1973) 'L'Image du corps dans la psychose hystérique', *Revue française de psychanalyse*, 37, pp. 415–38; Gisela Pankow (1974) 'The Body Image in Hysterical Psychosis', *International Journal of Psycho-Analysis*, 55, pp. 407–13. *Revue française de psychanalyse*, 37 (1973): 'Sur l'hystérie'.
17 David, 'A Discussion', p. 394.
18 Ibid., pp. 394, 395.
19 Jean Laplanche and J.-B. Pontalis (1973) *The Language of Psycho-Analysis*, London: Hogarth Press and the Institute of Psycho-Analysis, p. 465.
20 Sylvia Fraser (1989) *My Father's House: A Memoir of Incest and Healing*, London: Virago.

21 Ibid., p. x.
22 Ibid., p. 15.
23 Ibid., p. 153.
24 Ibid., p. 234.
25 See Nicolas Abraham (1987) 'Notes on the Phantom: A Complement to Freud's Metapsychology', *Critical Inquiry* 13 (Winter), pp. 287–92; E. Rashkin (1988) 'Tools for a New Psychoanalytic Literary Criticism: The Work of Abraham and Torok', *Diacritics*, 18 (Winter), pp. 31–52. The extension of interest in psychic transmission is signalled in the overall theme of the Sixth Conference on Psychoanalytic Research of the International Psychoanalytical Association, University College London, March 1996 being 'Delayed Effects of Trauma: The Transgenerational Transmission of Character and Pathology'. Cf. note 5, p. 131.
26 Rashkin, 'Tools', p. 39.
27 Ibid., p. 40.
28 It is difficult to write about this without giving the impression that the play shows that Freud 'should' have affirmed his patients' experience as real. I hope I have avoided doing so.
29 Steve Grant (1993) 'Move over Dali', *Time Out*, 1–8 September.
30 Didier Anzieu (1986) *Freud's Self-Analysis*, London: Hogarth Press and the Institute of Psycho-Analysis, p. 70.
31 Ibid.
32 Breuer and Freud, *Studies on Hysteria*, p. 55.
33 Nicolas Abraham and Maria Torok (1980) 'Introjection – Incorporation: *Mourning* or *Melancholia*', in Serge Lebovici and Daniel Widlöcher (eds), *Psychoanalysis in France*, New York: International Universities Press, p. 8.
34 Terry Johnson (1993) *Hysteria*, London: Methuen Drama, p. 91.
35 Jean Laplanche (reporter) (1974) 'Panel on "Hysteria Today"', *International Journal of Psycho-Analysis*, 55, p. 467.

7 *'Tied together, body to body': Anne Sexton, Linda Gray Sexton*

1 Jerome Bruner (1995) 'The Autobiographical Process', *Current Sociology*, 41, 2/3, pp. 161–77.
2 Diane Wood Middlebrook (1991), *Anne Sexton: A Biography*, London: Virago.
3 Ibid., p. 273.
4 See Roland Barthes (1979) 'From Work to Text', in José Harari (ed.), *Textual Strategies: Perspectives in Post-Structuralist Criticism*, London: Methuen, pp. 73–81.
5 Linda Gray Sexton (1995) *Searching for Mercy Street: My Journey back to Anne Sexton*, Boston: Little Brown.
6 Ibid., p. 291.
7 Ibid., p. 271.
8 Middlebrook, *Anne Sexton*, p. xvi.
9 The typographical devices of the ellipsis and the dash are used in the biography to capture pauses, omissions and ruptures in the clinical narrative. Cf. 'A Note on Punctuation', Middlebrook, *Anne Sexton*, p. xxiii.
10 Margaret Walters made a similar point in a television discussion with Diane Middlebrook: 'Can a third person ever know what's going on, because of the gaps between words?' *The Late Show*, BBC TV, 4 November 1991.
11 Middlebrook, *Anne Sexton*, p. 40.
12 Ibid., p. 114.
13 Ibid., p. 179.
14 Ibid., p. 19.
15 Ibid., pp. 167, 238.
16 Ibid., p. 224.
17 Ibid., p. 137.
18 Ibid., p. 59.
19 The ethical charges against Dr Orne were ultimately dropped. See Diane Wood Middlebrook (1996) 'Telling Secrets', in Mary Rhiel (ed.), *The Seductions of Biography*, New York: Routledge.
20 Quoted in W.J. Weatherby (1991) 'Into Verse – And Worse', *Guardian*, 17 July.

21 For commentary on the 'competing interests' in the privacy/publication frame, see Christopher Bollas and David Sundelson (1995) *The New Informants: Betrayal of Confidentiality in Psychoanalysis and Psychotherapy*, London: Karnac, pp. 9–11.
22 Dr Orne's 'Foreword' to Middlebrook, *Anne Sexton*, p. xvii. This view corresponds closely with that of Linda Gray Sexton, who thought the censure of Dr Orne 'sanctimonious' (*Searching*, p. xx).
23 The wider context of disclosure in the United States includes developments in managed care and mandatory reporting of suspected child abuse. See Bollas and Sundelson, *The New Informants*, passim.
24 *New York Times*, 26 July 1991.
25 Robert Stoller (1988) 'Patients' Responses to Their Own Case Reports', *Journal of the American Psychoanalytic Association*, 36, p. 390.
26 Jean Strouse, quoted in Alessandra Stanley, 'Fame and Privacy: The Sexton Tapes', *International Herald Tribune*, 16 July 1991.
27 Jacqueline Rose (1991) has argued that it is regrettable that the biography's reception concentrated on the disclosure issue, but also that it is hard to see how the decision to release the tapes could be defended. See 'Faking It Up with the Truth' (review of Diane Middlebrook, *Anne Sexton*), *Times Literary Supplement*, 1 November.
28 Middlebrook. *Anne Sexton*, p. 200; Diane Middlebrook discusses her countertransference, as a biographer, to Anne Sexton in 'Telling Secrets'.
29 Anne-Marie Sandler and Richard Holmes (1990) 'A Dialogue on Biography and Psychoanalysis', joint presentation, Institute of Psycho-Analysis, London, June.
30 The words quoted are Diane Middlebrook's (personal communication, 1996).
31 Stoller, 'Patients' Responses', pp. 381, 383.
32 Middlebrook, *Anne Sexton*, p. 45.
33 John Forrester (1989) 'Psychoanalysis: Gossip, Telepathy and/or Science?', in *The Seductions of Psychoanalysis*, Cambridge: Cambridge University Press, pp. 243–59.

34 Ibid., p. 246.
35 The phrase 'constructed eloquence' is Diane Middlebrook's (personal communication, 1996). I am indebted to Diane Middlebrook for sharing her thoughts in a way which has enabled me to clarify my own in this paragraph.
36 Linda Gray Sexton illustrates the point in *Searching*, closing the gap between everyday life and the consulting room: 'the pieces [Middlebrook] . . . chose to use did nothing more than elucidate text she had already established from other sources. Nothing particularly new was revealed in this private dialogue between doctor and patient' (pp. 238–9).
37 'Retrospective prose narrative': Philippe Lejeune, quoted in Bruner, 'Autobiographical Process', p. 164.
38 Linda Gray Sexton, *Searching*, p. 10.
39 Quoted in Carolyn Steedman (1986) *Landscape for a Good Woman: A Story of Two Lives*, London: Virago, p. 3.
40 Rosalind Delmar (1977) 'Feminism and Autobiography', paper presented at Durham University seminar, 'Women on Women', November.
41 Laura Marcus (1995) discusses '"the return of the subject"' and its link to a concern with personal pronouns, in 'Autobiography and the Politics of Identity', *Current Sociology* 41, 2/3, pp. 41–52.
42 Linda Gray Sexton, *Searching*, p. 300.
43 As in Steedman's notion of 'lives for which the central interpretative devices of the culture don't quite work', *Landscape for a Good Woman*, p. 5.
44 Linda Gray Sexton, *Searching*, p. 265.
45 Ibid., p. 71.
46 Ibid., pp. 99, 107.
47 Ibid., p. 160.
48 Ibid., p. 190.
49 Ibid., p. 235.
50 Ibid., pp. 238, 268.
51 Ibid., p. 301.
52 J.-B. Pontalis (1987) *L'amour des commencements*, translated as *Love of Beginnings*, London: Free Association Books, 1993. The point is drawn out by Adam Phillips in

his 'Foreword' to the English edition (p. viii), celebrating Pontalis's love of words.

53 I am contrasting this resistance with the idea of the invitation biography offers to *be* drawn into another's life, as discussed by Anne-Marie Sandler and Richard Holmes, 'A Dialogue on Biography and Psychoanalysis'.

54 Linda Gray Sexton, *Searching*, p. 276.

55 Richard Holmes (1994) *Dr Johnson and Mr Savage*, London: Flamingo, p. 5.

56 Louise de Salvo (1989) *Virginia Woolf: The Impact of Childhood Sexual Abuse on Her Life and Work*, Boston, MA: Beacon Press.

57 Cf. Cora Kaplan (1985) 'Psychoanalysis and Autobiography', seminar paper in History Workshop London seminar series, 'Psychoanalysis and History'. See Michael Vincent Miller (1994) Review of Linda Gray Sexton, *Searching for Mercy Street*, *New York Times Book Review*, 20 November.

58 Elizabeth Spillius (1985) 'The Kleinian Concept of Phantasy', University College London Freud Memorial Lecture, January.

59 Vivien Bar (1995), in a discussion of Kleinian and Lacanian readings of the acquisition of language, 'At the Edge of Reality', lecture in Philadelphia Association First Sunday lecture series, March.

8 *Unveiling and obscuring in the image of abuse*

1 See Andrew Barry (1995) 'Reporting and Visualising', in Chris Jenks (ed.) *Visual Culture*, London: Routledge, pp. 42–57.

2 'Forbidden Britain: Our Secret Past' (produced by Stephen Humphries), BBC TV, 1 December 1994; *Evening Standard*, 2 December 1994.

3 Sean Brierley (1995) *The Advertising Handbook*, London: Routledge, p. 243.

4 See Andrew Cooper (1995) 'Child Abuse' ('Britain in a Moral Panic: Part 4'), *Community Care*, 3–9 August (pull-out supplement).

5 Brierley, *Advertising Handbook*, p. 243.
6 Judith Williamson (1978) *Decoding Advertisements*, London: Marion Boyars.
7 Blake Morrison (1995) 'The Doctor's Children', *Independent on Sunday (The Sunday Review)*, 11 June, pp. 6–11.
8 Nick Hedges (1979) 'Charity Begins at Home: the Shelter Photographs', in *Photography/Politics: One*, London: Photography Workshop, pp. 161–4.
9 James Donald (1995) 'The City, the Cinema: Modern Spaces', in Jenks, *Visual Culture*, pp. 77–95.
10 Victor Burgin (1980) 'Photography, Phantasy, Function', in Burgin (ed.) (1982), *Thinking Photography*, Basingstoke: Macmillan, p. 203.
11 Brierley, *Advertising Handbook*, p. 179.
12 Andrew Cooper points out that some abuse ads do juxtapose 'naked revelation' with a form of obscuring. The spectator has to 'work a bit to grasp the full meaning of the communication. The wordplay – like in the NSPCC ad which depicts a girl with bruised, blackened eyes, and the caption "I've got my mother's eyes" – throws one off centre . . . and the whole family scene takes shape' (personal communication, 1996).
13 Brierley, *Advertising Handbook*, p. 158.
14 Barry Richards (1994) 'Goods and Good Objects', in *Disciplines of Delight: The Psychoanalysis of Popular Culture*, London: Free Association Books, pp. 87–107.
15 Roland Barthes (1964) 'Rhetoric of the Image', in *Image Music Text*, essays selected and trans. Stephen Heath, London: Fontana Press, 1977, pp. 38–9. The relationship between image and caption was made particularly vivid in Trevor Beatty's personal campaign against rape in the autumn of 1995. Beatty had previously run the Wonderbra campaign, but donated his time and influence to a fascinating series of hoardings in which the image and the caption were ostensibly in direct contradiction. The images depicted a delicate kiss between a man and a woman, a table napkin with a woman's phone number on it invitingly placed next to a coffee cup and empty wine glass; the morning dress of a wedding ceremony. All had the caption, in incongruously

small type, 'this is not an invitation to rape me'. The effect was not transparent. As one interviewee commented: 'They're quite mysterious – you'd need to look around town for it to make sense.' Another said: 'The images are great, especially when you see them from a distance – but then you can't read the slogan.' See 'Advertising Poster Points (Kate Withers Finds the Real Connection between Wonderbras and Rape)', *Arena*, Autumn 1995, p. 32.

16 Simon Watney (1982) 'Making Strange: The Shattered Mirror', in Burgin, *Thinking Photography*, pp. 154–76.

17 As was pointed out at the seminar at which I first presented this chapter as a paper: 'If it wasn't for the caption you'd think it could be poverty in Bombay.'

18 The image was also used by British Telecom in *Update* (Winter 1994) as part of its Community Programme, appealing for donations and offering a lo-call number.

19 Roland Barthes (1981) *Camera Lucida: Reflections on Photography*, trans. Richard Howard, London: Vintage, 1993. See Louis-Jean Calvet (1994) *Roland Barthes: A Biography*, Cambridge: Polity Press, pp. 235–7.

20 John Tagg (1988) 'Introduction', in *The Burden of Representation: Essays on Photographies and Histories*, Basingstoke: Macmillan, p. 1.

21 Barthes, *Camera Lucida*, p. 89.

22 Tagg, *Burden of Representation*, p. 2.

23 Quoted in 'Forbidden Britain'; see n. 2.

24 Barthes, *Camera Lucida*, p. 89.

25 Chris Jenks, 'Introduction' to *Visual Culture*, p. 22.

26 Suzanne Moore (1995) 'Look What's Under the Patio', *Guardian*, 18 May.

27 *Newsnight*, BBC TV, 7 July 1995.

28 As reported on ITN News, 18 July 1995.

29 'It's the most talked-about trial since O.J. Simpson', *What's On TV*, 8–12 May 1995.

30 'Right to Reply: *Brookside* Special', Channel 4, 20 May 1995.

31 Phil Redmond (1995) 'Why I Had to Find Beth and Mandy Guilty', *Guardian*, 18 May.

32 See, for example, *Brookside Special*, Channel 4, 2 October 1994.

33 Stuart Jeffries, 'Court in the Act', *Guardian*, 13 May 1995.
34 Quoted in *TV Times*, 6–12 May 1995. As *TV Quick* put it, in an interview with 'Chris Brown, a Professor of Psychology at London University: "She is suffering repression. This normally occurs when people don't talk to anyone about what's happened to them. It may be because they've been threatened by their abuser and have subconsciously forgotten what happened as a way of dealing with it . . . in time Rachel may begin to remember things".'
35 See, for example, *Brookside* episodes of 11, 12 and 14 July 1995.
36 The debate about lying vs. repression – which takes the form: 'what is the truth?' – was mirrored in the huge interest taken at the time in the actress who played Beth, Anna Friel. The interest had its undercutting, as one of the interviewees in 'Dyke TV's' portrait of Beth Jordache observed: 'Beth is a lesbian but Anna Friel is a heterosexual woman, so people can mentally insert that' (Channel 4, 2 September 1995). Anna Friel also commented on the canonisation of Beth, in the shoot for *Brookside* magazine's cover story on her, wearing a crown of thorns and dressed in a white robe. 'They wanted me to be looking angelic' (*Brookside: The Magazine*, 1, 1995).
37 Mark Cousins (1993) 'Psychosis and Truth', paper presented at THERIP annual conference on 'The Utterances of the Mad', London, March.
38 Roland Barthes (1961) 'The Photographic Message', in Barthes, *Image Music Text*, p. 17; Burgin, *Thinking Photography*, p. 17.
39 Tagg, *Burden of Representation*, p. 4.

Bibliography

Abraham, N. (1987) 'Notes on the Phantom: a Complement to Freud's Metapsychology', *Critical Inquiry*, 13 (Winter), pp. 287–92

Abraham, N. and Torok, M. (1980) 'Introjection – Incorporation: *Mourning* or *Melancholia*', in Serge Lebovici and Daniel Widlöcher (eds), *Psychoanalysis in France*, New York: International Universities Press

Adams, Mary (1990) 'The Couple and the Group: Co-therapy with Incest Survivors', *British Journal of Psychotherapy*, 7, pp. 25–37

Adams, Parveen (1995) *The Emptiness of the Image: Psychoanalysis and Sexual Differences*, London: Routledge

Adams-Silvan, Abby and Silvan, Mark (1994) 'Paradise Lost: A Case of Hysteria Illustrating a Specific Dynamic of Seduction Trauma', *International Journal of Psycho-Analysis*, 75, pp. 499–510

American Psychiatric Association (1984) *Diagnostic and Statistical Manual of Mental Disorders (Third Edition)* [DSM-III], Washington, DC: American Psychiatric Association

American Psychiatric Association (1994) *Diagnostic and Statistical Manual of Mental Disorders (Fourth Edition)* [DSM-IV], Washington, DC: American Psychiatric Association

Anderson, Perry (1968) 'Components of the National Culture', *New Left Review*, 56; reprinted in Alexander Cockburn and Robin Blackburn (eds) (1969) *Student Power: Problems, Diagnosis, Action*, Harmondsworth: Penguin, pp. 214–84

Andrews, B., Morton, J., Bekerian, D.A., Brewin, C.R., Davies, G.M. and Mollon, P. (1995) 'The Recovery of Memories in Clinical Practice: Experiences and Beliefs of British Psychological Society Practitioners', *The Psychologist*, 8, pp. 209–14

Anzieu, Didier (1974) 'A Discussion of the Paper by Gisela Pankow on "The Body Image in Psychosis"', *International Journal of Psycho-Analysis*, 55, pp. 415–16

Anzieu, Didier (1986) *Freud's Self-Analysis*, London: Hogarth Press and the Institute of Psycho-Analysis

Arena (1995) 'Advertising Poster Points (Kate Withers Finds the Real Connection between Wonderbras and Rape)', Autumn, p. 32

Armstrong–Perlman, Eleanore (1993) 'The Zealots and the Blind', paper presented at Psychoanalytic Forum conference, 'Contemporary Psychoanalysis, Contemporary Sexualities', London, July

Ashplant, T. G. (1987) 'Fantasy, Narrative, Event: Psychoanalysis and History', *History Workshop*, 23 (Spring) pp. 166–73

Bachman, Kurt M. and Bossi, Jeannette (1993) 'Mother–son Incest as a Defence against Psychosis', *British Journal of Medical Psychology*, 66, pp. 239–48

Bar, Vivien (1987) 'Change in Women', in Ernst and Maguire (1987), pp. 213–58

Bar, Vivien (1995) 'At the Edge of Reality', Lecture in Philadelphia Association First Sunday lecture series, March

Barrett, Michèle (1987) 'The Concept of Difference', *Feminist Review*, 26, pp. 29–41

Barrett, Michèle and McIntosh, Mary (1982) *The Anti–Social Family*, London: Verso

Barry, Andrew (1995) 'Reporting and Visualising', in Jenks (1995), pp. 42–57

Barthes, Roland (1961) 'The Photographic Message', in Barthes (1977), pp. 15–31

Barthes, Roland (1964) 'Rhetoric of the Image', in *Image Music Text*, essays selected and trans. Stephen Heath, London: Fontana Press, 1977, pp. 32–51

Barthes, Roland (1975) *The Pleasure of the Text*, trans. Richard Miller, Oxford: Basil Blackwell

Barthes, Roland (1977) *Image Music Text*, essays selected and trans. Stephen Heath, London: Fontana Press

Barthes, Roland (1979) *A Lover's Discourse: Fragments*, Harmondsworth: Penguin, 1990

Barthes, Roland (1979) 'From Work to Text', in José Harari (ed.), *Textual Strategies: Perspectives in Post-Structuralist Criticism*, London: Methuen, pp. 73–81

Barthes, Roland (1981) *Camera Lucida: Reflections on Photography*, trans. Richard Howard, London: Vintage, 1993

Benjamin, Jessica (1988) *The Bonds of Love: Psychoanalysis, Feminism and the Problem of Domination*, London: Virago, 1990

Benjamin, Jessica (1993) 'Sameness and Difference: Like Subjects and Love Objects', paper presented to Psychoanalytic Forum conference on 'Contemporary Psychoanalysis, Contemporary Sexualities', London, July

Bennett, Catherine (1994) 'The Satanic Verses', *Guardian Weekend*, 10 September, pp. 13–20

Bentovim, Arnon and Tranter, Marianne (1994) 'Psychotherapeutic Work with Adult Survivors of Sexual Abuse in Childhood', in Petruska Clarkson and Michael Pokorny (eds) *The Handbook of Psychotherapy*, London: Routledge, pp. 403–30

Benvenuto, Bice and Kennedy, Roger (1986) *The Works of Jacques Lacan: An Introduction*, London: Free Association Books

Bernheimer, Charles and Kahane, Claire (eds) (1985) *In Dora's Case: Freud, Hysteria, Feminism*, London: Virago

Bollas, Christopher (1989) 'The Trauma of Incest', in *Forces of Destiny: Psychoanalysis and Human Idiom*, London: Free Association Books, pp. 171–80

Bollas, Christopher and Sundelson, David (1995) *The New Informants: Betrayal of Confidentiality in Psychoanalysis and Psychotherapy*, London: Karnac

Bowie, Malcolm (1991) *Lacan*, London: Fontana Modern Masters

Bowie, Malcolm (1995) 'Memory and Desire in Freud's *Civilization and Its Discontents*', *New Formations* 26, pp. 1–14

Bowlby, John, Figlio, Karl and Young, Robert M. (1986) 'An

Interview with John Bowlby on the Origins and Reception of his Work', *Free Associations* 6, pp. 36–64

Brenner, Charles (1955) *An Elementary Textbook of Psychoanalysis*, New York: International Universities Press

Breuer, J. and Freud, Sigmund (1893) 'On the Psychical Mechanism of Hysterical Phenomena: Preliminary Communication', in Breuer and Freud (1893–5), pp. 3–17

Breuer, J. and Freud, Sigmund (1893–5) *Studies on Hysteria*, in Freud, *Standard Edition*, Vol. 2 (For S.E. see Freud, 1896)

Breuer, Josef and Freud, Sigmund (1970) *Studien über Hysterie*, Frankfurt am Main: Fischer Taschenbuch Verlag

Bridge, The (1991) *Sukina: An Evaluation Report of the Circumstances Leading to her Death*, London: The Bridge Child Care Consultancy Service

Bridge, The (1995) *Paul: Death through Neglect*, London: The Bridge Child Care Consultancy Service

Brierley, Sean (1995) *The Advertising Handbook*, London: Routledge

British Journal of Psychotherapy (1996) 'Recovered Memories of Sexual Abuse' (special section), 12, 3, pp. 342–71

Britton, Ronald (1994) 'The Blinding of the Seeing Eye: Inverse Symmetry as a Defense against Reality', *Psychoanalytic Inquiry*, 14

Browne, Julie (1996) 'Unasked Questions or Unheard Answers? Policy Development in Child Sexual Abuse', *British Journal of Social Work*, 26, pp. 37–52

Bruner, Jerome (1995) 'The Autobiographical Process', *Current Sociology*, 41, 2/3, pp. 161–77

Burgin, Victor (1977) 'Looking at Photographs', in Burgin (1982), pp. 142–53

Burgin, Victor (1980) 'Photography, Phantasy, Function', in Burgin (1982), pp. 177–216

Burgin, Victor (ed.) (1982) *Thinking Photography*, Basingstoke: Macmillan

Burgoyne, Bernard (1990) 'Commentary by a Lacanian Psychoanalyst', in 'Clinical Commentary X', *British Journal of Psychotherapy*, 6, pp. 480–2

Butler, Judith (1990) *Gender Trouble: Feminism and the Subversion of Identity*, London: Routledge

Calvet, Louis-Jean (1994) *Roland Barthes: A Biography*, Cambridge: Polity Press

Campbell, Aisling (1995) 'Post-traumatic Stress Disorder and Accidents – A Psychoanalytic Perspective', paper presented to Greenwich Consortium conference on Post–Traumatic Stress Disorder, October

Campbell, Beatrix (1988) *Unofficial Secrets. Child Sexual Abuse: The Cleveland Case*, London: Virago

Chodorow, Nancy (1978) *The Reproduction of Mothering: Psychoanalysis and the Sociology of Gender*, Berkeley, CA: University of California Press

Clark, Ronald W. (1980) *Freud: The Man and the Cause*, London: Jonathan Cape and Weidenfeld & Nicolson

Collins, Jerré, Green, J. Ray, Lydon, Mary, Sachner, Mark and Skoller, Eleanor Honig (1983) 'Questioning the Unconscious: the Dora Archive', in *Diacritics*, 13, 1: *A Fine Romance: Freud and Dora*

Cooper, Andrew (1995) 'Child Abuse' ('Britain in a Moral Panic: Part 4'), *Community Care*, 3–9 August (pull–out supplement)

Cousins, Mark (1993) 'Psychosis and Truth', paper presented at THERIP annual conference on 'The Utterances of the Mad', London, March

Cousins, Mark and Adams, Parveen (1995) 'The Truth on Assault', *October*, 71 (Winter), pp. 93–102

Coward, Rosalind (1982) 'Erin Pizzey Adrift in a Misogynist Society', *Guardian*, 2 November

Cox, Murray (1970) 'Dynamic Psychotherapy with Sex-offenders' in Ismond Rosen (ed.), *Sexual Deviation*, Oxford: Oxford University Press, pp. 306–50

Crews, F. (1994) 'The Revenge of the Repressed', *New York Review of Books*, 17 November and 1 December

David, Christian (1974) 'A Discussion of the Paper by René Major on "The Revolution of Hysteria"', *International Journal of Psycho-Analysis*, 55, pp. 393–5

Delmar, Rosalind (1977) 'Feminism and Autobiography', paper presented at Durham University seminar, 'Women on Women', November

Delmar, Rosalind (1977) 'Afterword', in Agnes Smedley,

Daughter of Earth: A Novel (first published New York, 1929, reissued London: Virago, 1977) pp. 271–9
Department of Health (1995) *Child Protection: Messages from Research*, London: Home Office
De Salvo, Louise (1989) *Virginia Woolf: The Impact of Childhood Sexual Abuse on Her Life and Work*, Boston, MA: Beacon Press
Dinnerstein, Dorothy (1976) *The Mermaid and the Minotaur: Sexual Arrangements and Human Malaise*, New York: Harper & Row
Donald, James (1995) 'The City, the Cinema: Modern Spaces', in Jenks (1995), pp. 77–95
Dorey, Roger (1986) 'The Relationship of Mastery', *International Review of Psycho-Analysis*, 13, pp. 323–32
Ehlers, Hella and Crick, Joyce (eds) (1994) *The Trauma of the Past: Remembering and Working Through*, London: Goethe-Institut
Eichenbaum, Luise and Orbach, Susie (1982) *Outside In . . . Inside Out. Women's Psychology: A Feminist Psychoanalytic Approach*, Harmondsworth: Penguin
English, Deirdre (1984) 'The Masson–Malcolm Dispute', *Mother Jones*, 9, 10 (December), p. 6
Ennew, Judith (1986) *The Sexual Exploitation of Children*, Cambridge: Polity Press
Ernst, Sheila and Maguire, Marie (eds) (1987) *Living with the Sphinx: Papers from The Women's Therapy Centre*, London: The Women's Press
Felman, Shoshana and Laub, Dori (1992) *Testimony: Crises of Witnessing in Literature, Psychoanalysis, and History*, New York and London: Routledge
Fischer, Michael (1986) 'Ethnicity and the Post-Modern Arts of Memory', in James Clifford and George Marcus (eds), *Writing Culture: The Poetics and Politics of Ethnography*, Berkeley, CA: University of California Press, pp. 194–233
Fletcher, John (1994) 'Is the Superego a Psychotic Enclave? Problems in the Theory of Psychosis', paper presented at University of Warwick, July
Fletcher, John and Stanton, Martin (eds) (1992) *Jean Laplanche:*

Seduction, Translation, Drives, London: Institute of Contemporary Arts

Fonagy, Peter (1994) 'A Psychoanalytic Understanding of Memory and Reconstruction', *British Psychological Society Psychotherapy Section Newsletter*, 16 (December), pp. 3–20

Forrester, John (1989) 'Psychoanalysis: Gossip, Telepathy and/or Science?', in *The Seductions of Psychoanalysis*, Cambridge: Cambridge University Press, pp. 243–59

Fraser, Ronald (1984) *In Search of a Past: The Manor House, Amnersfield, 1933–1945*, London: Verso Books

Fraser, Ronald (1985) 'In Search of the Past: A Dialogue with Ronald Fraser', *History Workshop*, 20 (Autumn), pp. 175–88

Fraser, Sylvia (1989) *My Father's House: A Memoir of Incest and Healing*, London: Virago

Freud, Anna (1968) 'Indications and Contraindications for Child Analysis', in *Problems of Psychoanalytic Training, Diagnosis, and the Technique of Therapy*, London: Hogarth Press and the Institute of Psycho-Analysis, 1974, pp. 110–23

Freud, Sigmund (1896) 'The Aetiology of Hysteria', in *The Standard Edition of the Complete Works of Sigmund Freud*, 24 vols, ed. and trans. James Strachey, London: Hogarth Press and the Institute of Psycho-Analysis, 1953–73, Vol. 3, pp. 189–224

Freud, Sigmund (1905) 'Three Essays on the Theory of Sexuality', in *Standard Edition*, Vol. 7, pp. 123–245

Freud, Sigmund (1905) 'Fragment of a Case of Hysteria: "Dora"', in *Standard Edition*, Vol. 7, pp. 1–122

Freud, Sigmund (1909) 'Notes upon a Case of Obsessional Neurosis', in *Standard Edition*, Vol. 10, pp. 151–249

Freud, Sigmund (1910) 'A Special Type of Choice of Object Made by Men (Contributions to the Psychology of Love I)', in *On Sexuality (Pelican Freud Library, Vol. 7)*, Harmondsworth: Penguin, 1977, pp. 227–42

Freud, Sigmund (1914) 'Remembering, Repeating and Working-Through', in *Standard Edition*, Vol. 12, pp. 145–56

Freud, Sigmund (1916) Lecture 23 in *Introductory Lectures on Psychoanalysis* (1916), *Pelican Freud Library*, Vol. 1, Harmondsworth: Penguin, 1974, pp. 404–24

Freud, Sigmund (1937) 'Constructions in Analysis', in *Standard Edition*, Vol. 23, pp. 255–69

Freud, Sigmund (1938) 'Splitting of the Ego in the Process of Defence', *Pelican Freud Library*, Vol. 11, Harmondsworth: Penguin, 1984, pp. 457–64

Furniss, Tilman (1991) *The Multiprofessional Handbook of Child Sexual Abuse: Integrated Management, Therapy and Legal Intervention*, London: Routledge

Gabbard, Glen O. (1986) 'The Treatment of the "Special" Patient in a Psychoanalytic Hospital', *International Review of Psycho-Analysis*, 13, pp. 333–47

Gallop, Jane (1982) *Feminism and Psychoanalysis: The Daughter's Seduction*, Basingstoke: Macmillan

Gardner, Fiona (1990) 'Psychotherapy with Adult Survivors of Child Sexual Abuse', *British Journal of Psychotherapy*, 6, pp. 285–94

Gardner, Richard (1992) 'Belated Realization of Child Sex Abuse by an Adult', in *Issues in Child Abuse Accusations*, 4, 4, pp. 177–96

Grant, Linda (1995) 'A Past Imperfect', *Guardian*, 24 May

Grant, Steve (1993) 'Move Over Dali', *Time Out*, 1–8 September

Green, André (1995) 'Affects versus Representations: Or Affects as Representations?' Paper presented at *British Journal of Psychotherapy*/Freud Museum conference, 'How Do We Think About Feelings?', London, May; summary published in *British Journal of Psychotherapy* (1996) 12, 2, pp. 208–11

Grosskurth, Phyllis (1986) *Melanie Klein: Her World and Her Work*, London: Hodder & Stoughton

Hadjiisky, Elisabeth (1987) 'On First Contact with Child Abuse and Neglect', *Journal of Social Work Practice*, 3, 1, pp. 31–7

Hale, Rob and Sinason, Valerie (1994) 'Internal and External Reality: Establishing Parameters', in Sinason (ed.) (1994), pp. 274–84

Halsbury's Statutes of England and Wales (1994) *Fourth Edition, Volume 12, 1994 Reissue, Criminal Law*, London: Butterworth

Hanly, Charles (1986) 'Lear and his Daughters', *International Review of Psycho–Analysis*, 13, pp. 211–20

Hanly, Charles (1986) Review of Masson *The Assault on Truth* (1984) and Malcolm *In the Freud Archives* (1984), *International Journal of Psycho-Analysis*, 67, pp. 517–19

Hedges, Nick (1979) 'Charity Begins at Home: The Shelter Photographs', in *Photography/Politics: One*, London: Photography Workshop, pp. 161–4

Hetherington, Rachel, Cooper, Andrew, Piquardt, Rolf, Smith, Philip, Spriggs, Angela and Wilford, Gertie (1996) *Eight European Child Protection Systems: A Preliminary Report*, Twickenham: Brunel University College

Hinshelwood, R. D. (1989) *A Dictionary of Kleinian Thought*, London: Free Association Books (2nd, rev. edn, 1991)

History Workshop (1979) 'Editorial: Oral History', *History Workshop*, 8 (Autumn), pp. i–ii

Holmes, Richard (1985) *Footsteps: Adventures of a Romantic Biographer*, Harmondsworth: Penguin

Holmes, Richard (1994) *Dr Johnson and Mr Savage*, London: Flamingo

Horney, Karen (1967) *Feminine Psychology*, New York: W.W. Norton

International Journal of Psycho-Analysis (1986) 'Panel on Identification in the Perversions', 67

Jenks, Chris (ed.) (1995) *Visual Culture*, London: Routledge

Johnson, Terry (1993) *Hysteria*, London: Methuen Drama

Jones, Ernest (1967) *The Life and Work of Sigmund Freud*, Harmondsworth: Penguin

Jonsdottir, Gudrun (1990) 'Surviving Incest: Feminist Theory and Practice', *Journal of Social Work Practice*, 4, 3/4, pp. 56–70

Journal of Traumatic Stress (1995) Special Issue: 'Research on Traumatic Memory', 8, 4

Kaplan, Cora (1985) 'Psychoanalysis and Autobiography', seminar paper in History Workshop London seminar series, 'Psychoanalysis and History', May

Kaysen, Susanna (1993) *Girl, Interrupted*, New York: Vintage

Kempe, Ruth S. and Kempe, Henry C. (1984) *Child Abuse*, London: Fontana

Kendrick, Walter (1984) 'Not Just Another Oedipal Drama: The Unsinkable Sigmund Freud' (review of Masson, *The Assault on Truth*, 1984, Malcolm, *In the Freud Archives* and other new work on Freud), *Voice Literary Supplement*, June, pp. 12–16

Kennedy, Roger (1995) 'Bearing the Unbearable – Working with the Abused Mind', *Psychoanalytic Psychotherapy*, 10, pp. 143–54

Khan, Masud (1963) 'The Concept of Cumulative Trauma', in *The Privacy of the Self*, London: Hogarth Press and the Institute of Psycho–Analysis, pp. 42–58

King, Pearl and Steiner, Riccardo (eds) (1991) *The Freud–Klein Controversies in the British Psycho-Analytical Society, 1941–45*, London: Routledge

Klein, Melanie (1923) 'The Role of the School in the Libidinal Development of the Child', in *Love, Guilt and Reparation and Other Works 1921–1945*, London: Hogarth Press and the Institute of Psycho-Analysis, 1975, pp. 59–76

Klein, Melanie (1927) 'Criminal Tendencies in Normal Children', in *Love, Guilt and Reparation and Other Works 1921–1945*, London: Hogarth Press and the Institute of Psycho-Analysis, 1975, pp. 170–85

Klein, Melanie (1932) *The Psycho-Analysis of Children*, London: Hogarth Press and the Institute of Psycho-Analysis, 1975

Klein, Melanie (1957) 'Envy and Gratitude', in *Envy and Gratitude and Other Works 1946–1963*, London: Hogarth Press and the Institute of Psycho-Analysis, 1975, pp. 176–235

Klein, Melanie (1961) *Narrative of a Child Analysis*, London: Hogarth Press and the Institute of Psycho–Analysis

Klein, Melanie (1963) 'On the Sense of Loneliness', in *Envy and Gratitude and Other Works 1946–1963*, London: Hogarth Press and the Institute of Psycho-Analysis, 1975, pp. 300–13

Kraemer, Sebastian (1988) 'Splitting and Stupidity in Child Sexual Abuse', *Psychoanalytic Psychotherapy*, 3, pp. 247–57

Krell, David (1991) 'Wax Magic', in *Of Memory, Reminiscence and Writing: On the Verge*, New Haven, CT and London: Yale University Press, pp. 105–62

Krull, Marianne (1979) *Freud and his Father*, London: Hutchinson, 1986

Lacan, Jacques (1953) 'Some Reflections on the Ego', *International Journal of Psycho-Analysis,* 34, pp. 11–17

Lacan, Jacques (1953) 'The Function and Field of Speech

and Language in Psychoanalysis', in *Ecrits: A Selection*, trans. Alan Sheridan, London: Tavistock Publications, 1977, pp. 30–113

Lacan, Jacques (1973) 'Analysis and Truth or the Closure of the Unconscious', in *The Four Fundamental Concepts of Psycho-Analysis*, trans. Alan Sheridan, Harmondsworth: Penguin, 1979, pp. 136–48

Laplanche, Jean (1974) (reporter) 'Panel on "Hysteria Today"', *International Journal of Psycho-Analysis*, 55, pp. 459–69

Laplanche, Jean (1979) *Life and Death in Psychoanalysis*, Baltimore, MD: Johns Hopkins University Press

Laplanche, Jean (1989) *New Foundations for Psychoanalysis*, Oxford: Blackwell

Laplanche, Jean (1990) 'Implantation, Intromission', in *La Révolution Copernicienne inachevée: travaux 1967–1992*, Paris: Aubier, 1992

Laplanche, Jean (1992) 'Interpretation between Determinism and Hermeneutics: A Restatement of the Problem', *International Journal of Psycho-Analysis*, 73

Laplanche, Jean (1992) 'Notes on Afterwardsness', in Fletcher and Stanton (1992), pp. 217–23

Laplanche, Jean (1995) 'Seduction, Persecution, Revelation', *International Journal of Psycho-Analysis*, 76, pp. 663–82

Laplanche, Jean and Pontalis, J.-B. (1968) 'Fantasy and the Origins of Sexuality', *International Journal of Psycho-Analysis*, 49, pp. 1–18

Laplanche, Jean and Pontalis, J.-B. (1973) *The Language of Psychoanalysis*, London: Hogarth Press and the Institute of Psycho-Analysis

Laurent, Eric (1992) 'Phantasy in Klein and Lacan', lecture to THERIP in 'Phantasy' series, London, April

Leader, Darian (1994) 'Lacan and Phantasy', lecture to THERIP in 'Dialogues between Klein and Lacan' series, London, October

'Letter from the Women's Therapy Centre' (1979) *m/f* 3.

Levy, Allan (ed.) (1989) *Focus on Child Abuse: Medical, Legal and Social Work Perspectives*, London: Hawksmere

Lieven, Elena (1976) 'Patriarchy and Psychoanalysis', in Feminist Anthology Collective (ed.), *No Turning Back: Writings from the Women's Liberation Movement 1975–80*, London: The Women's Press, 1981, pp. 246–54

Lothane, Zvi (1987) 'Love, Seduction and Trauma', *Psychoanalytic Review*, 74, pp. 83–105

Luepnitz, Deborah (1990) 'Psychoanalysis and/or Feminism' (review of Nancy Chodorow, *Feminism and Psychoanalytic Theory*, 1990), *Women's Review of Books*, May, pp. 17–18

MacCarthy, Brendan (1985) University College London Freud Memorial Lecture

MacCarthy, Brendan (1988) 'Are Incest Victims Hated?', *Psychoanalytic Psychotherapy*, 3, pp. 113–20

MacKinnon, Stephen R. and Janice R. (1988) *Agnes Smedley: The Life and Times of an American Radical*, London: Virago

McRobbie, Angela (1988) 'An Interview with Juliet Mitchell', *New Left Review*, 170, pp. 80–91

Macey, David (1988) *Lacan in Contexts*, London: Verso

Maguire, Marie (1995) 'False Memories of Sexual Abuse', in *Men, Women, Passion and Power: Gender Issues in Psychotherapy*, London: Routledge, pp. 153–71

Major, René (1974) 'The Revolution of Hysteria', *International Journal of Psycho-Analysis*, 55, pp. 385–95

Malcolm, Janet (1980) *Psychoanalysis: The Impossible Profession*, London: Pan Books, 1982

Malcolm, Janet (1983) 'Annals of Scholarship – Trouble in the Archives – 1', *New Yorker*, 5 December, pp. 59–152. 'Trouble in the Archives – 2', *New Yorker*, 12 December, pp. 60–119

Malcolm, Janet (1984) *In the Freud Archives*, London: Flamingo, 1986

Mann, David (1989) 'Incest: The Father and the Male Therapist', *British Journal of Psychotherapy*, 6, pp. 143–53

Mannoni, Maud (1970) 'Psychoanalysis and the May Revolution', in Charles Posner (ed.), *Reflections on the Revolution in France: 1968*, Harmondsworth: Penguin, pp. 215–24

Marcus, Laura (1995) 'Autobiography and the Politics of Identity', *Current Sociology*, 41, 2/3, pp. 41–52

Masson, Jeffrey M. (1984) *The Assault on Truth: Freud's Suppression of the Seduction Theory*; with new Preface and Afterword, Harmondsworth: Penguin, 1985

Masson, Jeffrey M. (1984) 'The Persecution and Expulsion of

Jeffrey Masson as Performed by the Freudian Establishment and Reported by Janet Malcolm of the *New Yorker*', *Mother Jones*, 9, 10 (December), pp. 34–47

Meltzer, Donald with Stokes, Adrian (1978) 'Painting and the Inner World', in Lawrence Gowing (ed.), *The Critical Writings of Adrian Stokes*, Vol. 3, London: Thames & Hudson, pp. 219–35

Merck, Mandy (1987) 'Difference and Its Discontents', *Screen*, 28, pp. 2–10

Merck, Mandy (1987) 'The Critical Cult of *Dora*', in *Perversions: Deviant Readings*, London: Virago, 1993, pp. 33–44

Merck, Mandy (1988) 'The Fatal Attraction of *Intercourse*', in *Perversions: Deviant Readings*, London: Virago, 1993

Merendino, R. P. (1985) 'On Epistemological Functions of Clinical Reports', *International Review of Psycho-Analysis*, 12, pp. 327–35

Middlebrook, Diane Wood (1991) *Anne Sexton: A Biography*, London: Virago

Middlebrook, Diane Wood (1996) 'Telling Secrets', in Mary Rhiel (ed.), *The Seductions of Biography*, New York: Routledge

Miller, Alice (1979) *The Drama of the Gifted Child and the Search for the True Self*, London: Faber & Faber, 1983

Miller, Alice (1980) *For Your Own Good: The Roots of Violence in Child-Rearing*, London: Virago, 1987

Miller, Alice (1981) *Thou Shalt Not Be Aware: Society's Betrayal of the Child*, London: Pluto, 1986

Miller, Alice (1987) *The Drama of Being a Child and the Search for the True Self*, London: Virago

Miller, Jacques-Alain (ed.) (1988) *The Seminar of Jacques Lacan, Book 1, Freud's Papers on Technique, 1953–1954*, trans. John Forrester, Cambridge: Cambridge University Press

Miller, Jonathan (ed.) (1983) *States of Mind: Conversations with Psychological Investigators*, London: BBC Books

Miller, Michael Vincent (1994) Review of Linda Gray Sexton, *Searching for Mercy Street*, *New York Times Book Review*, 20 November

Milton, Jane (1994) 'Abuser and Abused: Perverse Solutions Following Childhood Abuse', *Psychoanalytic Psychotherapy*, 8, pp. 243–55

Mitchell, Juliet (1974) *Psychoanalysis and Feminism*, London: Allen Lane

Mitchell, Juliet (1984) *Women: The Longest Revolution. Essays in Feminism*, London: Virago

Mitchell, Juliet (ed.) (1986) *The Selected Melanie Klein*, Harmondsworth: Penguin

Money-Kyrle, Roger (1978) 'Melanie Klein and her Contribution to Psychoanalysis', in Donald Meltzer (ed.), *The Papers of Roger Money–Kyrle*, Strath Tay, Perthshire: Roland Harris Educational Trust

Money-Kyrle, Roger (1982) *Man's Picture of His World*, London: Duckworth

Moore, Suzanne (1995) 'Look What's Under the Patio', *Guardian*, 18 May

Moore, Suzanne (1995) 'For the Good of the Kids – and Us', *Guardian*, 15 June

Morrison, Blake (1995) 'The Doctor's Children', *Independent on Sunday (The Sunday Review)*, 11 June, pp. 6–11

Morton, John (1996) 'The Dilemma of Validation', *British Journal of Psychotherapy*, 12, 3, pp. 367–71

Morton, John, Andrews, B., Bekerian, D.A., Brewin, C.R., Davies, G.M. and Mollon, P. (1995) *Recovered Memories*, Leicester: British Psychological Society

Nava, Mica (1988) 'Outrage and Anxiety in the Reporting of Child Sexual Abuse: Cleveland and the Press', in *Changing Cultures: Feminism, Youth and Consumerism*, London: Sage Publications, pp. 146–61

Nava, Mica (with Orson Nava) (1990) 'Discriminating or Duped? Young People as Consumers of Advertising/Art', in *Changing Cultures: Feminism, Youth and Consumerism*, London: Sage Publications, pp. 171–84

Nava, Mica (1992) *Changing Cultures: Feminism, Youth and Consumerism*, London: Sage Publications

Nin, Anaïs (1994) *Incest*, Harmondsworth: Penguin

Orbach, Susie (1995) 'When It's All About Self, Self, Self', *Guardian*, 13 May

O'Shaughnessy, Edna (1987) review of P. Grosskurth, *Melanie Klein: Her World and Her Work* (1986), *International Review of Psycho-Analysis*, 14, pp. 132–6

Pankow, Gisela (1973) 'L'Image du corps dans la psychose hystérique', *Revue française de psychanalyse*, 37, pp. 415–38

Pankow, Gisela (1974) 'The Body Image in Hysterical Psychosis', *International Journal of Psycho-Analysis*, 55, pp. 407–13

Papers from the Patriarchy Conference (1976) London: Patriarchy Conference

Parsons, Michael (1986) 'Suddenly Finding it Really Matters', *International Journal of Psycho-Analysis*, 67, pp. 476–85

Perlow, Meir (1995) *Understanding Mental Objects*, London: Routledge

Phillips, Adam (1993) 'Foreword' to Pontalis (1987), pp. vii–ix

Pilkington, Bridget and Kremer, John (1995) 'A Review of the Epidemiological Research on Child Sexual Abuse: Clinical Samples', *Child Abuse Review*, 4, pp. 191–205

Pontalis, J.-B. (1987) *L'Amour des commencements*, translated as *Love of Beginnings*, London: Free Association Books, 1993

Pontalis, J.-B. (1992) 'Michel Leiris, or Psychoanalysis Without End', *Yale French Studies*, 81, pp. 128–44

Portelli, Alessandro (1981) 'The Peculiarities of Oral History', *History Workshop*, 12 (Autumn)

Quinn, Susan (1987) *A Mind of Her Own: The Life of Karen Horney*, London: Macmillan

Ramas, Maria (1980) 'Freud's Dora, Dora's Hysteria', in Bernheimer and Kahane (1985), pp. 149–80

Rashkin, E. (1988) 'Tools for a New Psychoanalytic Literary Criticism: The Work of Abraham and Torok', *Diacritics*, 18 (Winter), pp. 31–52

Redmond, Phil (1995) 'Why I Had to Find Beth and Mandy Guilty', *Guardian*, 18 May

Report of the Inquiry into the Removal of Children from Orkney in February 1991 (1992) Edinburgh: HMSO

Revue française de psychanalyse (1973) 'Sur l'hystérie', 37

Richards, Barry (ed.) (1984) *Capitalism and Infancy: Essays on Psychoanalysis and Politics*, London: Free Association Books

Richards, Barry (ed.) (1989) *Crises of the Self: Further Essays on Psychoanalysis and Politics*, London: Free Association Books

Richards, Barry (1994) 'Goods and Good Objects', in *Disciplines of Delight: The Psychoanalysis of Popular Culture*, London: Free Association Books, pp. 87–107

Rieff, Philip (1959) *Freud: The Mind of the Moralist*, 3rd edn, Chicago: University of Chicago Press, 1979

Robinson, Stephen (1984) 'The Parent to the Child', in Richards (1984), pp. 67–206

Rodman, F. Robert (ed.) (1987) *The Spontaneous Gesture: Selected Letters of D. W. Winnicott*, Cambridge, MA and London: Harvard University Press

Rose, Jacqueline (1983) 'Femininity and its Discontents', *Feminist Review*, 14, pp. 5–21; reprinted in Rose (1986) pp. 83–103

Rose, Jacqueline (1986) *Sexuality in the Field of Vision*, London: Verso

Rose, Jacqueline (1988) Panel discussion (unpublished) of *History Workshop*'s special feature on 'Psychoanalysis and History', Institute of Contemporary Arts, London

Rose, Jacqueline (1991) 'Faking It Up with the Truth' (review of Diane Middlebrook, *Anne Sexton*, 1991), *Times Literary Supplement*, 1 November

Rose, Jacqueline (1993) '"Where Does the Misery Come From?" – Psychoanalysis, Feminism and the Event', in *Why War? – Psychoanalysis, Politics, and the Return to Melanie Klein*, Oxford: Blackwell, pp. 89–109

Rose, Jacqueline (1993) 'Afterword' to Allon White, *Carnival, Hysteria, and Writing*, Oxford: Oxford University Press, pp. 178–86

RSJ Subgroup (1978) 'Marxism, Feminism and Psychoanalysis', *Radical Science Journal*, 6/7, pp. 107–17

Rustin, Michael (1982) 'A Socialist Consideration of Kleinian Psychoanalysis', *New Left Review*, 131, pp. 71–96

Rustin, Michael (1988) 'Shifting Paradigms in Psychoanalysis since the 1940s', *History Workshop*, 26 (special feature on 'Psychoanalysis and History'), pp. 133–42

Rycroft, Charles (1984) 'A Case of Hysteria' (review of Masson, *The Assault on Truth*, 1984), *New York Review of Books*, 12 April, pp. 3–6

Safouan, Moustapha (1983) *Jacques Lacan et la question de la formation des analystes*, Paris: Editions du Seuil

Sandler, Anne-Marie and Holmes, Richard (1990) 'A Dialogue on Biography and Psychoanalysis', joint presentation, Institute of Psycho-Analysis, London, June

Sayers, Janet (1983) 'Psychoanalysis and Personal Politics: A Response to Elizabeth Wilson', *Feminist Review*, 10, pp. 91–5

Sayers, Janet (1989) 'Melanie Klein and Mothering – A Feminist Perspective', *International Review of Psycho-Analysis*, 16, pp. 363–76

Schneiderman, Stuart (ed.) (1980) *Returning to Freud: Clinical Psychoanalysis in the School of Lacan*, New Haven, CT: Yale University Press

Scott, Ann (1987) review of Miller, *For Your Own Good* (1980) and *The Drama of Being a Child* (1987), *City Limits*, 21–8 May

Scott, Ann (1994) 'Childhood and the Forbidden', paper to Freud Museum conference, 'Psychoanalysis and Feminism: 20 Years On', London, May

Scott, Ann (forthcoming) 'Trauma, Skin: Memory, Speech', in Valerie Sinason (ed.), *Memory in Dispute*, London: Karnac

Segal, Hanna (1986) review of P. Grosskurth, *Melanie Klein: Her World and Her Work* (1986), *Sunday Times*, 22 June

Sexton, Linda Gray (1994) *Searching for Mercy Street: My Journey back to Anne Sexton*, Boston: Little, Brown

Sinason, Valerie (1993) 'Designed for Inconvenience', *Guardian*, 25 September

Sinason, Valerie (ed.) (1994) *Treating Survivors of Satanist Abuse*, London: Routledge

Sinason, Valerie (1994) 'Introduction' to Wright (1994), pp. vii–xx

Sinason, Valerie (ed.) (forthcoming) *Memory in Dispute*, London: Karnac

Smedley, Agnes (1929) *Daughter of Earth*, Old Westbury, NY: The Feminist Press, 1973

Smedley, Agnes (1943) *Battle Hymn of China*, London: Gollancz. Reissued as *China Correspondent*, London: Pandora, 1984

Spillius, Elizabeth (1985) 'The Kleinian Concept of Phantasy', University College London Freud Memorial Lecture, January

Stanley, Alessandra (1991) 'Fame and Privacy: The Sexton Tapes', *International Herald Tribune*, 16 July

Stanley, Liz (1992) *The Autobiographical I: The Theory and Practice of Feminist Autobiography*, Manchester: Manchester University Press

Steedman, Carolyn (1986) *Landscape for a Good Woman: A Story of Two Lives*, London: Virago

Steedman, Carolyn (1992) *Past Tenses: Essays on Writing, Autobiography and History*, London: Rivers Oram

Steiner, George (1984) 'The Fantasies of Freud' (review of Masson, *The Assault on Truth*, 1984), *Sunday Times*, 27 May

Stoller, Robert (1988) 'Patients' Responses to their own Case Reports', *Journal of the American Psychoanalytic Association*, 36, pp. 371–91

Sutton-Smith, Deirdre (ed.) (n.d.) *The Women's Therapy Centre: Groups for Incest Survivors – A Handbook Based on Practice at The Women's Therapy Centre*, London: Women's Therapy Centre

Symington, Neville (1993) Review of Bruno Bettelheim, *Freud and Man's Soul*, *Guardian*, July

Tagg, John (1988) 'Introduction', in *The Burden of Representation: Essays on Photographies and Histories*, Basingstoke: Macmillan, pp. 1–33

Trowell, Judith (1991) 'Fantasy in Child Sexual Abuse', unpublished lecture to THERIP, London, November

Trowell, Judith (forthcoming) 'Working with Child Sexual Abuse in Girls' in Joan Raphael-Leff and Rosine Perelberg (eds), *Female Experience*, London: Routledge

Trowell, Judith (forthcoming) 'The Psychodynamics of Incest', in Cleo van Velsen and Estela Welldon (eds), *Forensic Psychotherapy: A Handbook*, London: Jessica Kingsley Publishers

Van der Kolk, B. A. and van der Hart, Onno (1991) 'The Intrusive Past: The Flexibility of Memory and the Engraving of Trauma', *American Imago*, 48, pp. 425–54

Van Velsen, Cleo (1995) Review of Elaine Westerlund, *Women's Sexuality after Childhood Incest*, *British Journal of Psychiatry*, 166, 2, pp. 270–1

Wakefield, Hollida and Underwager, Ralph (1992) 'Uncovering Memories of Alleged Sexual Abuse: The Therapists Who Do It', *Issues in Child Abuse Accusations*, 4, pp. 199–213

Walters, Margaret (1988) 'The Infant Who Survives', Programme notes for Nicholas Wright, *Mrs Klein*, National Theatre, London

Walters, Margaret (1991) panel discussion with Diane Wood Middlebrook, *The Late Show*, BBC2, 4 November

Ward, Elizabeth (1984) *Father–Daughter Rape*, London: The Women's Press

Waterhouse, Hon Mr Justice (1989) 'Allegations of Child Abuse – the Court's Approach', in Levy (1989), pp. 1–7

Watney, Simon (1982) 'Making Strange: The Shattered Mirror', in Burgin (1982), pp. 154–76

Weatherby, W.J. (1991) 'Into Verse – And Worse', *Guardian*, 17 July

Welldon, Estela (1995) 'Female Perversion and Hysteria', *British Journal of Psychotherapy*, 11, 3, pp. 406–14

Wetzler, Scott (1985) 'The Historical Truth of Psychoanalytic Reconstructions', *International Review of Psycho-Analysis*, 12, pp 187–97

White, Allon (1993) *Carnival, Hysteria, and Writing: The Collected Essays and 'Autobiography' of Allon White*, Oxford: Oxford University Press

Williamson, Judith (1978) *Decoding Advertisements*, London: Marion Boyars

Wilson, Elizabeth (1981) 'Psychoanalysis: Psychic Law and Order?', *Feminist Review*, 8, pp. 63–78

Winnicott, D. W. (1961) 'Varieties of Psychotherapy', in *Home is Where We Start From: Essays by a Psychoanalyst*, Harmondsworth: Penguin, 1986, pp. 101–11

Wolff, Heinz, Bateman, Anthony and Sturgeon, David (eds) (1990) *UCH Textbook of Psychiatry*, London: Duckworth

Working Together Under the Children Act 1989 (1991) revised version, London: Department of Health

Wright, Elizabeth (ed.) (1992) *Feminism and Psychoanalysis: A Critical Dictionary*, Oxford: Blackwell

Wright, Lawrence (1994) *Remembering Satan*, London: Serpent's Tail

Young, Robert M. (1988) 'Biography: The Basic Discipline for the Human Sciences', *Free Associations*, 11, pp. 108–30

Index

HAVERING COLLEGE OF F & H E
8573